falling for you

falling for you

LISA SCHROEDER

SIMON PULSE

New York   London   Toronto   Sydney   New Delhi

This book is a work of fiction. Any references to historical events,
real people, or real places are used fictitiously. Other names, characters, places, and
events are products of the author's imagination, and any resemblance to actual
events or places or persons, living or dead, is entirely coincidental.

◊

SIMON PULSE

An imprint of Simon & Schuster Children's Publishing Division

1230 Avenue of the Americas, New York, NY 10020

First Simon Pulse paperback edition December 2013

Text copyright © 2013 by Lisa Schroeder

Cover photograph copyright © 2013 by Corbis

Book design by Karina Granda

All rights reserved, including the right of reproduction in whole or in part in any form.

SIMON PULSE and colophon are registered trademarks of Simon & Schuster, Inc.

Also available in a Simon Pulse hardcover edition.

For information about special discounts for bulk purchases, please contact Simon &
Schuster Special Sales at 1-866-506-1949 or business@simonandschuster.com.

The Simon & Schuster Speakers Bureau can bring authors to your live event.

For more information or to book an event contact the Simon & Schuster Speakers
Bureau at 1-866-248-3049 or visit our website at www.simonspeakers.com.

The text of this book was set in Adobe Caslon Pro.

Manufactured in the United States of America

2 4 6 8 10 9 7 5 3

The Library of Congress has cataloged the hardcover edition as follows:

Schroeder, Lisa.

Falling for you / Lisa Schroeder. — 1st Simon Pulse hardcover ed.

p. cm.

Summary: Very good friends, her poetry notebooks, and a mysterious "ninja of nice"
give seventeen-year-old Rae the strength to face her mother's neglect,
her stepfather's increasing abuse, and a new boyfriend's obsessiveness.

ISBN 978-1-4424-4399-0 (hc)

[1. Family problems—Fiction. 2. Dating (social customs)—Fiction.
3. High schools—Fiction. 4. Schools—Fiction. 5. Poetry—Fiction.
6. Stepfathers—Fiction. 7. Florists—Fiction.] I. Title.

PZ7.S3818Fal 2013

[Fic]—dc23

2012012993

ISBN 978-1-4424-4400-3 (pbk)

ISBN 978-1-4424-4401-0 (eBook)

Lucky number seven is for Sara Crowe,
because I am so lucky you loved my
odd little manuscript all those years ago.
I hope there are at least seven more!

the hospital—4:05 p.m.

At last I can breathe.

"Has anyone reached her family?"

Before they got to me, I felt like I was suffocating.
I can feel them working on me. Hear them.

"Rayanna? My name is Dr. Lamb. We're going to take care of you."

Dr. Lamb. I like the sound of your voice. I want to believe you'll take care of me. Except you can't do that forever. I mean, for now, maybe. But after that, what happens?
There's a light far, far away. I can feel it. It's warm.
Is it wrong to want the light?
Maybe the light doesn't want me.
All I want is to be wanted by someone. Just as I am.
That may be the only thing I've ever wanted.

six months earlier

it hurts

I WAS MAKING HAMBURGERS FOR DINNER. DEAN, MY STEPDAD, loves hamburgers, although I wasn't making his favorite out of a deep devotion for the guy. Grease kept spraying up from the frying pan, burning my hands, like tiny electrical shocks. It was a small price to pay. Once I got him fed, I could retreat to my room, like always, where he'd leave me alone for the rest of the night.

When the meat was done, I put the patties and buns on two plates, then rushed around grabbing the chips, a Coke for me, and a beer for him.

"Dinner's ready," I called.

"Good. I'm starving," Dean said as he got up off the couch. He took a seat at the old butcher-block table and scrutinized his dinner plate along with the condiments I'd set out earlier. I waited. There was always something.

"Shit, Rae," he yelled. "Where's the onions?"

Right. His beloved onions. "Sorry. Hold on. I'll get them."

"Damn right you will," he muttered.

I sliced through the onion, pretending it was his head.

I looked up. He handled his hamburger so gently. Putting on ketchup, mustard, and pickles with such tender care, you'd have thought he was a mother dressing her newborn baby.

I sliced harder. Faster.

"Ow!" The knife fell to the counter with a rattle. "Sh—" I pinched my lips together, keeping the promise to myself to be nothing like my foulmouthed stepfather. I blasted the water in the sink and thrust my hand under the stream, wincing because it stung.

Dean said nothing.

The reddish-pinkish water swirled down the drain, and I imagined a sink full of blood. It'd overflow onto the floor. Creep across the linoleum to his oil-stained boots.

How much blood before he'd notice?

How much blood before he'd care?

No doubt in my mind. He'd let me bleed to death. Years ago, when I'd hoped he might be the dad I'd never had, his nonreaction probably would have bothered me. Not anymore. I'd learned to keep my expectations low. There's less disappointment that way.

Because one thing I really didn't need any more of? Disappointment.

My mother definitely didn't marry Dean for his compassion. She married him for money, what little of it he had, anyway. It was more than we had, which was nothing, and that was all that'd mattered.

I turned off the water and grabbed a paper towel, wrapping it tight around my finger, afraid to look too closely at the cut.

Dean got up with his plate and marched to the counter, cussing under his breath. He picked up a handful of sliced onions and put them on top of his burger.

Blood seeped through the towel. I squeezed it tighter.

He went back to the table. Sat down. Took a bite of his burger.

"Now, that's better," he mumbled.

The whole scene reminded me of the time I'd heard two DJs on the radio talking about a survey some researchers had conducted on memories. The results showed there are three things people remember most from their childhood: family vacations, holiday traditions, and mealtimes.

I had to laugh. Yeah, I'd remember mealtimes at my house, and immediately wish I could forget them.

I spent the evening in my room, doing homework. Mom got home around ten, like always. She worked the swing shift as a checker at the Rite Aid. I heard her in the other room, exchanging words with Dean. Their voices got louder, and my name was mentioned a time or two.

I turned up the music on my laptop in response, doing

my best to fight the world with Foo. The Foo Fighters, that is. I traced my finger along my ankle, imagining the tattoo I'd designed in my head with a circle of musical notes and lyrics from my favorite song, "Everlong." If I make it to eighteen with my sanity intact, I figure I'll owe it to the Foo Fighters. Well, and to my job at Full Bloom. Might need to incorporate a couple of flowers into that design.

I picked up my book, trying to read like a good junior should. *The Crucible*. Ms. Bloodsaw (yes, that's really her name) said it was a perfect example of irony. If you denied you were a witch, they hanged you. If you admitted you were a witch, they set you free. But you had to live every day with the lies you told. What kind of life would that be? I'd thought about it a lot. Probably too much.

Mom poked her head into my room. "Rayanna, how come the dishes aren't done?"

I held up my bandaged finger for her to see.

"Well, it's not broken, is it? Get out there and wash 'em. 'Cause I sure as hell can't do 'em. I've been on my feet—"

"For over eight hours. I know, Mom. But I cut it really bad."

"You'll live," she said. "Though you may not if you don't get off your ass and get those dishes done. You know how Dean likes things kept neat around here."

Grandma used to say, "The road to happiness is paved with good deeds for others." Clearly my mother had taken a detour. Would it kill her to do just *one* nice thing for me?

I got up off my bed. "Why don't you make him—"

"Go. Wash." She walked over and pointed her finger in my face. "The damn. Dishes."

I don't know why I even tried. She always took his side. Just what I needed—another reminder of how I should expect nothing from either one of them.

My mother had never been an easy person to live with. I tried my best to be empathetic toward her. Grandma told me once that Mom had a lot of bad things happen to her when she was younger, and it left her angry at the world. When I pressed Grandma for more information, wanting so desperately to understand my mother, she said it wasn't her place to tell me. And then she told me I should try not to take it personally, which is pretty much impossible to do when it *feels* personal.

After Grandma died from cancer six years ago, I told myself not to worry, because there was no way my mother could get any angrier.

Turned out I was wrong.

I DON'T BELONG HERE

I feel like
an obstacle stuck
in your way.

You kick me
to the side of the road
in order to get
where you need to go.

Where are you going?
Do you even know?

Seems like you
go around
and around
and around,
always coming back
to the same place.

And always,
I am in the way.

You push me
this way
and that way
and all I can think
is I don't belong here.

Nowhere
is nowhere
near the place
I want to be.

meet the new kid

THE NEXT MORNING I APPROACHED THE JUNIOR BENCHES IN THE common area inside the main entrance of the school. Alix saved me a spot, like she's supposed to. Just like I do for her when I get there first. It's our meeting place. I took my seat. Alix was talking to Felicia on the other side of her. I nudged her, causing Alix to whip around and put her arm around me, her hand getting tangled in my dark blond hair as she gave me a squeeze. "Yay! Rae's here, Rae's here."

"Hi, Rae," Felicia said, leaning forward, her elbows on her knees and her head propped in her hands. "Cute sweater. The pink really brings out the blue in your eyes. Where'd you get it?"

I smiled. That's exactly why I bought it. "Thanks. The City Girl had a sale last week."

It was a little white lie. I wanted my friends to think I was just as good as they were. I rarely bought new clothes. I shopped at the Goodwill store. I'd become a genius at thrift-store shopping. You wouldn't believe some of the stuff people give away.

"Love that store," Felicia said. "God, I want to go shopping so bad. Mom won't have any of it though. Says she's given me enough money lately. Whatever."

"Well, you could get a job, like Rae," Alix said. "Though it'd be hard to find one as fun as hers. Which reminds me, are you working after school? Want to grab a bite before the game?"

"Game?" I teased. "What game?"

"Very funny," Alix said. "Don't let Santiago hear you say that. He is so stressed about this one. Thinks it's gonna be the toughest game of the season."

"Alix, don't get mad, but I don't know if I want to go. I have to work. And I'm tired. It's been a long—"

"What?" Alix scowled at me. "You are not saying this right now. The team needs you. Santiago needs you. I need you!" She turned to Felicia. "Can you believe this girl?"

"You have to go!" Felicia said. "It wouldn't be the same without you."

It felt good to be wanted. If I stayed home, I'd probably sit in my room, listening to my music, feeling sorry for myself. That didn't exactly sound like a good time. Sometimes I felt a little left out of all their boy talk, but they didn't do it on purpose.

Alix took my hand in hers and pleaded with her eyes. "Please go. Please?"

"Fine. But I'll have to meet you there."

"Not a problem. I can spend a couple of hours helping Dad. The sixty-seven Mustang he brought in a few days ago needs a lot of work, but it's gonna be amazing when it's finished."

"Alixandria, stop it," I deadpanned. "You know how your car talk turns me on."

She smiled as she raised her eyebrows. "Yeah? Well, come over anytime and you can get greasy with me."

I grimaced. "I think I'd rather scale Mount Everest. With no clothes on."

Felicia laughed. "Totally agree with you on that one."

Alix crossed her arms over her chest. "You guys, it's fun! And must I remind you, Rae? Where would you be if it weren't for me, your faithful grease-monkey friend?"

I leaned into her. "Riding on two wheels instead of four, that's where. You know my love for your mechanical aptitude runs deep. But as for me, I'll keep my job with purdy flowers, *thankyouverymuch*."

Just then, Santiago, Alix's boyfriend, walked up along with a cute guy I'd never seen before. I figured he was new, since Crestfield isn't very big.

Alix jumped up and threw her arms around Santiago. She was affectionate, that girl. We'd met in eighth grade, at homework club after school. Two girls among many, who were trying to bring up their grades. Fate sat us together. For once, I'd had a lucky break.

When we started hanging out, it seemed kind of strange how she often wanted to hold my hand while we talked or link arms when we walked down the hall. It's just who she is. Once I got used to it, I liked it. My mom had stopped hugging me a long time ago. As for Dean, well, thank God he kept his hands off me.

After a couple of quick kisses, Santiago wrangled Alix to his side then gestured to the mystery guy. "Hey, girls, this is Nathan. Maybe you've seen him around. Just started here a couple days ago. You won't see him in a uniform until spring, but he's one to watch on the baseball field."

Alix gave him a little wave. "Hey, good to meet you. I'm Alix. That's Felicia and Rae."

Nathan gave us both a nod. "Hey."

He was really cute, with dark blond hair sticking every which way, electric blue eyes, and a little dimple in his chin. I love dimples.

He started to say something else, but then Tyler, Felicia's boyfriend, showed up, and the couples started whispering sweet nothings to each other. I stood up to head to class.

Nathan stopped me. "You going to the game tonight?"

It was a simple question. Yet, for some reason, it felt important. I fiddled with Grandma's antique ring on my finger, hoping I didn't say something stupid. "Yeah. I'm meeting Alix and Felicia there. Santiago and Tyler play best when we're all cheering for them. Or so my friends tell me."

He stuck his hands in his jeans pockets and smiled at me. I swallowed hard, because, sweet mother-of-pearl, the way he looked at me sent a little shock wave from the top of my head to the tips of my toes.

"Well, maybe I'll see you there?" he said.

"Yeah. Sure. Come find us if you want."

I mentally kicked myself as soon as the words were out of my mouth. I wasn't good with guys. I got tongue-tied and self-conscious, and in trying to avoid all the parts of my life I didn't want to talk about, conversations usually ended up being weird and awkward.

The five-minute bell rang and I'd never been so happy to hear that thing go off. Left for another minute, who knows what I might have said that I'd regret.

"See you later," I told him before I bolted.

At least Alix and Felicia would be with me at the game. And, I told myself, if things got too uncomfortable, I could just head to the concession stand for a snack. Of course there'd be a really long line. Like miles long. I'd be gone forever.

Oh, who was I kidding? If he came and found us, I'd want to stay and hang on to every word. Maybe I was afraid of guys and getting close and revealing too much of myself, but that didn't mean I wasn't curious.

And as far as Nathan was concerned? I was more than a little curious.

i want to be brave

ENGLISH IS THE CLASS I LOVE THE MOST, WITH THE TEACHER I love the most. Lucky for me, Ms. Bloodsaw is as awesome as her name.

I sat down at my desk and flipped open my notebook. Felicia came in and took the desk in front of me. She turned around and raised her eyebrows at me. "So. The new guy. Initial reaction?"

I shrugged. "Don't really have one."

Her mouth dropped open. "Are you serious right now? Come on. Don't play hard to get before you've even given him a chance."

"I'm not playing anything. I just don't think I should be too quick to judge a book by its cover, so to speak."

She leaned in, her eyes like a doe's, big and round. "But you can't deny it. He's hot, right? And the way he looked at you? Rae, I'm telling you, do not mess around. You have to show a little interest or you'll lose him."

I held up my fist as if I was holding a microphone, although I kept my voice fairly quiet. "Welcome to the Dr. Felicia show, ladies and gentlemen. Relationship advice from the number one expert on love."

Felicia leaned back. "Fine. Mock me all you want. But you know I'm right. He could be the one."

And that was exactly why I hadn't given her any indication of what I thought about the guy. If she knew how I really felt, that I was secretly dying to know more about him, I'd never hear the end of it.

"Good morning," Ms. Bloodsaw said, entering the class-room right before the final bell rang. "Before we begin, I have an announcement. As most of you probably know, due to a generous donation by the late Mrs. Enid Scott, a retired teacher from Crestfield High, this year marks the first year we'll be publishing an anthology of students' poetry. Enid adored poetry, and it was her dream to have Crestfield students experience the thrill of seeing their work in print.

"Every month, the newspaper will print a pull-out section of student poetry. Most anything submitted will be included, as long as it's appropriate. No foul language, no sexual refer-ences, that kind of thing. In April a panel of teachers will select the best poems to be included in the anthology, which will be available for purchase.

"The deadline for the first pull-out issue will be in one week. If you have questions, please see me after class."

It felt strange to have her speak to us like that. Like writing poetry was as normal as breathing. Was it possible that I wasn't the only one who had more poetry journals than pairs of pants?

I couldn't help but wonder who would be brave enough to publish poems for everyone to see. Not me. No way. I had too much to hide.

If I submitted some of my writing, wouldn't people be ruthless? Wouldn't they look beneath the beauty of the words, hoping to find a poor, hurting soul to obliterate?

Maybe not.

Maybe a poet's pain, or pleasure, would reach out and touch a reader's heart.

Maybe the sky would open up and pour golden light into someone's soul.

Maybe, just maybe, a reader would feel a little less alone in the world.

That thought right there? It sent shivers up and down my spine.

After class I told Felicia to go on without me. I took my time gathering up my things. By the time I stopped at Ms. Bloodsaw's desk, everyone else had left.

"Hi, Rae. What can I do for you?"

"I was wondering, um, could I submit a poem anonymously? For the newspaper? Would that be all right?"

Ms. Bloodsaw tilted her head and squinted her pretty green eyes a bit. "It wouldn't be considered for the anthology, but if that's what you're most comfortable with, sure, go right ahead."

It was definitely what I was most comfortable with. Writing poetry was my way of dealing with the sad and ugly parts of my life. My friends knew very little about those parts, and I wanted to keep it that way.

Grandma told me once, keeping feelings locked away isn't good for a person. They need to go somewhere, or they can be damaging. It frightened me when she said that, because I had a lot of feelings, which meant there was the potential for a whole lot of damage. And so I started writing.

I wasn't sure how I would choose a poem out of the hundreds. Or was it thousands? All I knew is that I wanted to do it, because when I thought of possibly helping someone with my words, it made me feel something I hadn't felt much in my life.

Powerful.

home away from home

AFTER SCHOOL ALIX WALKED WITH ME TO THE PARKING LOT. The warm autumn air smelled like exhaust, as car after car left the school grounds. A lot of the cars had kids hanging out the windows as they went in search of some fun before the game.

Alix patted the hood of my little black Nissan pickup. "Glad to see you're still treating her well."

I found my old truck on Craigslist last year for five hundred bucks. It didn't run when I bought it, but Alix and her dad took care of that.

"I wonder what kind of car Nathan drives," Alix continued, looking around the parking lot. "Maybe he'll ask you out tonight, and you'll get to find out."

I rolled my eyes. "Alix, please. Not you, too. Felicia practically married us off in first period."

"We just want good things for you, that's all. And Nathan?"

She smiled deviously. "He looks like a very good thing. He's got to be interested, right? Why else would he ask if you were going to the game?"

I shook my head. "Whatever. You know how it is with me and guys. I'm the nice girl it's fun to be friends with. Or something."

"Rae, I'm pretty sure that's because you never *want* to be more than friends. As soon as things start moving in that direction, you pull away. Wait. Scratch that. You run away. Why is that?"

I reached into my pocket for my phone, checking the time. "Sorry, I need to cancel this therapy session or I'm gonna be late for work."

I opened the door and started to climb in, but she grabbed my hand. "You really need to give him a chance. Santiago thinks he's a great guy."

"Okay, okay. If he's even interested, which is a pretty big 'if.' Did you see the way all the girls looked at him today?"

She winked. "He only had eyes for you. Trust me."

"See you tonight," I said as I hopped into the truck. She blew me a kiss as I drove off and it made me laugh. The girl could be relentless, but I sure did love her.

I went a few blocks down Fifth Street and then pulled onto Pacific Road. The town of Crestfield isn't much. At all. Pacific Road takes you from one end of town to the other, with grocery stores, gas stations, banks, and other businesses along the way. Old downtown is where I work, which isn't so old anymore. New stores have replaced the old ones, although the buildings are original, so it still has that homey feel people love.

The good thing about a small town is it doesn't take you very long to get someplace. After one and a half Foo Fighters songs, I pulled into the parking lot behind the building where I work. The parking lot is shared by three businesses: a hair salon called Cutting Edge, Full Bloom, and a coffee shop, Mack's Bean Shack.

Nina keeps the back door locked, so I walked around to the front, past Cutting Edge, and through the door of Full Bloom. The sweet-smelling shop has walls the color of sunshine and shelves filled with potted plants and flowers. It gave me a warm, fuzzy feeling when I walked in, like always.

I could see Nina in the back workroom through the large picture window behind the long front counter. She sat with a pile of paperwork in front of her and her laptop.

"Hey, Nina. How's it going?" I asked as I walked through the workroom door.

"It's been quiet all day," she said, glancing up at me. "So I'm paying bills. Man, do I *hate* paying bills. But Uranus is finally leaving my second house, which rules earned income. Uranus is volatile, so it's a good thing it's leaving. More money should start coming in now, right?"

I curled my lips in, trying not to giggle. "Nina, I'm sorry, but I'm still back at 'Uranus is volatile.'" She could talk astrology to me all she wanted, but as soon as she mentioned Uranus, it was over.

"All right, all right. I'll keep my thoughts about Uranus to myself."

"Much appreciated. So, what's my horoscope say? Do I have anything to look forward to? If not, don't tell me. I don't want to know."

Nina regularly checked a bunch of online sites to get her daily, weekly, and monthly horoscopes. I thought she took it a bit too seriously sometimes, but I'd never tell her that. Mostly I joked with her about it, hoping to remind her it should be for fun, not something to plan her life around.

"Romance," she said as she typed numbers into her spreadsheet. "Something big is supposed to happen soon."

I took my sweater off and hung it on the coatrack. "Since I'm sixteen, wait, I mean, newly seventeen, and have never been kissed, that's even funnier than saying Uranus is volatile."

The bell above the front door jingled.

"Where's Spencer?" I asked. He usually sat at the counter, greeting people and answering the phone.

"I gave him the afternoon off. It's Kevin's birthday today, so they're going up to Portland to celebrate."

"Okay, I'm on it."

I walked out and greeted the young, pretty woman. "Can I help you?"

"My name is on your board out there. You know, the name of the day?"

Nina has a sign outside:

IF YOUR NAME IS _____, COME IN FOR A FREE FLOWER.

Every day she changes the name on the board. It's a fun way to get new people into the shop. And I'm amazed how often we get new business because of it.

"Sorry," I said. "I forgot to look at the sign as I walked in. You are—?"

"Grace." She reached for her purse. "Do you want to see my driver's license?"

"Nah. It's okay. I trust you."

I walked to the cooler, where I picked out a red rose and some baby's breath. "Let me wrap this for you."

As I finished with the flower, the bell rang again. It was my friend Leo. He works for his dad next door at Mack's Bean Shack. He's homeschooled, so I only see him when I'm working.

The woman thanked me and grabbed one of our business cards before she left.

Leo stepped up to the counter. He smelled like coffee and his brown eyes looked tired. "Hi, my name is Grace. I'd like my free flower please?"

"Now, that's a first. Come back tomorrow when the name is Fred, and I'll hook you up."

"Fred?" He looked shocked. "You think I look like a Fred? With this incredible head of hair?"

Leo and his hair. He's kind of obsessed with it. Yes, it's nice—the color of chocolate, shiny and soft-looking—but it's kind of become a joke now.

"Well, you look like a Fred a helluva lot more than you look like a Grace."

He smiled. "Actually, my dad needs some tape. Can we borrow some?"

"Scotch or masking?"

"Not sure. Uh, Scotch, I guess."

"Coming right up."

"You sound like a bartender. Not that I've been to many bars. Just seen 'em in the movies."

"Why do you sound like you're trying to cover something up, Mr. Martin? Hmmm? Been sneaking out when Daddy's not looking?" I pulled open the shop's junk drawer. No tape.

It was always like this with Leo. Fun. Easy. I was always happy when I got the chance to see him.

"All right. You caught me. There's this twenty-three-year-old girl who is smoking hot and scored me a fake ID. The things we do for love, you know?"

I pulled a bunch of paperwork out of the in/out basket. There it was. "Ooooh, a secret life. The stuff good books are made of." I handed him the tape. "Speaking of which, I'm almost done with *The Crucible*. My teacher called it 'chilling and delicious.' Chilling, yes. Delicious, I'm not so sure. But I need something else to read. Any suggestions?"

"I've heard *Catcher Eats a Pie* is pretty tasty."

"Oh, that sounds good," I said, my mind racing. "Or maybe *Pecan with the Wind*?"

"*Pride and Asparagus*?" he quipped back.

I laughed. "Oh no, chilling and disgusting. Okay, seriously. You always have your nose in a book. Help me out here."

"Do I look like a librarian?" He walked toward the door. "I'm a barista, Rae. Big difference."

"But you're a barista who reads! Actually, I think you're my only friend who likes to read. Think about it and get back to me, okay?"

He grinned. "I will. Next time I see you, I'll be ready. Just can't think of anything right now. You know how it is when your brain is screaming, 'Work to do, work to do!'"

I did know. That was another thing about Leo. He was my only friend who understood what it's like to juggle life and school with a job. My other friends didn't need to work. I was glad I had him to talk to about that sometimes.

"Bye!" I called out.

He waved before he hustled out the door, and I thought, *There should be more guys like Leo.* I hoped Nathan was as nice as him. Maybe I'd get lucky and Nathan would like to read too. Or he'd confide in me that he secretly wrote poetry in notebooks that he kept hidden in his room.

What was I doing? I didn't even know if Nathan and I

would be able to carry on a decent conversation, and here I was hoping he'd share his deepest secrets with me?

I felt butterflies in my stomach at just the thought of Nathan. I wanted to blame Alix and Felicia for getting my hopes up, but I knew it was all me. I couldn't deny that I often envied my friends, with their boyfriends who lavished them with love. I wanted a little lavishing too.

late for dinner

BUSINESS PICKED UP, AND I ENDED UP STAYING LATE TO HELP NINA finish some bouquets. It was six thirty when I pulled into the driveway, and I knew a certain someone would not be happy with me.

I got out of my truck, the smell of cut grass and twilight all around me. Dean stood at our faded picket fence with the lawn mower, talking with one of the neighbors, Mr. Pulley. Each had a beer in his hand. Well, how nice. Dean actually knew how to share.

Dean smiled and waved. "Hey, sunshine, good to have you home. I'll be inside in a minute."

"Sunshine?" What the—are you kidding me? Mr. Pulley smiled and waved, so I did the same. What a picture-perfect scene. We'd become experts at creating magical illusions.

I hurried inside to get Dean's dinner going. What could

I make that would be fast? A frozen dinner would be the quickest, but I couldn't remember if we had any. My mom hadn't been shopping lately. She was probably waiting for payday.

I opened the freezer door, hoping for the best. "Oh, thank God," I whispered. There was one Hungry-Man left. Even better, it was his favorite, Classic Fried Chicken.

Dean lumbered in as I tossed the plastic tray into the microwave and set it to cook for five minutes. "I count on you for dinner at six thirty, Rae. You know that. It's really not too much to ask."

"Something came up at work," I told him. "It'll be ready in a few minutes."

I wanted to ask if he'd somehow managed to break his hands while mowing the lawn. God forbid he should make himself something to eat for a change. But I kept my pissy thoughts to myself and pulled another beer out of the fridge for him.

"Look, I'm sorry I'm late. I couldn't help it." I handed him the beer and took his empty one. He wiped the top of the can with the edge of his Blue Streak Auto Shop work shirt before he popped the tab.

"What do you do with all that money you make, anyway?" he asked.

I threw the can into the recycle bin next to the fridge. "It pays for my gas and insurance. Clothes. You know, girl stuff."

I swallowed hard. I did not like this conversation. "And it's not very much, since I only work part-time."

What Dean didn't know, and hopefully never would, was that I had a savings account. I called it my Get Out of Crestfield fund. After I paid my bills and bought whatever else I needed, the rest of the money went into my savings.

Dean took a swig of beer. "You get tips?"

"Sometimes. Not today though." I looked down at my hands and picked at the ugly bandage on my finger.

I glanced at him as he leaned against the counter and took a deep breath. There was something in his eyes I hadn't seen before. He almost looked . . . sad.

"I got laid off today," Dean said quietly. He cleared his throat. "When I tell your mother, she won't be happy."

He looked at me expectantly, like I was supposed to reassure him. I bit my lip, trying to figure out what to say. It was all so strange. Wasn't *he*, as the adult, supposed to reassure *me* that we'd be all right? Then I remembered who I was talking to. There was nothing normal about our family. "She'll probably understand. These things happen sometimes," I said, not very convincingly. "At least Mom still has her job. And you'll find work. Right?"

He shook his head. "I don't know. You know what Crestfield's like. Small. Tight. It may be a while. And your mom don't make shit." He took another swig of beer. Then his face changed. The Dean I knew and despised returned.

He came closer to me. "You'll give me your paycheck on paydays. The first and the fifteenth, isn't it? I'll decide how much money you get for your girl crap."

I couldn't believe this was happening. "Why should I hand it over to you?" I waved my hand at the empty cans. "You'll just throw it away on beer."

Dean reached out and slapped me hard across the face. I tottered back and landed against the stove. My cheek burned. Tears pushed against my eyelids, wanting to escape. Too bad. I wouldn't let them. If I was trapped, so were they.

"If you want to keep living here, you will help pay for your living expenses. This is my house, remember? Now, lucky for you, I'm going to make you look like a good girl to your mother. As far as she knows, you offered up your paycheck happily. Don't let me hear any different. Are we clear?"

I nodded, covering my cheek with my hand. Dean had never slapped me before. He yelled at me all the time, raised his hand and threatened me a couple of times, but this was a first. It scared me. Obviously he was serious about this money thing.

Usually I didn't make waves. I tried to keep the peace, always doing what he asked of me. This, though—handing over my paychecks? *My* money? It wasn't fair. And yet, it didn't look like arguing about it would get me anywhere.

The microwave started beeping. Dean sat down at the kitchen table. I removed the brownie from the tray, then stuck the rest of the dinner back in for another couple of minutes, like the instructions said to do.

I paced the floor, trying to think of what I could do to change his mind. Maybe I could talk to Mom before he did, and explain to her why I needed my paychecks. She had a better chance of changing his mind than I did. No. Of course that wouldn't work. She always took his side.

When the microwave beeped again, I took the tray over to Dean with a fork. I had to try. Just one more time.

"I, uh . . ."

"What?" His gnarled, ugly hand gripped the fork as he peeled the skin away from the breast meat. I thought of him reaching up and hitting me again. "Spit it out, Rae."

"I'm going to the football game. I'll be back later."

I started to go into the bathroom, to brush my hair and change the bandage on my finger. But with anger boiling up inside me, I decided I had to do something else first. I headed to my bedroom, shut the door, and picked up my favorite pen.

ON THE MENU

I made you
a special
casserole
for dinner tonight.

It's full of
all the ingredients
you seem
to love.

Two cups of selfishness,
a half cup of spite.

Three cups of greed,
and four tablespoons of grudge.

I mixed them all together,
then poured them in a pan.
Baked it for an hour;
now I'll serve it nice and hot.

You think it looks
delicious?
I'm so glad, 'cause
it's *all* yours.

Though
I think it needs
one
more
thing.

Please, take a seat
while I finish
up your meal.

I add a pinch
of poison.

Now, won't that
hit the spot?

strangers no more

I STOOD AT THE BOTTOM OF THE BLEACHERS, SCANNING THE crowd. They must have spotted me, because Alix and Felicia began waving their arms frantically from the middle of the student section. I trudged through the mountain of people, and thankfully a few kind souls let me squeeze in between my friends. Two big zeros lit up the scoreboard, so although I'd missed some of the first quarter, I obviously hadn't missed much.

"Did you get my texts?" Alix asked. "We thought maybe you were ditching us."

"Yeah, sorry I'm late." I shivered a little from the cool night air, so I buttoned the top button of my jacket. "Work stuff."

"It's okay," Alix said, slipping her arm through mine and pulling me close to her. I took in the familiar scent of her green apple shampoo and felt myself relax a little. "All that matters is you're here now."

Apology accepted. Exactly how it should be. If only it could be that easy in my own home.

At the thought of Dean and the ugly scene that had played out, I instinctively reached up and touched my cheek. It still stung a little when I touched it, although no one would ever know what happened. Thankfully nothing showed, and I sure didn't plan on telling anyone.

I turned to Felicia. I could feel her eyes on me. "You okay?" she asked. "Have you been crying?"

"I'm fine!" I said, probably a little too enthusiastically. "It's just the cool air. Makes my eyes water."

I try not to let things get to me. But after I'd scribbled in my notebook for a while and replayed the whole thing over and over, there was no stopping the tears. I didn't let it go on too long, since I had a game to get to. And now I felt happy to be here, a normal girl at a normal football game with a bunch of other happy, normal people.

The ref blew his whistle, indicating the end of the first quarter. Everyone stood up and cheered. Had to give the boys on the field a little love. Or in Felicia's and Alix's case, a lot of love. They didn't simply cheer, they screamed.

When we sat back down, Alix motioned a few rows below us. "Nathan's turned and looked up here, like, six times. I think he's been waiting for you."

"Yeah, right. And Santa Claus is bringing me a pony this year."

But as soon as I said that, Nathan turned and looked right at me. Our eyes met. A shiver went down my spine, and this time it wasn't because I felt cold. Quite the opposite.

Feeling weird that he'd caught me looking at him, I glanced away, but not before he flashed me a grin.

"I think he likes you," Alix whispered in my ear.

"He doesn't even know me."

"Well, I think he wants to *get* to know you."

What if he did? Could I let him in? Alix and Felicia, Nina and Spencer—they knew I'd never met my dad, that my mom and I lived in the ugly part of town with my stepfather, and that I couldn't stand him. I think they respected how hard I worked at the flower shop so I could make a better life for myself someday. My friends also knew that I didn't like talking about my family, and unless I brought something up, they shouldn't ask.

I'd told each of them, ever so briefly, about my mom and Dean after I felt comfortable with them and trusted them. Still, it was hard. It probably would always be hard, giving people a glimpse of the family I felt ashamed of. And when it came to a potential love interest, it seemed pretty much impossible.

Maybe it was better to just get it out of the way. This is who I am, this is the family I'm not proud of, and if you ask me anything about it, then it's over between us. Yeah, right. That's the way to build a close, loving, trust-filled relationship.

Part of me wondered if maybe, like my mother, I simply wasn't capable of one.

I tried to imagine what kind of family Nathan might have, playing out different scenarios in my head. Then the game got interesting. Santiago scored a touchdown with five minutes left in the half. The crowd stayed on their feet for the rest of the quarter, and we held the lead through halftime.

"I need a coffee," Alix said as the crowd began dispersing. "Want anything?"

"I do," Felicia said. "I'll go with."

I stood up to join them, but as I did, Nathan also got up.

"No," Alix said, leaning in close so Nathan couldn't hear her. "You're staying right here. Tell me what you want and I'll bring it back for you."

So much for the safe harbor of friends.

"I'm starving. Can you get me some Peanut M&M's?" I fished some money out of my pocket as Nathan made his way up the bleachers toward us. I felt my heart speed up.

"Absolutely," Alix said with a smile.

"Hey, girls," Nathan said. "Good game, huh? Thanks to Santiago!"

"Yep, he's the man," Alix said. "Here, take a seat, Nathan. Felicia and I were just leaving."

Wow, obvious much? My friends hopped down the bleachers as Nathan and I sat down. "Your little town sure loves football, huh?" he said.

I wrapped my arms around myself. I felt cold. Or maybe nervous. Or both. "Yep. Although I think it's the Crestfield Warriors they really love. Gives people something to do besides sit home on a Friday night watching TV."

"So, not a lot of nightlife happening here? Is that what you're telling me?"

I smiled and finally looked at him. His eyes were like pools of water, begging me to dive in. "That would be correct," I somehow managed to say. I nervously looked away, back to the crowds of people mulling around down below.

"What about you?" he asked. "Do you like football?"

I shrugged. "It's all right, I guess. Mostly I like how it brings people together. Here, in the stands, with everyone cheering for the same thing, it feels nice. Safe, in a way." I took a deep breath and looked at him again. "So, how'd you end up in Crestfield, anyway?"

"I hate that question," he said. "I pretty much sidestep it as much as possible. But . . . I'll tell you."

I waited as he stared at the field. It seemed like he was having a hard time opening up, for some reason. Was he ashamed about something? I was actually a little excited by that prospect. Maybe we'd have something in common right off the bat.

"We moved here so my dad could immerse himself in small-town life." He made quotes in the air with his fingers. *"For research."*

"What does he do?"

"He's an author, working on his next series. And what Gary Sharp wants, Gary Sharp gets."

Mother-of-pearl, is he kidding me? His dad is Gary Sharp? The Gary Sharp? He was the most popular author of horror and thriller novels in the past ten years. I stared at Nathan. I couldn't believe I was actually talking to Gary Sharp's son.

Nathan turned back to me and leaned in a little. His breath smelled like bubble gum, and I swear my heart dropped to my stomach. What was I doing with this guy?

"I'm actually nothing like my dad," he said playfully. "I hate creepy stuff."

"But you've read his books, right?"

He shook his head.

My eyes got big. "Not one?"

He shook his head again.

"Wow. I read three of them last summer. He's a really good writer!"

He laughed. "Yeah. That's what I've heard." He glanced over at the scoreboard. "Okay, five minutes of halftime left. Quick, tell me something about you. Or even better, two or three things. Before your friends come back."

After hearing about his dad, just thinking about telling him anything about my pathetic life made me feel slightly ill. I couldn't tell him anything really personal. Not yet, at least.

"Okay, well, let's see. I'm pretty sure I'm the Foo Fighters' number one fan."

He crinkled his face. "Really?"

I sat back. "What? You don't like them?"

"Aren't they some old, washed-up band?"

"Are you kidding? Every album they make gets nominated for at least one Grammy Award. I don't even know how many they've won, and quite a few recently."

He scratched his nose and got quiet for a second, like he was trying to think of a good response. All he said was, "Okay, what else?"

I nervously tucked my hair behind my ears. I wasn't used to this much interest in myself. And from a boy, no less. "I have the best job ever, at a flower shop called Full Bloom."

"Wow, a working girl," he said. "That's impressive. How often do you work?"

"After school most days, and almost every Saturday. But it's not even like a job, because I love it there so much, you know? Most of the time I get to deliver flowers, and it's such a great feeling, bringing people a little bit of joy in a vase. Plus, I adore my boss and coworker. Honestly, I'd much rather be there than hanging out at home with nothing to do."

Nathan sat back, leaning his elbows on the bleachers behind him. "But when do you have time for fun?"

"I don't know. I make time, I guess."

The cheerleaders finished their halftime routine, and I

watched him eye them as they left the field. I felt like I was on a love-gone-wrong episode on a bad reality TV show. According to him, I loved a washed-up band and I never had fun. Wow, we were off to a *great* start.

As Alix and Felicia ambled up the steps, carrying drinks and candy, I wanted to jump up and kiss them, I was so happy they'd come back. Alix laughed at something Felicia said, causing Nathan to turn and notice them. I guess their approach prompted him to get to the point.

"Go out with me?" he asked as he stood up. "You don't work Saturday nights, right?"

Seriously? Like, this was so much fun you can't wait for more? I tried to think of an excuse. Maybe I already had plans. Maybe my mom and I were doing something.

"Right, I don't work," I said. "But—"

"Good," he interrupted. "Meet me at the Mushroom tomorrow night at seven."

It wasn't a question. More of a demand. My friends stood behind him now, and Alix had obviously heard him, because she gave me a look that said, *Do it or I'll kill you*, as she nodded her head like a madwoman. Pressure was coming at me from all sides, and so, I caved.

"Yeah. Sure. I'll see you at seven."

A look of satisfaction came over his face. "Perfect. I can't wait." And then he returned to his seat.

Alix sat down next to me shoving two yellow packages of M&M's into my hands before she threw her arms around me and gave me a hug.

"You did it, you did it!" she said. "You didn't run away!"

She was right. I didn't. But why did a small part of me feel like that's exactly what I should have done?

first date

SEVEN O'CLOCK. I WAS ON TIME. HE WASN'T. I SAT IN MY FAVORITE booth and waited, spinning Grandma's ring around on the table. She'd given it to me shortly before she passed away, like she knew she'd be gone soon. The simple silver band with three tiny diamonds was my favorite thing.

An old Creedence Clearwater song, "Have You Ever Seen the Rain," came on the classic jukebox. In eighth grade Alix and I would come here on Sunday afternoons, when the place was empty, to drink cherry Cokes and sing along with our favorite songs. We'd put our quarter in, make our selection, and then perform for a room full of tables and chairs. Sometimes the owner, Mr. Ladd, would come out and watch us. I'd get shy then, but not Alix. She's a ham, that girl.

The place buzzed with activity as I slipped the ring back on my finger and checked my phone for the twentieth time.

A group of kids sat at a large table with a pile of gifts in the middle and a big sheet cake. Balloons were tied to every chair. Family after family strode through the door, the moms' faces all aglow because they'd been given the night off from cooking.

I thought of my mom going out to dinner with Dean tonight. He hadn't told her about being laid off yet. He'd planned to do it this evening. When he told her about my paycheck, a small part of me wanted to believe she'd tell him I could keep my money. Logically, I knew that was about as unlikely as Dean making his own dinner. It wasn't that my mom didn't love me. She did, in her own way. But Dean was her savior and what he said was law. If he told her they needed my money, then it must be true.

I checked my phone again. Ten minutes late. What kind of guy makes a girl wait for him, especially on their first date? I should have gotten his phone number. I started to text Alix when Nathan slid into the seat across from me.

He smiled at me and it was like someone had opened the blinds and let in the sunshine. "Hey, beautiful. Good to see you."

I didn't know whether to laugh or cringe. "I was beginning to think you'd stood me up."

He reached across the table and took my hand. "Nah. I'd never do that to you. It'd be a crime to leave a gorgeous girl like you alone."

I sat there, speechless, because what was I supposed to say to that?

"I should order our pizza. Combination okay with you?" Nathan asked.

"Um, no onions. Please. I can't stand onions. Just the smell of them makes me nauseous."

He smiled again. His voice came out smooth and soft, "You can just pick off what you don't want, how's that?"

I started to reply, but I didn't get a chance. He was already on his way to the counter. He was probably right, though. I could pick them off.

When he came back, Nathan brought drinks. I took a couple sips of the one he set in front of me. Diet Coke. Blech.

"Most girls I know drink Diet. Figured you probably do too, since, you know . . ."

"What?" I asked, puzzled how someone could assume something like that. I took another sip out of nervousness.

"Because," he said, leaning back in his seat, "you're pretty damn hot."

I choked, literally started choking. He laughed. "You okay? Do I need to do CPR?"

My hand went to my chest as I somehow managed to compose myself. "I'm fine. It's just—I'm not used to all the compliments. How about we talk about something else?"

He leaned forward, his eyes trying to seduce mine. "They're all true, you know. Everything I've said about you. I feel like I've won the lottery. A million dollar lottery."

Now I laughed. I couldn't help it. I held my hand out like a crossing guard trying to protect innocent children from being run over. "Nathan, seriously. Stop it!"

He leaned back, a slight grin on his face. "Okay. Fine. I'll stop. But how will I know when it's okay to start up again? Will you give me a signal or something?"

"How about when you find a Foo Fighters song that you can sing to me?"

He put his hands to his chest, like someone had just stabbed him. The idea clearly pained him. "No. No way. Impossible." He raised one of his eyebrows, looking a little bit sinister. "Wait. I've got it. After you kiss me, anything goes. How's that?"

"Well, that'll probably be a—"

Before I could get the rest of the words out, he leaned across the table, took my head in his hands, and pulled me to him.

The kiss was fast. Race-car fast. But he was smooth. Like he knew what he wanted and nothing was going to get in his way. It was incredibly flattering.

Was it a good kiss? It was too quick to tell. But it was my first *real* kiss. And the way he looked at me? The way he held my hand across the table afterward? The way he made me laugh as he got up and did a jig to get the pizza when they called our number?

I couldn't help but hope more kisses were in my future.

a little unreal

AS I PICKED THE ONIONS OFF MY PIZZA, HE ASKED ME, "SO WHY the fiery hot passion for the Foo Fighters?"

I figured there was no harm in telling him the story. Absentee parents seemed to have become as common as pesky dandelions. Besides, I didn't feel ashamed or embarrassed about my dad the way I did about my mom or Dean. Talking about him seemed a little bit like talking about a movie star I admired from afar.

"I never knew my dad. He left before I was born, and my mom hated talking about him. So she never did. Whenever I asked, she simply told me he left us and I was better off without him.

"One day five or six years ago, I was helping my mom put away groceries and she was barking orders at me. My grandma had recently died, which meant my mom was the only family

I had left. I found myself thinking about my dad a lot—wondering what my life would have been like if he'd stuck around. And I don't know why, but I suddenly had this strong desire to know something about him. Anything.

"So I held out the box of doughnuts she'd just bought and I asked her, 'Did my dad love doughnuts as much as I do?' Mom looked at me like I'd gone insane. Probably because my question came out of nowhere. But I didn't let up. I begged her to tell me something about him."

Nathan put his piece of pizza down and wiped his mouth with his napkin. "Seems kind of cruel to have never told you anything about him. Why would she do that?"

I didn't want this to be about her. Talking about my dad was one thing, talking about my mother, and her pathetic parenting skills, was a different thing entirely. I treaded carefully. "I don't think they went out, if you can even call it that, very long. A relationship based on lust, if you will. I think, in her mind, it was just easier to write him off. Pretend he never existed.

"So, back to the original question. After lots of begging, Mom told me three things about my dad." I ticked them off on my fingers as I went through the list. "His nickname was Buzz. His favorite movie at the time was *Clerks*. And he was a huge fan of Nirvana. Specifically, Dave Grohl, the drummer. So Dave kind of became my obsession. He's the lead singer for the Foo Fighters now."

Nathan picked up another piece of pizza. "So his favorite

musician became yours too? That's . . . different. I don't like anything my dad likes. I don't even like the way he makes cereal."

I took a bite of my pizza. Despite my efforts, the taste and smell of onions lingered. I wanted to spit it out, but I made myself chew. "In a way, when I listen to their music, I feel close to my dad. It's the only thing I can share with him, you know?"

Nathan stared at me intently. I felt my cheeks get warm. "I know," I said, looking down at my lap. "It's weird."

He reached over, cupped my chin in his hand, and lifted my face until our eyes met. I felt that electric buzz again. "Actually, it's really sweet." After a few seconds he let go and picked up his soda. "And I think you should check out my favorite band, Blue October. That way, when I'm not with you, they'll remind you of me."

I smiled. "Okay. I will."

He pointed to my pizza. "Hey. You're not eating. So, eat already. Because I sure as hell can't eat this whole thing by myself."

"I can still taste the onions. Sorry." I pulled the crust off and took a bite to make him happy. He didn't say anything. It felt like he should, though I wasn't sure what. "Anyway, I feel like I've done all the talking. What about you? What do you like to do besides play baseball?"

"You mean there's life beyond baseball?" he teased.

"I think so. Isn't there?"

He scooted out of his seat. "I have to use the restroom. I'll be right back."

And just like that, he was gone. It was kind of weird. Maybe I was getting too personal for a first date.

I checked my phone. Alix had texted me: HOW'S IT GOING?

I replied back: IDK, I'M NOT GOOD W/GUYS.

Her response: YOU ARE SO! TOO SOON TO GIVE UP K?

When Nathan returned, he stood at the table and pulled out a pack of gum. He offered me a piece. "You ready to go?"

That's it? Date over? I figured I'd messed up big-time. I'd talked too much and, in the process, scared him away. It was probably for the best, although a small part of me felt disappointed. Maybe with more time, we could have smoothed out the awkward bumps between us.

"Oh. Sure." I stood up, not sure of the protocol in this situation. "Uh, thanks for the pizza. I guess I'll see you—"

"No, no." He shook his head and smiled. "I'm not ready to let you go home yet. I thought maybe we could drive around and you could show me the town."

I looked outside. "In the dark?"

He leaned in and whispered in my ear. "Yes. Just the way I like it."

I don't think I'd ever felt such a roller coaster of emotions. One minute he left me breathless, the next I wanted to dump the disgusting diet soda all over him. Did he do it on purpose, because he liked to keep me guessing? Or was he a self-absorbed jerk and clueless about how to treat a girl? Or maybe he was a bundle of nerves, like me, and actually had no clue what he was doing.

I decided to assume the latter. After all, he *had* just moved here. Starting over, making friends, figuring out where to fit in—all of that had to be difficult.

He took my hand and led me through the parking lot to his fancy red VW Jetta with New York plates. So that's where he was from. I hadn't even asked him and I realized I should have.

We drove around Crestfield, and I pointed out places as we drove past. Like the park where I used to play when I was little. The library where I get most of the books I read. The middle school where Alix and I met. The flower shop where I work.

When we approached the cemetery, I told him my grandma was buried there. He turned and drove in.

"Are you hoping to scare me?" I asked.

"Rae, I'd never do something like that." I felt his hand on my thigh. "You're safe with me. I promise."

Maybe it was supposed to make me feel better, but it actually caused the nerves I'd forced down earlier to come rushing back. If he wasn't trying to scare me, what were we doing in a dark, secluded cemetery?

He followed the road that wound through the place until he eventually pulled over onto the side of a narrow lane. After he parked, he turned the engine off but kept the radio on.

Thank goodness for the dashboard lights and the soft glow from the moon, or it would have been pitch-black.

"Nathan, I don't know . . ."

"Don't tell me you don't kiss on the first date, Rae. You wouldn't do that to a guy, would you? Besides, we already did, remember? It's done and out of the way." He kissed my neck. Nibbled on my ear. His warm breath gave me goose bumps. Everywhere.

"There's nothing to worry about," he whispered. "Okay?"

Then, as his fingers combed through my hair, his lips were on mine. Soft. Warm. Nice. He tasted good. Sweet, like Coke and bubble gum.

And so it went. Music playing. Us kissing. My heart beating wildly. Every once in a while, he'd tell me how beautiful I was. The most beautiful girl he'd ever known, he said once.

I couldn't believe it was happening. A guy actually liked me. Everything else that had happened between us faded away, and all that remained was the warmth and attraction. Kissing him was like nothing I'd ever felt before. I felt alive and special. Extraordinary, even. And that feeling, it was something I wanted to wrap around myself, like a soft shawl, and wear forever.

Finally, totally out of breath, and not sure how much longer it could go on before clothes started coming off, something I definitely wasn't doing on a first date, I managed to find my voice.

"I should, uh, get home," I said. I stroked his cheek, liking how the stubble felt on my hand. He was so incredibly good looking.

He twirled a lock of my hair around his finger, seeming to be fascinated with it. "What if I don't want you to go?"

I smiled. "I think you're supposed to push those feelings down, be the gentleman I know you can be, and take me to my car anyway."

His hands dropped to his lap and he leaned back into the leather seat with a big sigh. "Yeah. But that's no fun."

"No. But I really should go," I said softly. "I'm sorry."

He nodded and started the car. We didn't say anything on the ride back. I could feel the attraction between us lingering, could almost see it, shimmering, in the darkness. I didn't want to lose it, but I wondered, would it still look the same, feel the same, tomorrow in the daylight?

When we pulled into the Mushroom's parking lot, I felt butterflies in my stomach. What came next? I wasn't sure, except that I somehow had to get out of his car and into my own. And I should probably say something before I did that.

"Thanks. That was . . . fun."

He leaned in and kissed me. "Yeah. It was. Can I call you later?"

"Uh, okay. Sure."

We pulled out our phones and exchanged numbers. As I was keying his in, he said, "You're going to delete any other guys you have in there, right?"

"Sorry, what was that?" I asked.

"Any other guys. Their numbers. You'll delete them?"

I shook my head, still not entirely clear I was following him. "There, uh, aren't any other guys. I mean, no one—"

He chuckled. "Okay, good. I wasn't sure. I mean, Santiago told me you were available, but . . . I never really asked you if there was anyone else. It's just, I think we're good together, you know?"

I was so confused about what all of this meant. Why would he ask me to delete people in my phone after one date? Did all guys do that? Maybe I was supposed to feel flattered that he wanted me all to himself.

He kissed me again, quickly, and said, "Good night, Rae. Thanks for a good time."

I got out of the car as I said, "Bye."

He waved and took off, while I stood there, both excited and terrified about what had just happened with Nathan Sharp.

really and truly

ALL THAT KISSING MADE ME HUNGRY. OF COURSE, THREE BITES of pizza isn't much of a dinner, either. Nathan called me as I was inhaling a peanut butter sandwich. I let it go to voice mail because I just wanted to eat and go to bed. When I played back the message, it said, "I was hoping to hear your voice one more time. Hopefully tomorrow. Sweet dreams, Rae."

I went to bed feeling dazed and confused.

On Sunday, Nathan called me three times. The first time, we didn't say a whole lot, and it was pretty awkward. I hung up worried that last night's magic had been lost forever. He must have been worried too, because he called back a little while later and asked me questions about English. He also had Ms. Bloodsaw for a teacher, though in a different period. The conversation went much better that time. The third time he called, he spent twenty minutes telling me about his old school and all the friends he'd left behind and missed.

"Why don't you call a couple of them and say hey?" I asked him. "They'd probably love to hear from you."

"No," he said firmly. "I'm not gonna do that. People move away. Things change. Life goes on. I'm making a new life here. A good one. A better one." He lowered his voice. "Mostly thanks to you."

It sounded so strange—like we'd been going out for weeks, not for a day. I didn't know how to respond, so I changed the subject and we talked about Blue October. I'd listened to a few of their songs earlier, and although I could tell they'd never be my favorite, they were all right. He thanked me a bunch of times for listening, and I knew it made him happy that I'd taken the time to check them out.

Finally, he said he should go, since he needed to help his mom with something. Maybe I shouldn't have felt relieved, but I kind of did.

We hung up, and I went to the kitchen to get some food. Mom and Dean were talking. I hadn't seen them yet, since they'd slept in, like they did most Sundays. I stopped at the edge of the hallway and peeked around the corner. They sat on the couch in the family room. Mom had her arms around Dean, whose back was toward me. She was using what I call her quiet-the-baby voice. I hadn't heard it since the morning we got the news that Grandma had died. When Mom told me that Grandma had slipped away during the night, her battle with the cancer finally over, I was devastated. I couldn't imagine what my life would be like without Grandma in it. So Mom held me in her arms, and tried to quiet me down. Just like she did with Dean now.

"Shhh, it'll be all right now, don't you worry, honey."

He sobbed as she rocked him ever so slightly back and forth. "I'm so sorry," he managed to get out.

"I know, Dean," she said. "You've already said that at least a half a dozen times. You need to pull yourself together and start looking for work. Tomorrow you'll get yourself to the unemployment office, and you'll find something real soon. I just know it."

They sat there, quietly, until he finally sat up, wiping his face with the back of his hands. He looked so small. Pathetic.

I continued on into the kitchen. Mom saw me and called out my name.

I peeked my head out. "Yeah?"

"Dean here, he feels real bad about losing his job. We need to make sure he knows we support him and believe in him. All right?"

"Sure," I said, heading back to the kitchen, where I could roll my eyes in private.

Their voices became whispers, and I felt like an intruder. I grabbed a couple of slices of cheese from the fridge along with a box of Wheat Thins and snuck back to my room, leaving them alone, the way they liked it best.

. . .

On Monday, Nathan was waiting for me by my locker. It took me by surprise. Even more surprising? He kissed me before I even had a chance to say hello.

"I missed you," he said, his eyes searching mine after I pulled away. What was he looking for? School wasn't really the place to see if we could make sparks fly again.

I went to work on my locker combination, trying to ignore the funny feeling in my stomach. "But we talked three times yesterday," I told him.

"You can't do this on the phone." He kissed my neck and then whispered in my ear, "Did you miss me?"

It tickled. I raised my shoulder to my ear, gently pushing him away. "Maybe." The truth was, I had thought about our evening together all day long. One minute I was sure we belonged together, and the next I wanted to send a cowardly text, telling him maybe we'd be better off as friends. Alix's voice kept playing in my head, though. *As soon as things start moving in that direction, you pull away.* I kept telling myself I needed to give it more time. It was too soon to know anything.

Once I had my locker open, Nathan spun me around and kissed me again. This time, slower. Softer. "You must have missed that," he whispered. "Right?"

He gently tucked a strand of hair behind my ear. Good thing I had the wall at my back, because the way he looked at me in that moment? I'm not sure my legs would have been able to hold me up.

Okay, so he was right. I *had* missed that.

After I grabbed my books, Nathan took my hand, weaving his fingers in with mine, and walked me down the hall toward the benches. It felt like every pair of eyes in Crestfield High was watching us. Girls smiled at us in that aren't-they-so-adorable way. And when I saw a couple of them whispering about "that hot, new guy" and *me*, any doubt I'd felt earlier slipped out the front doors. Being with Nathan suddenly felt as right as Grandma's ring on my finger.

Alix and Felicia could hardly contain their excitement. I watched as they squirmed in their seats, beaming at us.

When Santiago came up and slapped Nathan on the back, Nathan turned to greet him. The girls used that opportunity to pump their fists in the air and give each other a high five.

I leaned into Nathan and put my arm around him. He did the same. I had to admit, it felt really good to have someone to lean on like that. I felt safe. Cared for. And I didn't usually feel that way.

When the bell rang a few minutes later, he kissed me good-bye. "See you at lunch?"

I nodded slightly. Felicia pushed me toward English class. "Bye," I said as I waved back at him.

"See you later, beautiful."

"Are you kidding me?" Felicia squealed. "One date and

you guys are holding hands at school and *kissing* good-bye first thing in the morning? That must have been some first date."

I tried to play it cool. "Yeah. I guess you could say that."

She laughed. "It's okay, Rae. You don't have to be modest. I'm proud of you. Seriously, you two make a *sweet* couple." She reached over and squeezed my arm. "I'm really happy for you."

"Thanks," I told her.

We took our seats and I felt myself relax. People were happy for us. We were good together. Everything was going to be okay. Nathan was just . . . enthusiastic. And I was inexperienced. We'd figure things out. Together.

Settling into my seat, I noticed a reminder on the board about the looming poetry deadline for the newspaper. I'd forgotten to look for something to submit. When Ms. Bloodsaw started lecturing on literary devices, I flipped through my poetry journal. I landed on one I'd written a few months back, and I loved how well it summarized the contrasts in my life. It reminded me, too, of how life is often a wide range of emotions, and I felt comforted in that knowledge. Of course a new relationship was going to be that way too.

I knew which poem I wanted to submit for the first issue.

The Colors of Me

by Anonymous

Black like the ace of spades
when you yell my name,
cussing in the next breath,
like I'm as dirty as the word.

Red like a painful sunburn,
lingering for days,
the anger never cooling
between you and me.

Gray like bits of gravel
as I walk along the path,
barefoot and alone,
my voice never heard.

Yellow like a baby chick
free from its confining shell,
when I'm busy at work,
surrounded by joy.

Pink like a rosebud
ready to bloom into greatness,
nurtured with tender care
when friends are near.

White like a cloud,
flying free, lined with hope,
drifting and dreaming
of a life without darkness.

the hospital—4:08 p.m.

I can't turn off the memories.

They just keep coming, one after the other after the other. Is this what it means to have your life flash before your eyes?

"Her mother is on her way. Should be here soon."

When I wrote that poem, the contrast in my life was so clear. Some parts were dark and dreary, while other parts were bright and colorful.

The dark and the light.

It used to be they were always separate.

"Good. We're almost ready to take her up."

When did the darkness sneak into the light?

It happened so slowly, I didn't even notice.

I was on my cloud, drifting and dreaming.

Drifting and dreaming.

Drifting and dreaming.

Kind of like . . . now.

five months earlier

not quite the happiest place on earth

NATHAN'S HAND CREPT UNDER MY SWEATER, UP MY STOMACH, and into my bra. His mouth pressed on mine, impatient, as he laid me down on his bed.

I turned my head and pushed his body away from mine, sitting back up. "No, Nathan, stop. Please."

He caressed my cheek. "Rae, come on. It'd be so good."

When he leaned in for more kisses, I answered with a quick one and gently pushed him away again. "I'm not ready. How many times have I told you that?"

He looked at me like a sad kitten. "Rae, you are everything to me. You know that, right? I don't know what I'd do without you. Still, a guy can only make out for so long. It's not fair. Kissing might be enough for you, but it's not for me."

I sighed. I loved his kisses that tasted like bubble gum. Loved being in his arms, where I felt safe and cared for. He wanted me like no one had ever wanted me, and, yeah, it felt good to be wanted. But we hadn't been going out that long. I didn't want to be like my mom, always jumping into bed with the first guy who came along. I'd promised myself my first time would be with someone I loved.

And although I loved his kisses, I didn't think I loved Nathan.

I got up to go home. He grabbed my arm. "Rae, please, don't be mad." I shook my arm free and kept walking. "Wait. Where are you going?"

"Disneyland," I quipped. I glanced back and saw the hurt on his face. My heart softened. I didn't want to upset him. "The bathroom, okay?"

He moaned. "Who needs Disneyland? We could have all kinds of fun if you'd just let it happen."

In the bathroom, I patted my hair down and straightened my sweater. Maybe I should have just gone home after we'd met up for ice cream. As I licked my cone, he'd looked at me with such longing. He'd raised his eyebrows and whispered, "No one's home at my house. Want to come over?"

"Where are they?" I'd asked.

"Mom's out with a new friend. My dad's away on tour. At least that's what he said. He never tells us where he's at or what his schedule is or anything. Just calls us occasionally to say hi and to let us know that he's still alive. Like I even care."

"Nathan." I'd lightly slapped his arm. "Of course you care. He's your dad."

He'd laughed. Actually laughed. "I'm sorry to break it to you, but Gary Sharp is not a nice guy. He doesn't give a shit about anyone else but himself. It's hard to care about someone like that."

I thought of Dean. Of my mom, at times. Of course he was right, and I knew better than anyone what he was talking about. It *was* hard to care about someone like that. Still, whenever his dad came up, I saw sadness in his eyes. I could tell he tried to push it down and bury it. But I saw it, peeking out, like the first signs of spring.

"Does that bother your mom?" I'd asked.

"I think so. I mean, she'd never say it does. But how could it not?"

"So why does she stay with him?"

He'd chuckled, playing with his cone wrapper. "And do what if she left? She's never worked a day in her life. No, she'll never leave. She knows she's nothing without him."

After that he'd begged me to go home with him. And because I'd felt sorry for him, I said yes. Besides, I'd figured it'd be a nice change of pace to make out somewhere other than the cemetery.

But lately we always seemed to end up fighting, because he wanted more than I did. The attraction between us was strong, no doubt about it. I loved the way everything faded around us when we were together, until there was nothing but me and him and the moment. Why couldn't the closeness we shared be enough for him?

Sometimes I wondered if Nathan and I were really a good match. We often struggled to find things to talk about. So he'd fill the awkward moments with kissing. That was what we did best.

When I'd talked to Alix about my concerns, she'd said I was crazy. Everyone adored Nathan. It seemed like I should too.

I took a deep breath and went back to Nathan's room. He stood at the window, looking outside.

"I'm ready to go," I said as I looked around, searching for my purse. "Your mom will probably be home soon anyway."

"Nah. When she goes out, she stays out late." He came over and pulled me to him. "I'm telling ya, it's the perfect opportunity, right here." He kissed my neck in the spot below my ear that makes me quiver. It felt like a last-ditch effort to get me to change my mind and fall into bed with him.

I untangled myself from his arms. "Stop it. I can't believe how persistent you are. Maybe this isn't working, Nathan. Maybe I'm not the right girl for you, if that's all you want."

His mouth dropped open. "What? What do you mean?"

I crossed my arms and looked at the floor, to avoid his eyes. "I'm tired of saying no all the time. What I mean is, I'm tired of you asking all the time. I'm not ready." My eyes met his, and I saw something that looked like fear. "I'm tired of every date ending like this. That stuff you told me about your dad? That's the first *real* thing you've told me. I feel like I don't know you, Nathan. Like we talk, but not really. It's all just . . . noise. A means to an end for you."

He shook his head, his eyes pleading with me now. "No. No, that's not true. I love hanging out with you, being with you, and not just in a physical way." He came closer. "Please, Rae. You gotta believe me. We're good together. Maybe I'm pushing you a little too hard, but I'm a guy. You can't condemn me for that."

Before I could respond, he kissed me. His solution to everything, it seemed. But I was tired of doing what he wanted simply because I didn't want to upset him.

What I wanted to do in that moment was leave. And that's exactly what I did.

WHO AM I?

I'm the girl
keeping secrets,
bottled up tight.

The girl
with the parents
who yell day and night.

The girl
who's never been
quite good enough.

The girl
crying inside
but acting all tough.

But something strange happens
when I'm with you.
I forget who that girl is,
because what do you do?

You tell me sweet things
that I've never heard.
Suddenly "beautiful"
is more than a word.

When we walk down the hall,
holding hands, you and me,
I'm the cute guy's girlfriend,

the one
other girls
wish they could be.

a way with words

TUESDAY MORNING, AND I WAS RUNNING LATE. AGAIN. I CRAMMED my books along with my poetry journal into my backpack and hustled out to the kitchen. I grabbed the last banana out of the fruit bowl.

"Yesterday was the fifteenth, Rae."

I hadn't heard him coming, so it startled me. I spun around. Dean stood there wearing one of his flattering wife-beater T-shirts and a pair of boxer shorts.

"I don't do business with people who aren't wearing pants," I said, disgusted by his greediness more than his appearance.

"Give me the damn check," he barked. "You were asleep when I got home last night, so I didn't bug you for it then. Next time I might not be so considerate."

Considerate? What a joke. "Where were you anyway? I made dinner for you and you never showed."

"None of your business."

I reached into my backpack and pulled out my wallet along with a pen. He watched as I signed my paycheck over to him. It was the second one since our little "agreement."

"Where's my share?"

He snatched the check from my hand and dropped the bills he'd been holding onto the floor. I picked them up as he retreated back to his bedroom.

"Forty bucks?" I yelled. "Are you kidding me? How am I supposed to pay my insurance? This will barely pay for my gas!"

I wanted to jump on him. Slam him into the wall. But I knew even yelling at him could make things worse. Last time he'd given me a hundred, and I'd objected, loudly, since my checks are usually around three hundred. He'd told me I better watch it, because I was lucky to be getting any at all.

"Dean, come on," I said, with all the sweetness I could muster as I chased after him. "Please? Can't I have forty more? Or even twenty?"

He glared at me. "You want to eat or not? Now get your ass to school."

I gathered my stuff and trudged to my truck. Something told me it was going to be a long day.

At school Nathan met me at my locker, like he had every morning for the past few weeks. I'd get my stuff for my morning classes, then we'd walk to the benches together. When I eyed him standing there like our disagreement the night before had never happened, I found myself wishing for the days I didn't have a boyfriend to worry about on top of everything else.

"I'm kind of surprised to see you," I said. "Thought you might want a little space today."

He pulled me to him. "Please don't be upset with me. Please? Let's pretend it never happened. You came to my house and we played Scrabble. Wasn't it fun? Sorry I beat you, but I'm good with those triple word scores." His eyes searched mine for a trace of forgiveness, though he hadn't even apologized for how he'd behaved. Not really.

His finger traced my jaw. "It's so good to see you, beautiful." His blue eyes kissed me before his lips did. And then we were at it, doing what we did best.

Kissing.

More kissing.

And yes, more kissing.

When I pulled away, he whispered, "Everything's cool with us, right?"

I put my finger on that dimple I loved so much. "You have to back off trying to get me horizontal. Okay?"

"Whatever you say."

I wasn't quite convinced, but I could feel people's eyes on us as they walked by. I didn't want to talk about it anymore. Not here.

"You know, I have Saturday off," I said as I moved around

him to get to my locker. "Want to go to Portland? Maybe go to the art museum or something?"

He groaned and slumped against the wall. "The art museum? You're kidding, right?"

I stopped midspin and turned to him. "No, I'm not kidding. I thought it'd be fun. I want to get out of here. Have an adventure, you know?"

"An art museum is not an adventure, Rae. It's more like a prison sentence. Maybe we could catch a college game or something. That'd be fun."

Typical Nathan. I grabbed my books and slammed the door closed. Suddenly, I didn't want to spend my day off with him.

I pretended to be sad. "Oh, you know what? I just remembered, I promised Alix we'd go shopping. Sorry. Maybe you and Santiago can go to a game."

As we walked, holding hands, girls stopped what they were doing and stared at us. Would it ever stop? We should have been old news. Although maybe his good looks would never get old.

When we got to the benches, a few guys leaning against the wall called out to Nathan, and he headed over to say hi. I sat down next to Alix and whispered in her ear, "I told Nathan we have plans on Saturday. So, can we do something?"

She gave me a concerned look. "Sure. What's going on?"

I mouthed, "Later."

Felicia sat next to Alix, reading a newspaper. "Hi, Felicia," I said.

She looked up and smiled. "Hey. How's it going?"

"Fine. Is that the school paper, by chance?"

"Yeah. There's some over there in the rack."

I jumped up, snagged one, and came back to my seat. I thumbed through the paper until I found the pull-out section. They'd titled it "Poetry Matters." Alix looked over my shoulder.

After a minute she pointed at one and laughed. "Oh my God. Michael Montgomery. I'm pretty sure he's the only guy in the school who would feel compelled to write a poem comparing boxer shorts to tighty whities."

I chuckled and kept reading. Some were good. Some, not so much.

Alix pointed to my poem. "What's the deal with anonymous? Everyone else included a name. Embarrassed, maybe?"

I blinked, trying not to show my surprise at her pointing to my poem. "Maybe. Who knows?"

"It's pretty good," Alix said. "Sad, though."

Felicia looked up from reading. "Rae, how come you didn't submit a poem? Didn't you tell me once you love writing poetry?"

"Yeah. I do. It's just . . . Robert Frost I am not." I elbowed Alix, wanting to turn the attention away from myself. "What about you? You should write about that Mustang you've been working on."

She sat up straight and smiled. "Hey. Maybe I will. I mean, if Michael Montgomery can do it—"

"Anyone can do it," we said at the same time, then laughed.

The bell rang, so I let Nathan kiss me good-bye before Felicia and I scurried off to English.

Felicia motioned to the board as we took our seats. "Deadline for the next issue is coming up. You should write something, Rae."

"I don't know. Between work and school and Nathan, I don't have any time."

"You could use something you've already written. You must have some, right?"

Thankfully, I didn't get a chance to respond. The bell rang and Ms. Bloodsaw started talking. My friends didn't really know about my poetry journals. I was afraid if they knew, they'd want to read some of the stuff. And that was the problem—most everything I wrote was just too personal to share. Maybe other people could write about underwear or trees or their dog, but to me it was like, what's the point? It should matter. It should say something. Mean something.

With class well underway, I slipped out my poetry journal and paged through it. I stopped when I landed on one I'd rewritten a few months ago, after I'd found it in one of my earlier journals. I'd do that sometimes—find one that needed work, pull it out, and spend time searching for better words. I loved getting lost in the process of revision. Maybe lots of things in my life were out of my control, but when it came to my words, I had all the authority.

I'd written the first draft soon after we'd moved in with Dean. What was I? Twelve? I remembered how I had felt when I'd written it. My illusions of what "a new man" and "we're getting married" meant shattered like a broken window. I'd believed my mom when she told me our life would be so much better with Dean around. Not only did I believe her, I'd let myself imagine a happy family, like I used to dream about as a little girl.

For the girl who had longed for just a little happiness at home and never got it, I chose that poem.

In My Imagination

by Anonymous

Most kids imagine
castles and dragons
and knights wielding swords.
Or fairies with pixie dust,
making wishes come true.

Not me.

I liked to imagine
one happy family,
taking trips to the zoo.
Packing lunch in a basket
for a day at the park.

Happy me.

I can hardly believe
how different life is
from those childhood dreams.
No zoo trips, no picnics,
just harsh words and spite.

Disappointed me.

Alone in my room,
I feel trapped,
and forgotten.
What I'd give for a fairy tale
and wishes come true.

Why me?

So I'll imagine
my real dad, a knight,
riding up on a horse,
with lunch in a basket
and me in his heart.

Rescue me.

it's personal

SCARLETT WAS SITTING ON THE WHITE BENCH IN FRONT OF
Cutting Edge when I arrived for work after school. I admired
her darling red-and-white vintage dress. Scarlett's a genius
when it comes to thrift-store shopping. She took me shopping
with her one time and I learned so much about how to scour
the racks for the best finds.

"Rae!" she said in her raspy voice. "Haven't seen you in a
while. You staying out of trouble?"

"I'm trying, Scarlett. I swear, I'm trying."

She took a long drag of her cigarette, then blew it out and
smiled. "Good girl."

"What about you?"

"I have a cut and color in a couple of minutes with Mrs.
LaBlanc. I'm telling you what, I could hardly sleep last night

because I was so damned excited to hear all about her hip replacement surgery."

I laughed. "You love your clients and you know it." I motioned toward Mack's. "I'm gonna get myself a tea before I head to work. You want anything?"

She raised her coffee mug. "I'm good, sweetie, thanks for asking. Have a nice afternoon, okay?"

"You too."

My stomach growled as I opened the door to Mack's. I hadn't eaten lunch. I told my rumbling stomach to shut up. Only three hours until dinner. I could wait.

Mack's Bean Shack is a cute coffee shop with regular tables in the center of the café and big, comfy chairs along the walls. It's an inviting place and does good business, but the place was empty that afternoon. Leo stood behind the counter, his back to the front door, as he ground beans. The strong smell made me blink a few times. I definitely prefer the sweet smell of flowers to the pungent aroma of coffee.

When he turned the noisy grinder off, I said, "Hey, Leo."

He startled, but smiled when he saw me. "Rae! How you been? You want your usual?"

"Yes, please. And I'm okay. Busy with school."

He grabbed a cup and started filling it with hot water. "I'm glad you came in. I brought a book I think you might like. Have you read *Through the Wilderness*?"

"No. What's it about?"

He rummaged around in the basket of tea bags until he found my favorite, green tea with jasmine. I do love flora, even in my tea. "It's about this sixteen-year-old kid who travels back in time," he explained, "and ends up riding for the Pony Express. The writing is unbelievably good."

"Hmmm. Okay. I'll have to check it out." I pulled the newspaper and a couple of books out of my backpack as I searched for my wallet. Leo slid the mug of hot water and the tea bag over to me.

"Don't worry about it, Rae. I've got it covered."

"Thanks, Leo."

He snatched up the school paper. "Hey, can I read this?"

"Sure. Take it home, if you want. I can pick up another copy for myself tomorrow. You worried you're missing out on some top-notch journalism or something?"

I put the tea bag in my mug. Leo tucked the newspaper under his arm as he went to the glass case and pulled out two oatmeal chocolate chip cookies, another of my favorites. Clearly, Leo was my snack-time hero.

"I just like reading it. For a few minutes I can pretend I'm a regular kid going to high school like everyone else." He walked around the counter and came over to where I stood, then handed me one of the cookies. "Take a seat and I'll get that book for you."

I sat at one of the tables in the middle of the café. When he came back, I had only one bite of my cookie left.

"You were hungry." It was a statement, not a question, but I nodded anyway. He sat down and pushed his cookie, along with the book, toward me. "You can have mine. I'm kind of sick of them anyway."

Yep. Hero. "Thanks again. For the tea. The cookies. The book." I sighed. "You're like the sweet whipped cream alongside the dry, burnt cake."

He chuckled. For the first time I noticed a dimple on the left side of his face. I loved his smile, how had I missed his dimple?

"Rough week?"

I blew on my tea then took a sip. "Understatement. But I don't really want to talk about it. What about you? What are you doing for fun these days? Besides sneaking into bars with older women?"

Leo flipped open the newspaper, his eyes skimming the headlines. "Right. Besides that." He looked up at me, his eyebrows raised. "You really want to know?"

I smiled. "I don't know. Do I?"

He turned the pages of the newspaper again, stopping at "Poetry Matters." "It might sound weird, but I love making crazy videos. I go outside, down the street where there's a patch of woods, or to a park, or anywhere, really, and I'll shoot random things. Then I edit the clips into one piece, set it to music, and upload it."

"Do you have a channel?" I asked.

"Yeah."

"I'd love to check it out."

"Nah. I think, for now, I want to remain anonymous." He looked at me. "I mean, no offense. It's just—"

"It's okay. I get it. It's personal. Kind of like your diary or something."

"Yeah. In a way." His eyes returned to the paper. I could tell he was reading one of the poems.

I don't know why I did it. Did I hope he'd confide in me if I confided in him? Or did I want someone to know pieces of the hidden truth? I'm not sure. Leo just had a down-to-earth quality that made me feel like I'd known him forever. If I was going to hand my trust over to someone on a silver platter, something told me Leo would not only accept it, he'd take care of it.

I reached over and pointed to my poem. "I'm actually quite familiar with wanting to be anonymous."

He followed my finger. Then I sat back, picked up the second cookie, and let him read.

When he finished, he looked at me. The expression on his face wasn't one of pity or disgust, which I half expected, even from someone as kind as Leo. Instead, he looked at me in a way that simply said, *I hear you.*

"It's really good," he said.

I felt my cheeks get warm and suddenly I felt very shy. I'd just let someone into my life as well as my writing, neither of which I did much, if at all. "Thanks," was all I could manage to say.

"Does it help? Getting the words out like that?"

I set the remainder of the cookie down, staring at it, afraid of the vulnerability I felt. "Yeah. It does. I have journals filled with them, so that tells you how screwed up my life is."

I meant it to be kind of funny, but it didn't come out that way.

"Rae, if you ever want to talk—"

I let out a little nervous laugh, suddenly kicking myself for thinking it was a good idea to show him that poem. "No, I'm fine, really." I stood up and tossed the book into my backpack. "I should get to work. Nina's probably wondering where I am."

He stood up too. "Oh. Right. Well, let me know what you think of the book, okay?"

"I will." I looked at him before I turned to leave. I wanted to say something. Let him know how much it meant that he'd said just the right things. But all I could say was, "Thanks again."

His warm smile reassured me that I didn't need to say anything else. "Anytime."

How come I never noticed that dimple before?

desperate

"WHAT ARE YOU DOING HERE?" I ASKED.

Nathan got up from the bench where I'd seen Scarlett ten minutes earlier and stormed toward me. "Who is he?"

"What? Who?"

He grabbed my arm and pulled me past the front door and window of the Bean Shack. Before I knew what was happening, Nathan had me pinned against the wall, his face inches from mine.

"I saw you," he hissed. "With that guy in there. You think I wouldn't find out?"

I tried to shake free. "Nathan, stop it. What is wrong with you?"

"Tell me who he is."

"He's a friend. That's all. I went in there to get a tea. He works there, and business was slow, so he sat and talked with me for a few minutes."

Nathan didn't say anything. He just stared at me, like he was trying to figure out if he should believe me or not.

"Look, you'd better let go of me before I knee you where it hurts." He slowly loosened his grip. As he did, I shook him off and took a few steps away, grabbing my backpack, which I'd dropped in the scuffle. His face changed at the realization of what he'd done. He looked like a lost little boy. Sad. Confused.

"Damn it. Rae. Are you okay?" He took a step toward me.

I held out my hand for him to stop. "Don't come near me. You need to go. Now."

"Let me explain first, okay?" He looked like he was going to cry. He took another small step toward me. "I really needed to see you. It's my dad. I saw him with another woman on my way home. He kissed her, and then he helped her into a car. I'd always suspected that he's been lying to us. But it made me sick, seeing it, you know? I didn't know what to do. Where to go. So I came to find you. Your truck was in the parking lot, so I knew, when you weren't at work, you had to be around here somewhere. I looked through the café window and when I saw you, I freaked. It was like seeing my dad all over again."

Nathan put his face into his hands. His shoulders shook as he let out the quiet sobs. I took a deep breath. The guy was obviously not himself. Hesitantly, I went to him. He pulled me to him and wrapped his arms around me. He cried into my neck.

When his sobs finally subsided, he pleaded, "Please don't be mad at me. Please. I need you, Rae. You're the only good thing in my life."

"Nathan, I—I don't know." I pulled away, thinking back to when I first spotted him sitting on that bench, waiting for me. I should have been happy to see him. He was my boyfriend, after all. But that's not what I'd felt. I'd felt smothered. And now, after what he'd done? Yes, he was hurting, but that didn't mean he had the right to take it out on me.

"I have to go to work, okay? I'm late."

He wiped at his cheeks. "Can't you call in sick? I don't want to be alone right now."

I shook my head.

He started pacing, waving his arms around. "If you don't give a shit about me, like everyone else, what's the point, Rae? Huh? Why should I keep trying? What is there to live for, then?"

I felt like I was inside some kind of horrible nightmare. What was I supposed to do? He was obviously in a lot of pain, but he might be playing it up now, just to get his way. On the other hand, if I left him alone and something awful happened, to him or to someone else, I'd never forgive myself.

"All right. Go wait in your car. I'll talk to Nina. I'll tell her I have a family emergency or something."

He bent down to kiss me. I moved my face so his lips

landed on my cheek. I wasn't in the mood. "Thanks, beauti-ful," he whispered. "Thank you so much."

Because I have the most awesome boss in the world, Nina didn't even blink when I asked if I could have the afternoon off because of a family emergency. She told me to go and said, "If I can do anything to help, you let me know, okay?"

As I walked to the parking lot, I thought about Nathan and his dad. I certainly understood messed-up parents. But I didn't know what to say or do to make Nathan feel better. I racked my brain. Where could I take him? What did he need right now to help him feel better? I thought of the one thing he loved more than anything: baseball. I decided it was worth a shot.

I found Nathan leaning against the hood of my truck. His face was blotchy and red. He rushed to greet me, but I held my arm out again. He stopped. I wrapped my arms across my chest and looked at him. This was my boyfriend. I should have felt sympathy, and all I felt was anger. Lots and lots of anger.

"You know, you never apologized. For what happened back there."

"I didn't?"

"No. You didn't. And let's get one thing straight. That will never happen again. I'm not your father. And I'm not anyone from your past who may have hurt you. It's not fair to assume the worst. I don't deserve that."

His blue eyes looked dull. Their normal sparkle had com-pletely vanished. "I'm sorry," he whispered.

I think it was the first time I'd ever heard Nathan say those words. I wondered, was that because he didn't hear them at home? Neither did I, but it made me understand their power even more. With Nathan, it seemed like they simply didn't matter.

"Please believe me," he said. "I'll make it up to you. I promise."

I forced myself to let the anger go as I gave him a hug. "Come on. I'm going to take you someplace fun."

On the way to the batting cages, I drove and he talked. He said he'd had a hunch that the reason they'd moved to Crestfield was because of another woman.

"Even though I suspected an ulterior motive, a part of me didn't want to believe it. I wanted this to be a fresh start. I let myself imagine he'd be home more. Doing family stuff again. Maybe he and I would do things together like we used to, before he became so famous."

As he talked, I realized how much he sounded like me. Yeah, Nathan had a lot more money than I did. He had a beautiful home, with a mom and a dad who were married. But beyond that, what we felt inside, what we longed for from our families—it was the same.

The difference was, I'd found things to do with those feelings. I let them out through my poetry. And I'd promised myself to be different from my mom and Dean.

I thought of my grandma and one of her favorite sayings.

The first time I heard it, I was staying the night at her house when the electricity went out. Together, we lit candle after candle throughout the house until warm light embraced us and I didn't feel scared anymore.

She told me that night, and again many times later, "Where light shines, darkness disappears." As I got older, she explained to me that in life, all kinds of darkness exists, and we can create light in more ways than simply lighting candles.

I looked at Nathan. I don't think he'd ever learned that. And I couldn't help but wonder if maybe it might be too late.

wish i could be a cat

HITTING A BUNCH OF BASEBALLS SEEMED TO HELP. AT LEAST, I hoped it did. When Nathan's arms seemed to grow heavy and he started to miss more than connect, we left. The ride back to Full Bloom was peaceful and quiet, as he seemed to be lost in his own thoughts.

I pulled into the parking lot, next to his car. "So where will you go now?" I asked him.

He shrugged. "I'll go home. See my mom. Act like nothing's changed. Like my dad is out touring the country, promoting books, when he's right here in town, sleeping with another woman. I guess if my mother wants to live in a bubble, I will too."

"Doesn't she check online to see where he's at?"

He shook his head. "Not that I know of. Like I said, it's a bubble, Rae."

I couldn't help but wonder what would happen when that bubble popped.

I let Nathan give me a quick good-bye kiss, and then I went home. Dean was glued to the TV, watching his beloved wrestling. As I fried up the meat for a taco dinner, the phone rang. Dean answered, and I leaned in to listen.

"Oh, come on now, Bill. It's a sure thing. I should do three times that. In fact, maybe I will." He laughed. "Hell, yeah. Let's do it. No pain, no gain—isn't that what they say?"

Dean said something else I couldn't hear and then hung up. I tried to figure out what he meant by no pain, no gain. Was he going to start working out? He certainly had the time. I wanted to tell him he should be using that time to find a job, but I kept quiet.

When the tacos were done, he took his plate and went back to the family room and I took my plate to my room. I watched some YouTube videos on my laptop while I ate, and then I gave Alix a call.

"Hey," she said. "What's up?"

"I had the weirdest afternoon ever," I told her.

"At work? What happened?"

I leaned back against my bed. "No. Before work. Nathan came to the shop and saw me talking to my friend Leo, who works at the coffee shop next door, and he flipped out. I mean, seriously, Alix. It scared me."

"He wouldn't hurt you, though. You know that."

Did I? "You should have seen him. It was ridiculous. I mean, Leo and I, we were just talking."

"Stupid jealousy. Why do boys have to get like that?"

"Part of it is he's having trouble at home." I paused. "Alix, I think I want to break up with him. But I'm not sure he can handle it. He keeps saying stuff like he needs me and I'm all he has."

"Well, if he's having a hard time right now, he probably does need you. It's not very nice to kick the guy when he's down, you know?" She wasn't being mean, just honest. And I could tell by her tone she was concerned, for both of us.

I sighed. "I know. Still, it's not right. Nothing feels right with him anymore."

"Aw, Rae. That sucks. You guys are so cute together. Maybe things will get better. You never know. I'll bet he feels really bad."

Just then, my phone beeped with another call. It was Nathan.

"That's him," I said.

"See? He's probably calling to apologize again. Go talk to him. It'll be all right. I'll see you tomorrow, 'kay?"

She made it sound easy. Like another apology would solve everything, and with a snap of my fingers, I could forget what happened. But it was *so* not easy.

"Yeah. Bye, Alix."

I watched the phone buzz. Then I turned it off. Because as far as I was concerned, there wasn't anything left to say.

The next day I took a tardy, on purpose. Anything to avoid seeing Nathan.

While we worked on an in-class essay, Ms. Bloodsaw called me up to see her. I took a seat in a chair by her desk. I wasn't worried. She wasn't the type to get upset.

"What's your cat's name?" I asked, admiring the picture of her tabby with green eyes.

"Eddie," she said.

"He's beautiful. You should enter one of those contests they have. You know, where you submit a picture of you and your pet and the ones who look most alike win a huge prize."

She smiled. "I'll take that as a compliment."

"It is," I assured her.

"Do you have any pets, Rae?"

I shook my head.

"Eddie is a wonderful companion. He loves curling up on my lap while I read a good book." She chuckled. "He loves to sleep, that cat." And then her tone changed. I could see concern on her face. "Is everything all right in your world, Rae? Your poetry, it's amazing. Really. And I don't want to say anything that might keep you from submitting more in the future. But I also—well, I simply need to know you're okay."

Another teacher might have said something judgmental. Made me feel like a loser. But not Ms. Bloodsaw.

"I'm fine," I said softly. "I promise. The poetry? It helps."

She nodded and I could tell she understood. "Good. I think that's wonderful. Keep it up. And please, if there's anything I can do for you, don't hesitate to ask, okay?"

I looked at the picture of her cat again. She obviously loved Eddie a lot. Ms. Bloodsaw was a kind person, and I knew she really meant what she said. Of course, there wasn't anything she could do for me, but I wasn't going to tell her that. "Sure. Okay. And I'm sorry I was late today. I had something I needed to take care of."

"It's all right. I won't mark you tardy. I'm just glad everything's all right."

I stood up. "Thanks a lot."

When I got back to my desk, Felicia discreetly tossed me a note, then went back to her essay.

Trying not to make any noise, I opened the note carefully.

> Where were you this morning? Nathan was so
> worried about you. Like, frantic. It was really
> freaky. We tried to tell him that you probably
> just overslept, but he wouldn't have any of it.
> How come you didn't pick up your phone?

Nathan had called me four times and texted me five that morning. I didn't answer because I didn't want to talk to him.

You'd think he might catch a clue. I needed to figure out what to do about him.

I wrote back:

You're right. I overslept. Nathan needs to chill out.

But would he? That was the question.

I tried to avoid Nathan at lunchtime, but I had to go to my locker to get some books, and that's when he pounced on me.

"Finally, Rae," he said, coming up from behind and putting his arms around me. "I was worried about you."

His presence was like a weight around my neck. I felt myself slipping down into a place I didn't want to go.

I wriggled free. "Look, Nathan. I need to ask you a favor. I need you to give me some space, okay? I'm still a little freaked out about yesterday. I need some time to think things over."

"No," he said pitifully. "No, Rae, please."

I hugged my books to my chest and pushed myself to keep going. "Don't call me every five minutes. Don't come to my locker every chance you get. Don't show up unexpectedly at my work. I need some space," I pleaded. "Show me you can give me something I need for a change. Please?"

I could tell pushing him away tore him apart. But I didn't feel like I had any other choice.

Nathan was quiet. People walked by, staring at us. School was the absolute worst place to try to have a serious conversation.

"Okay," he said finally. "As long as it's temporary. If that's what you really want." He touched my arm. Begged me with his gorgeous blue eyes. "Please know how sorry I am. I want to make it up to you. Just let me know when you're ready, and I promise, I'll make it up to you."

Then he turned around and headed off down the hallway. A wave of relief washed over me. Until I remembered what he'd said.

As long as it's temporary.

that's a first

AT WORK AFTER SCHOOL, MISTER, SPENCER'S GOLDEN RETRIEVER, greeted me at the door, his tail wagging. Sweetest dog ever. The customers love him.

I leaned down to pet him and realized I felt lighter than I had in a while. It felt *so* good to be in the one place I could relax, surrounded by people (and a dog) I adored.

"Hey, boy," I said, stroking his silky soft head. "How ya doin'?"

"Our Rae of sunshine's here," Spencer announced. He was tallying credit card receipts at the front counter.

I admired the scarf hanging around his neck, full of rich autumn colors—burgundy, gold, and forest green. "Make this yourself?" I asked, reaching out and taking the tassels at the end of the scarf in my hand. "It's beautiful."

"Thank you. Just finished it last night. I had every intention of giving it to my sister for Christmas. But, Rae, I love it so much! I'm just too selfish, aren't I?"

"You are," I said, sliding behind the counter. "So make me one for Christmas and the universe will forgive you." I checked the box marked "deliveries." Nothing.

"Rae. Dinner with Hitler or Stalin?"

"Are you kidding?"

"Come on. You know you have to choose one. That's how the game works."

I don't remember exactly how it got started, but we play "This or That" on a semiregular basis, to entertain ourselves. I took a seat on the stool next to Spencer's. "Okay, Hitler. And I would serve hamburgers and french fries with a lovely side of arsenic."

Spencer laughed. I love his laugh. It's deep and hearty, which is kind of surprising since he's fairly petite. We have so much fun together, and he's one of my favorite people in the world.

"Snakes or spiders?" I asked him as a spider scurried across the counter. I grabbed his copy of *People* magazine, rolled it up, and . . . good-bye, spider.

"Oh, dear God. Please. Two of the most loathsome creatures on the planet."

As I put the magazine back in its spot, after wiping it with a tissue, I noticed an envelope with my name on it. "Oh, yeah," Spencer said. "Found that outside the door when I ran an errand for Nina earlier."

I ripped it open. "You didn't answer, Spencer. Spiders or snakes?"

He shuddered. "Fine. Snakes. Only because I love that scene with Indiana Jones and the snakes. He's adorable covered in fear, isn't he?"

I laughed. "That he is."

Inside the envelope was a note and some cash.

Please deliver a nice flower arrangement to
this address:

1925 Swiffer Street, Apt. 35D

The flowers are for Maddie. Sign the card
"From a Friend."

I knew that apartment complex. I knew it because I used to live there. A shiver ran down my spine.

"Spencer, have we ever gotten one of these before?"

He stopped what he was doing and took the note from me. "No, I don't think so. But you know what they say. There's a first time for everything."

"I want to show Nina."

In the workroom, Nina looked up from her bouquet. "Hon, I've been worried sick about you since yesterday. Is everything okay?"

"I think things are back to normal now. For the most

part. Thanks for giving me the afternoon off." I walked over and handed her the envelope. "Why would someone want to deliver flowers and not sign their name?"

She set a yellow rose down on the table. "I don't have the foggiest idea." She read the note, then said, "Well, I'm happy to take the business. If I make up a bouquet, would you leave a little early and deliver it on your way home?"

"Sure."

She gave me back the envelope. "Rae? What's wrong? You look worried."

"I'm not sure why my name is on the envelope. What do I have to do with this?"

Nina went back to the bouquet. "I don't know. But if you're concerned, I can have Spencer make the delivery."

"I think I'm supposed to do it, though. Why else would it have my name?"

"Well, there's no law that says you *have* to do it."

I read it again. What if it was Nathan, setting some kind of trap? Maybe he'd come up with some elaborate plan to freak me out so I'd go running back to him.

I tried to tell myself I was being paranoid. It didn't even look like his handwriting. It was a random act of kindness. Like when my grandma would pay for the person's order behind us in the drive-through line. I could still hear her voice as she told me that the road to happiness is paved with good deeds for others. That's all this was—a good deed.

"No, it's all right. I'll do it. Unless my horoscope says to avoid strange situations or something." I winked at her.

She smiled. "Nothing like that. Watch your wallet, though. It said finances could be a problem for you this month."

Wow. Right on the money. So to speak.

"Did it say what to do about it?" I asked, trying to sound casual.

Concern filled her eyes anyway. "You okay? Anything I can do? Besides give you a raise, which you know I'd do if I could."

"I've just had some unexpected expenses, that's all. It'll be okay." I said it to reassure myself as much as her.

"Rae?" Nina called out as I walked toward the door.

"Yeah?"

She pointed a daisy at me. "I'm really glad you work here. I know the pay isn't much, darlin', but money isn't everything, right?"

I smiled. "You and Spencer. The flowers. Making people happy. Those are the reasons I work here. The money's just a bonus."

She spun the bouquet around, taking it in. The blues and yellows were so pretty together, and I could tell she was proud of the work she'd done.

"I couldn't agree with you more," Nina said.

When Dean started taking most of my money, I probably would have quit if I'd worked anywhere else. But this was more than a job. It felt like home.

special delivery #1

AS I DROVE UP TO THE GLENN RIDGE APARTMENTS, MEMORIES assaulted me. My mother, lost in a fog of grief after Grandma died, calling in sick to work and sleeping for days. Men, walking up our steps, carrying brown paper bags, eager to ease her pain. Eleven-year-old me, sleeping on a friend's floor, out of sight, out of mind, just the way my mother liked me.

I'd dream of my dad coming back for us, driving up in a shiny red Mercedes, and taking us to live in a fancy house in a big city. I was sure if he could only find us, all of our problems would be solved.

We didn't get a Mercedes, or a fancy house, or my dad. Instead we got Dean.

The place was full of memories, and none of them good. I was anxious to make the delivery and get out of there. After I snagged a visitor spot, I grabbed the arrangement and made my way to the apartment. Nina had chosen such a lovely combination of flowers: red roses, lilies, and pink and white daisies. I kept my nose close to the roses and breathed in their fragrance as I walked.

When I reached the door, I couldn't help but wonder who was on the other side. My heart pounded inside my chest. I held my breath and knocked. A baby cried. I waited.

Finally, a large girl wearing sweats and a stained, pale blue T-shirt opened the door. She was young. Like my age young. She cradled the crying baby in her arms, while the angry infant punched and kicked the air. The girl stuck her pinky in the baby's mouth, quieting the baby's cries for a moment.

"Are you Maddie?" I asked.

She nodded.

"I'm from Full Bloom, and these flowers are for you!"

She looked at the arrangement, then back at me, like she didn't quite believe it.

I kept talking. "I'm sorry, I don't know who they're from. The card says 'a friend.' Can I come in and set them down, since you've got your hands full?"

She pushed the door open wider with her body, and stood to the side so I could walk past her. I glanced around for a place to put the arrangement. The kitchen's countertop was covered with dirty dishes.

Past the kitchen was a square card table with junk all over it. I pushed a pizza box along with an empty formula container aside and set the flowers down.

The baby started crying again. Maddie closed her eyes, took a breath, and opened them.

"Thanks," Maddie yelled over the baby's cries. "They're . . . pretty."

That was my cue to leave. The flowers had been delivered. My job was done.

And yet, something pulled at me. My job didn't feel complete. I mean, she didn't seem happy.

"I know this is going to sound weird," I said, "but is there something I can do for you? Like, anything?"

Tears sprang to her eyes. She flipped the baby up onto her shoulder and bounced him around. Or was it a girl? I couldn't tell. She looked at the floor, biting her lip. I could tell that she wanted to say no, that everything was fine. But she knew that I knew she'd be lying.

"I need formula," she finally said. I could barely hear her as the baby cried. "He can't eat flowers, you know?"

It was a boy. A hungry little boy.

"Let me go get you some." I picked up the empty formula can. "Do you want this kind again?"

She nodded, a tear slowly making its way down her cheek.

"Okay. I'll be right back."

As I rushed out the door, she called out, "Thank you!"

Her words replayed in my head. *"He can't eat flowers, you know?"*

It was getting dark. I'd be late for dinner. Again. Dean would chew me out. Well, maybe he'd let a baby go hungry, but I sure couldn't.

stuck

I LUCKED OUT. DEAN WASN'T HOME, SO I MADE MYSELF DINNER
and took it to my room. I turned on my laptop and checked
e-mail. Nathan had sent me one. I groaned as I opened it
reluctantly. I thought we'd had a deal.

It read:

> I'm really sorry, Rae. He got the best of me.
> It won't happen again. I need you so much.
> You're all I have.

He'd included a link. I clicked through to one of my favorite Foo Fighters songs, "Best of You." It's a song that makes
you want to stand up and fight, no matter how much pain you
might be in. I was glad Nathan had found it. I'd often listen
to it when I was feeling down, to remind myself that maybe

I couldn't control everything that happened around me, but I could control how I reacted. Maybe it'd help Nathan like it helped me.

After that I did some homework, wrote a new poem, and read the book Leo had given me. Around ten I started getting ready for bed.

I'd just gotten back from the bathroom, my face clean and my teeth brushed, when Mom came barging into my room.

"Where is he?" she yelled. "Where's Dean?"

"How should I know? I'm not his keeper, Mom. I haven't seen him since yesterday."

She paced my room, still wearing her blue Rite Aid smock.

"Something's going on. I can feel it. He keeps disappearing and not telling me where he's going."

I sat down on my bed. "You know he took most of my paycheck yesterday?"

She stopped. "It's because we need it, Rae. We're hurting something fierce."

"But what if he's just drinking it away?"

My mom looked so old. Like years of stress and unhappiness were pulling on her skin. She wasn't even forty yet, but you'd never know it. She stood there, panicked over a man who'd done nothing but treat both of us badly. And yet, to her, it was better than being alone.

"He's not drinking it away," she spit out. "He wouldn't do that. He knows we need the money to pay bills."

"So what, then?" I asked. "Where do you think he is?"

Her bottom lip started to tremble. Was she going to cry? My mom didn't cry much. She was usually so tough and matter-of-fact about everything. I hated how nothing seemed to matter to her. Except him. Always him.

She quietly said, "I'm worried he might be seeing someone else."

I wanted to say, *Good riddance.* But she looked so incredibly sad, I didn't say anything. I walked over and gave her a hug. She rested her head on my shoulder. "Mom," I whispered. "I'm sure it's not that. He's just stressed. He's probably out with friends trying to forget about it. It's hard being unemployed, you know?"

Mother-of-pearl, has an alien taken over my body? But I felt her head nod a little bit, and I knew I'd said the right thing. It was what she needed to hear. I rubbed my hand in big circles around her back, like Grandma used to do when I was upset.

"I was thinking of Grandma today," I told her. "Missing her."

Mom sniffled and pulled away. "Me too. I miss her every day. She helped me be a better person. Rae, I don't even know who I am anymore. I can't remember the last time I was happy. How is that possible?"

"So leave him, Mom," I said. "You have a job. I have a job. We don't have to stay here if he makes you that miserable."

I hadn't even gotten all the words out when Mom's expression changed. Before I turned around, I knew. Dean was home.

"Do I make you miserable, Joan?" he asked from the doorway. "Huh? Do I?" He walked in and grabbed her arm.

"No," she said, trying to smile. "Rae was just joking around. You know how she can be." She rubbed his hand. "I'm so glad you're home. Come get a snack with me?"

I did my best to smooth things over. "She was worried about you. We didn't know where you were."

"I'm a big boy," he quipped back. "I can take care of myself."

Dean marched out, pulling her along with him.

"Good night, Mom," I called out. Then I whispered, "When you're ready to go, just say the word."

THE UNWANTED GUEST

He visits when you least expect him.
You open the door and there he is.
He doesn't wait for an invitation,
just barges in with his
greasy hair and bloodshot eyes,
smelling like a garbage dumpster.
If you aren't home, he sneaks in
through the window and quietly waits
for the perfect moment
to JUMP out and scare you.

You try to get rid of him.
Threaten him.
Bribe him.
Feed him one day.
Starve him the next.
Offer him a drink.
Or five.
A hit.
A pill.
A razor.
Anything to get him to
leave
you
alone.

Sometimes he disappears for a while.
But he always comes back,
stronger than before.
You feel like you'll never get rid of him.

So you finally deal with him, straight up.
You look him in the eye and tell him
he can't hide there with you, forever.
You tell people about him.
Through words. Through music.
As much as possible, you share.
Because if there's one thing that'll
make him leave and go hide somewhere else,
it's being exposed
for the whole world to see.

Be strong when you feel
like the strength is gone.

It takes work.
It takes time.

But Pain,
the unwanted guest,
doesn't have to stay forever.

when it rains, it pours

"HEY, I DIDN'T SEE THIS ONE," ALIX SAID, GRABBING A PURPLE AND black T-shirt off the rack.

I couldn't believe my best friend. Most of the time she was content in jeans and T-shirts, helping her dad fix up cars. But we'd been shopping at the City Girl for over three hours. When she set down the monkey wrench and let out the girly girl, there was no stopping her.

I reached over and pried the hanger out of her hand and put it back on the rack. "We are done, Alix. Remember? That bag in your hand? It's filled with two hundred dollars' worth of stuff you already paid for." I pulled her toward the door. "Come on. I need some caffeine or I'm going to fall over."

"Isn't it so fun, the whole shop till you drop thing? Let's do it again tomorrow." Yeah, she would think it's fun. It's fun when your adoring father hands you a wad of cash and says,

"Have a great time, sweetheart." It's not so fun when your wallet is emptier than a flower shop after Mother's Day.

"Rae, are you sure you don't want to go back and get something? Those jeans you tried on looked amazing, I'm telling you. It's your day off! You need to live a little."

"I am living, trust me. This is the most fun I've had in a long time." I opened the door and pushed her out into the rainy evening.

"Hurry!" I yelled. We ran toward my truck, which was parked a few blocks down the street. Alix held her shopping bag above her head to shield her from the rain, but I had nothing. I felt like I needed to be squeezed out like a sponge by the time I climbed into the truck.

Alix slid in next to me, laughing hysterically. "Holy monsoon, that was insane."

I reached into the glove box, pulled out some napkins, and squeezed the ends of my hair into them. Then I tilted the rearview down so I could see myself. Mascara streaked down my face, so I tried to wipe it away with one of the napkins.

Alix squeezed my forearm.

"What?" I said, still occupied with the napkins and wanting the use of my arm back.

"Rae. Look out your window," she whispered.

I jumped. It was like something out of a horror movie. A guy stood a few feet away, with no coat or hat or umbrella, in the pouring rain, just staring at us.

The window was fogged. "Is that—?"

"Yes," Alix said, her warm breath on my neck. "I'm pretty sure it's your boyfriend."

As I searched for the keys I'd tossed onto the seat, Nathan tapped on the window.

"Are you going to open it?" she asked.

"I don't think I want to," I said.

She pinched my elbow. "Rayanna Lynch, that's your boyfriend out there and something's obviously wrong with him. Open the flippin' window!"

I did as she said. "What are you doing here?" I asked, more annoyed than sympathetic.

"I need to talk to you."

I shook my head. "Nathan, I asked you to give me some space." I put the keys in the ignition and started the truck.

"Can you call me later?" he asked. His hair was plastered to his head and rain dripped down his face, like he was crying a bucket of tears. "I need your advice about something. That's all."

Alex piped up before I had a chance to reply. "Of course she'll call you. Do you need a ride somewhere?"

"Nah. I got my car." I could feel his eyes on me, but I kept mine straight ahead.

Alix waved good-bye as I rolled up my window and pulled out into the street.

"He must have followed us, right?" I shivered.

She blasted the heat. "He probably heard us yesterday, when we were talking about shopping." Then she said quietly, "You didn't have to be so mean."

"He was being creepy. Besides, how was I supposed to know that he wasn't going to go ballistic on me again, like he did the other day?"

I shivered again just thinking about it.

The rain started to let up a bit and I turned the wipers down a notch. I gripped the steering wheel tight. "I told him I needed some space. I asked him to leave me alone for a while—which he refuses to do. He keeps sending me e-mails. And running into me in the hall, even though his class is nowhere near mine. And now this?" I pushed my damp bangs out of my eyes. "I don't know what to do. Alix, what should I do?"

"Did you know Santiago and Nathan went out last night after Santiago got home from his away game?"

"No."

"It was late, but Santiago told me Nathan had begged him to go. He said they went to the cemetery. Nathan had a six-pack in his car, and apparently started crying after he downed a few. He wouldn't tell him why."

I pulled into the parking lot behind Full Bloom and Mack's. The rain had let up. It was just sprinkling now.

"It's such a freaking mess," I said after I turned off the truck. I rested my elbows on the steering wheel and put my head in my hands. "If I break up with him, I'm afraid he'll go off the deep end. If I stay with him, he's going to suffocate me. And after his outburst the other day? I'm kind of afraid of him, to be honest."

I turned and looked at Alix. Her eyeliner was smudged and her hair was super frizzy. I couldn't help it. I started laughing.

"What? What's so funny?"

"You're such a sight," I said.

"And what? You're Miss America?" She reached over and stroked my wet, stringy hair.

"Think we should go in, looking like this?"

"Yes. If anyone deserves a hot drink, it's us. Maybe the caffeine will clear your brain and help you figure out what to do."

I could only hope.

Inside Mack's, a few people sat in the comfy chairs, but it wasn't very busy. We went to the counter, where Aaron, Leo's brother, took our order.

"Got caught in the downpour, huh?" he asked.

I smoothed my hair and acted offended. "What!? Why would you say that?" I smiled. "Yeah. We practically swam here. Which is why we need some warm beverages. Can I have a green tea with jasmine please? What do you want, Alix?"

"I'd like a mocha. And give us two of those oatmeal chocolate chip cookies, please." Before I could hand over any money, Alix thrust a twenty toward Aaron. She looked at me. "I got it. You were very patient while I worked hard at spending all of Dad's money. It's the least I can do."

I wrapped my arm around her shoulder and half hugged her.

Leo walked in through a back door carrying two pans of freshly baked cookies. "Oh, can we have the ones fresh from the oven?" Alix asked. "Please?" She pointed behind Aaron at Leo.

Aaron handed her the change. "Sure. Take a seat and I'll bring everything out to you."

After Leo set the pans down, he came to the counter. "Hey. You girls out for a stroll on this gorgeous day?"

"Yeah, you like our new hairdos?"

"Very nice." He swept his bangs out of his eyes. "Though I've still got you beat."

"Leo, this is my friend Alix. I don't think you guys have met before."

They shook hands and exchanged greetings. Leo was warm and charming, like always, and I wanted to talk to him some more. I asked him to join us, hoping Alix wouldn't mind.

"Let me get these cookies off the pans," he told us, "and then I'll take a quick break."

We sat at a table, and Leo joined us a minute later. When Aaron brought our order over, Alix said, "Ah, much better. Food, drink, and no drenched boyfriends sneaking up and giving us a heart attack."

I glared at her, as Leo looked at her curiously. "Drenched boyfriends? Sounds kind of kinky."

Alix laughed. "Well, I don't think Rae's that kind of girl. Though, what do I know? Are you, Rae?"

I wanted to crawl inside the coffee grinder and die. I tried to think of a way to quickly change the subject, but it seemed impossible.

"I didn't know you had a boyfriend," Leo said. "And why was he sneaking up on you?"

"Long story," I quickly said, before Alix had a chance to blurt out the whole ugly truth.

Alix blew on her mocha. "You're gonna call him soon, right?" she asked. "Make sure Nathan's okay? You're acting like he's some kind of a monster, and he's not. He's just a guy. A guy with some troubles at home."

I instantly felt guilty. Troubles at home. Of all people, I should understand what that was like.

"Leo, I need your help, man," Aaron called out.

He stood up. "Sorry, girls. I'd love to hear more, but duty calls." He looked at me. "I hope everything's okay. Let me know if I can do anything."

I gave him a little smile, appreciative of his kindness, although it was embarrassing. First I showed him my stupid poem, and then he finds out my boyfriend is acting like a crazy person.

"Let's get out of here," I picked up my tea and cookie.

"What? Why? Where are we going?"

I shrugged. "Your place? It's normal there, isn't it? I really need some normal about now."

She stood up. "You gonna call him?"

With a deep sigh I said, "Yes."

I glanced at Leo as we left, thinking about his offer to help. Just like Ms. Bloodsaw had done a few days ago. Did they do that with everyone? I decided they must. After all, that's what nice, normal people do.

the hospital—4:15 p.m.

I've heard it said normal is overrated.

How can anyone say that?

When things are normal, you don't worry so much.

You don't cry so much.

You don't make mistakes again and again and again.

I've made so many mistakes, I can't even count them all.

"Her mom's here. Admitting has her. Can we wait?"

Right now, it feels like there isn't a person in the world who's made as many mistakes as I have.

"Yes, let's wait. Her mom probably wants to see her."

My mom? Okay, maybe one person.

I'm not sure I can go back to that place.

A place where all I do is screw up.

I always thought that I'd kept a level head.

That at least I'd stayed normal, despite everything.

But look at me.

If that were true, would I even be here?

four months earlier

the season of giving

WINTER BREAK WAS RIGHT AROUND THE CORNER. TEACHERS were piling work on at school, cramming our brains with information, trying to make up for the fact that soon we'd have two weeks with nothing to do but eat frosted reindeer cookies and watch *A Christmas Story* seven or eight times.

After school on Thursday, Nathan walked me to my truck. It was one of those clear December days where the sky is ice blue and the sun is shining, but you can't even feel it because it's so dang cold. I had three shirts on plus my coat and I was still freezing.

Nathan took my face in his chilly hands and kissed me softly. "Call me later? After work?"

"Sure," I said. "But I thought you were going out with your parents tonight. To celebrate?"

"Oh. Right. Well, we should be home by eight. It's just

dinner. I mean, the guy's hit the bestseller list before, so it's not like it's *that* exciting."

A cold wind whipped past us. I pulled my coat around me tighter. "I hope everything goes all right. You feeling okay about it?"

"Yeah. Things have been much better lately."

"Good. I gotta go. Talk to you later, okay?"

As I hopped in the truck, he waved at me, grinning from ear to ear. He'd been a perfect gentleman the past few weeks. After that day in the rain, I'd called him and we'd had a heart-to-heart. I'd told him showing up out of the blue like he'd done wasn't okay. He said he'd just been so desperate to talk to me. That he needed help figuring out how to confront his dad about the woman he'd seen him with in the parking lot. He said he couldn't pretend with his parents that everything was fine when it wasn't.

I'd told him he should tell his dad what he saw, and then wait for his dad's response. Confrontation was never easy, but sometimes necessary.

After that, we'd talked about us. I made sure he understood how I felt. I told him he couldn't be so needy with me. The constant calling and texting, the surprise visits—all of it had to stop. He'd promised to back off, and told me how much I meant to him. He'd sounded so sincere, and remorseful. I felt like I had to give him one more chance.

The conversation with his dad wasn't pretty, but it went

all right, and it accomplished what Nathan had hoped for. His dad promised to stop seeing the woman immediately and he'd begged Nathan for forgiveness. Since then things had apparently been going well, and now they were going out to celebrate his tenth book hitting the *New York Times* bestseller list. As a family. Nathan had been the picture of happiness all day.

I was almost to work when I noticed my fuel light had come on.

"Aw, man," I exclaimed. It seemed like I'd just filled the thing up a few days ago. There'd been a lot of deliveries lately. Full Bloom had a van, but sometimes I'd use my truck when necessary.

Payday was yesterday. Soon Dean would make me sign over my check and most likely give me forty dollars, just like the past few times. My heart sank at the thought. I needed to ask Nina for some gas money.

I found her and Spencer hunched over the worktable, twisting and folding silver ribbon, making bows.

"Hey," I said when I entered the back room. "Are those for the wedding on Saturday?"

Spencer looked up. "Hi, Rae! Yes, they are. We are planning to turn that little Methodist church into a winter wonderland for the two lovebirds. It's going to be fabulous!"

"Are you doing all white flowers?" I hung up my coat.

"White with a touch of blue," Nina said. "I special ordered

some hydrangeas that'll be arriving by airmail tomorrow. The bouquets are going to be exquisite! Just wait."

"Oh, Rae," Spencer said, "before I forget, there was an envelope outside the door again this morning. You know, with your name on it? I left it by the register."

My mouth fell open. I couldn't believe there was another one.

> Please deliver a nice flower arrangement to this address:
>
> 825 Englewood Avenue
>
> The flowers are for Ella. Sign the card "From a Friend."

I went back to the workroom. "Fifty dollars and a delivery from a *friend*," I told them.

"You know, I like this floral philanthropist, whoever it is," Spencer said, standing up and reaching his hands to the sky to stretch. "I love the idea of sneaking around, making the world a better place by sending flowers, and not wanting anything in return."

"Like a ninja of nice," I said. "But aren't you dying to know why?"

"I doubt we'll ever know," Nina said. "Spencer, will you do the arrangement? You okay with delivering it, Rae?"

"Yeah, of course," I said. "Except my tank is on empty. I

hate to ask, Nina, but since I've done so many deliveries in my truck lately, I was wondering if you could help me out with some money for gas?"

"Rae, absolutely! You should have said something sooner."

She walked over, took the envelope from my hand, and took out the money. She handed me forty. "There. I'm so embarrassed. Forgive me?"

"It's fine," I said, touching her arm. "And thank you. That's more than enough. You sure you want to give me that much?"

"I'm sure, hon." She turned to Spencer. "So what should we do for this one?"

"Her name is Ella." I'd never quite understood why, but they liked to know the person's name. Maybe certain names scream certain flowers?

Spencer clapped his hands together. "Let me whip up something Ella will adore. I'm thinking lots of red holly berries, white roses, and maybe some lilies. Rae, you want me to see if I can find a Santa suit for you to wear for this one?"

"Uh, no, think I'll pass. I'm not really good at the whole ho-ho-ho thing."

"That, my friend, is a very good thing in my book." He winked at me. *Oh, Spencer.*

While he went to work on the bouquet, I examined the handwriting. Young or old? Male or female? Friend or stranger? Impossible to tell.

Maybe Ella would give me a clue. I could only hope.

special delivery #2

ENGLEWOOD AVENUE ISN'T FAR FROM THE FLOWER SHOP. IT'S in one of the nice older neighborhoods near the hospital. Nina says it has character. Most new houses kind of look the same. But the older houses around Englewood are quaint and charming, and have lovely yards with big trees.

As I drove, darkness had just begun to fall, and I noticed that, unlike in newer housing developments, fancy Christmas displays didn't greet me at every turn. I pulled up to the little gray house with white shutters. A FOR SALE sign stood in the front yard. I walked up to the front door, adorned with a giant wreath, and knocked. A minute passed before a petite lady with short white hair and very wrinkly skin opened the door. She wore navy slacks and a blue sweatshirt with two large red ladybugs on it.

"Hello. I'm from Full Bloom. I have a delivery for Ella."

The woman didn't crack a smile. "Yes, that's me. Who are they from?"

I drummed up as much enthusiasm as I could. "It's a secret! From a friend. That's all I know. But isn't that nice?"

She scowled. "I don't want them."

"Oh, don't say that. They're pretty, aren't they? Can I come in? I'll help you find the perfect place to put them."

The lines on the woman's face seemed to grow deeper before my eyes. She shook her head slightly. "You don't understand. I'm only here for a few more days. On Sunday they move me out."

Clearly she wasn't happy about moving, and I couldn't help but want to know more. "Where are you going?"

Moisture filled her eyes. "Park Place Assisted Living." Ella took a deep breath. Anger covered her next words. "I've lived here for forty-two years. And then one day my son thinks I'm an invalid and tells me I have to move."

I didn't know what to say. "I'm sorry."

We stood there for a few seconds, neither of us quite sure where flowers fit into the equation.

"So, don't think of the flowers as celebrating the move," I said. "Think of them as a good-bye gift. Maybe one of your neighbors wanted you to know that you'll be missed but was too shy to say so." Ella didn't say anything, so I kept talking. "They'll make your last few days here special. When you look at them, maybe you'll think, 'Someone cares about me.'"

Her posture relaxed a bit. "All right. You can bring them in."

I followed Ella through the family room, where moving boxes sat against the walls, to an old dining room table. The table looked out a big picture window, into her backyard. And what a yard. Even in the twilight I could tell Ella had a serious green thumb. Trees in all different shapes and sizes stood against the fence line, with low-lying shrubs and colorful winter pansies filling the flower beds.

"Your yard is amazing," I said.

"Thank you. It's my pride and joy. I've always loved the outdoors, getting my hands dirty. And when it's too cold to be outside, I can sit here with a cup of coffee and a good book and enjoy the view."

"You like to read?" I asked.

"Yes. Very much. I worked as a school librarian for many years."

"Really? I want to be an English teacher."

It made me smile, the thought of her helping kids find books they'd like to read. I liked Ella. I could imagine myself sitting down at the table with her and talking books for hours.

Just then, Ella scurried by me, into the nearby kitchen. She went to the stove, turned the dial, and picked up a pan with steam rising out of it.

"It's my dinnertime," she explained.

"Oh, right. Well, I should go then. I hope you enjoy the flowers. And good luck with your move."

I had started for the front door when Ella called out to me. "I'm sorry, I don't know your name, but . . . well, would you like to stay? For dinner?"

I stopped. Nina was expecting me back at the shop to finish up a few things before I went home. But something told me Ella needed me more than the flowers did.

"It's nothing fancy," she continued. "Just some leftover spaghetti. There's enough for both of us, if you'd like to join me."

I smiled. "My name is Rae. And I'd love to stay and have dinner with you."

GRANDMA

Every other Saturday,
we'd head to the library,
she and I.

"How many can I get?"
I'd ask each time.

"As many as we can carry!"
she'd reply.

Our arms full of
faraway places,
we'd go back to her house,
where she'd dish up
steaming bowls of
tomato soup and
grilled cheese sandwiches
for lunch.

I'd count out the crackers
before I crumbled them
into my soup.

"One, two, three, four."

"Who's the girl I most adore?"
she'd reply in her singsongy voice.

"Me?"

"You!"

I miss those days
of books,
of soup,
of Grandma and me.

Those days of sweet, sweet love.

enough is enough

I FORGOT TO CALL NATHAN.

I got caught up in thinking about Ella and how she reminded me a little bit of my grandma and ended up writing a poem after I got home.

We'd had a really nice dinner, slurping our spaghetti noodles like old friends. She'd told me all about her son and how he constantly worried. Since her eighty-fifth birthday, it'd gotten even worse. He'd call her three or four times a day, just to check on her. She said the move was more for him than for her. It made her angry, how he didn't seem to have any regard for how she felt about the situation.

"Why can't he just let me be?" she'd asked me. "If something happens, well, it happens. I am an old lady, after all."

I could see her point. And she seemed pretty capable to me.

"He loves you, that's all," I'd told her.

As I got ready to leave, I'd asked if I could come and visit her at her new place. She'd said she'd like that. I was already looking forward to it.

At nine my phone rang. I turned down the volume on my music before I answered.

"You didn't call me" were the first words out of Nathan's mouth.

"Oh, sorry. Lost track of time. See, I got this envelope—" I wanted to tell him about meeting Ella.

"Dinner was a total disaster," he said. "Mom found out about Dad's affair. She found texts on his cell phone."

I sat straight up on my bed. "Are you serious? And she confronted him at dinner? With you there?"

He sniffled a little bit, and I wondered if he'd been crying. "Yeah. I could tell something was up. She stayed quiet the whole way there. Dad tried to talk to her, but she wouldn't have any of it. After we ordered, she let him have it. It's like she wanted to humiliate him in public or something. I don't know. Rae, I wanted to die."

"So what'd you do?"

"She left before our food arrived. Told Dad she was taking a taxi home and if he had any sense at all, he'd get a hotel room. He and I stayed and tried to eat, but our appetites were gone."

"Nathan, I'm so sorry." And I did feel bad for him. It was bad enough having parents argue behind closed doors, but in public? I couldn't even imagine.

"I need to see you. Can I come over?"

"Now? It's late and my stepdad is home for a change. Trust me, you don't—"

"Come on. I need you, Rae. If I can't go over there, could you come here? Mom is holed up in her room, so we'd be alone."

I was torn. I didn't doubt for a second he did need someone. But I didn't really know what to do for him. He probably needed to see his mom more than he needed to see me. I'm sure he felt betrayed, like the one family member he could count on had turned on him, in a way.

"Like I said, it's late. I'll stay on the phone with you for a while, if that will help."

"Don't you get it? I need you right now. You're the only one who gives a shit about me. The only one who cares how I feel. I have to see you. I'll be there in a few."

He hung up before I could protest. I tried calling him back, but he didn't answer. I decided I'd better go out and warn Dean we'd be having a visitor.

Nathan had been to my house to pick me up a few times, but he'd never been inside. What would he think? His house was nice. Really, really nice. Ours? Not so much.

Dean was sitting on the couch, a tower of empty beer cans on the coffee table. "Hey, Rae, can you make me a sandwich? I'm starving."

I went to work picking up his cans. "A friend of mine is

coming over. He's kind of depressed and needs to talk to me. Please be nice to him, okay?"

"Make me a big ol' sandwich and I'll kiss the guy's stinkin' feet."

I took the cans to the recycling bin and went back to the family room to straighten up. Bills and junk mail were scattered everywhere. "Do these need to be paid?" I asked, starting to stack them.

"Hey, what are you doing?" He stood up and snatched the papers out of my hands. "Don't mess with my stuff. Go make me a sandwich, like I told you." He threw the papers on the coffee table.

"Can I please put all of that in your room or somewhere out of the way?" I asked.

"No!" He pointed to the kitchen. "Get in there. Now. I'm not gonna tell you again."

It was hopeless. He was wasted and in a foul mood. My best bet was to get Dean fed, then push Nathan into my bedroom when he arrived. Wouldn't Nathan love that?

I looked in the fridge for some lunch meat, but we were out. I grabbed a can of tuna fish from the cupboard and went to work cutting up pickles and onions. I wasn't quite finished putting it all together when the doorbell rang.

I rushed to get it, but Dean was already inviting Nathan inside.

"It's awful late to be visiting a girl, isn't it?" Dean asked as he closed the door. "Especially on a school night?"

"It's not that late," Nathan said, smiling. "We're not third graders, right?"

I winced. Arguing with the guy was not a good idea. "Nathan, come here. I was just making Dean a sandwich. Help me in the kitchen and then we can go to my room."

"No," Dean said. "He can stay here with me while you finish up." He motioned at the couch. "Take a seat. You like wrestling?"

Nathan sat on the couch. "Not really. But you do?"

"Hell, yeah. Check out who's matched up—"

I went back to the sandwich, hoping Dean wouldn't say anything to embarrass me. He could talk wrestling for hours, so if they stuck to that, everything would be fine.

Of course, that was wishful thinking. When I took the plate out, Dean was standing, his arms crossed. He looked at me accusingly. "Rae, this kid drives a brand-new Jetta? What kind of high school punk drives a car nicer than most adults' in Crestfield?" He looked at Nathan. "Are you dealing drugs, son?"

Nathan raised his arms like he was surrendering to the enemy. "No, I'm not dealing drugs." He chuckled. "Sorta wish I was, though."

I gave Dean the plate. "Stop it. His dad has a good job. So what? Maybe you could get one too if you tried a little harder."

I'd wanted to divert the attention away from Nathan. It

worked. Dean narrowed his eyes and glared at me. If Nathan hadn't been there, he probably would have let off a string of obscenities. "Shit, Rae, I'm trying. I really am."

I waved at Nathan. "Come on."

Nathan got up and followed me to my room.

"You okay?" he asked. "You were a little rough on him out there."

I crossed my arms. "Oh, no. Don't do that. Don't defend *him*. Unless you want me to hate you forever."

He came over and pulled me to him. "I definitely don't want that." He kissed me. "You're the only good thing I've got in this world right now." He tucked my hair behind my ear and kissed my neck. "The only one who makes me happy."

His lips moved up my neck, slowly, and then he nibbled on my ear. His hands moved underneath my T-shirt and caressed my back. I don't know why, but it annoyed me. Was *this* why he'd come over?

I wriggled out of his arms. "Nathan, come on. Dean could come in here any minute."

He pulled me to him again. "Nah. He wouldn't do that. He knows we want to be alone."

I pushed him away again, harder this time. "I thought you wanted to talk? About what happened at dinner?"

He sat on my bed and pulled me onto his lap. "No. That's the last thing I want to do. I want to forget about it." He kissed me. "Come on. Help me forget about it."

So we were back to this again. His promises conveniently forgotten. It was all about him. What *he* wanted. What *he* needed. I hadn't even wanted him to come over. But did he care? Did he care how I felt about anything?

I stood up and pointed at the door. "You need to go home."

Nathan laughed. "No, come on. I just got here."

Suddenly, everything about him infuriated me. The way he discounted everything I said. The way he needed me all the time. The way he tried to win me over with compliments.

What was I *doing* with him?

"Nathan," I said, gentler this time. "This isn't working. Me and you? I'm ending it. Right now. It's over. I'm sorry, I know you've got a lot going on, but I can't do this anymore."

He stared at me, like someone had just told him the earth was about to explode. He shook his head, slowly at first, then faster. "No. No, you don't mean it." He stood up, his eyes pleading with me. "We belong together, Rae. You know it. Maybe I shouldn't have come over here like this, I just—"

I backed toward the door as he talked, and he followed. "You need to go. Now. Or I'll call Dean and he'll make you leave."

It was like I'd flipped a switch. Nathan's shock turned to anger. I could see it all over his face. He looked like he wanted to punch something.

"I can't believe you're doing this to me."

"It's for the best. Really. I mean, we can still be friends. If you want," I said quietly, but firmly.

He flung open the door so it banged against the wall. "No thanks."

He stormed out. I listened as he and Dean exchanged a few words, but I couldn't hear what they said. And I wasn't about to go out there. After a minute or so I heard the front door open and close.

I waited, wondering if Dean would come and ask what had happened. But he didn't. I went to the bathroom and got ready for bed.

When I came back, my phone was buzzing.

It was Nathan. I turned it off and crawled into bed, trying to convince myself I had made things better for myself, not worse.

gone

I CAN'T EVEN DESCRIBE THE RELIEF I FELT WHEN NATHAN WASN'T waiting for me at my locker the next morning. I'd expected a big, ugly showdown. The kind the whole school buzzes about all day long. I was so glad I didn't get one.

I grabbed my stuff and headed to the benches to find Alix and Felicia. I wanted to tell them about the breakup before they heard it from someone else.

Alix jumped up when she saw me and pulled me over to a quiet corner. "Why is your phone off? What happened? Why'd you break up with him?"

"Who told you?"

"Santiago. I guess after Nathan left your place last night, he went over there. It was not a good scene. Santiago's dad had to ask him to leave. Nathan was apparently pissed off and letting the entire neighborhood know it."

I hugged my books tightly to my chest. "See, Alix? Something is seriously wrong with the guy."

"He was just upset." She gave me a hug. "Are you okay? I mean, he didn't freak out on you again, did he?"

"I didn't give him the chance. Luckily, my stepdad was there, so Nathan did as I asked." I looked past her. "Have you seen him yet today?"

"No. I don't think he's here yet."

We stood in the corner, waiting, until the bell rang. Nathan never showed up at the benches. Maybe he'd decided it'd be best to avoid the hangout spot. Or was he skipping school entirely? I felt a little tinge of worry. What if he'd done something terrible? No, I told myself. He's fine. Nathan's probably just playing games, hoping I'll get worried and call him.

Still, I turned on my phone to check for any missed calls. There wasn't anything from Nathan since the one last night. I didn't know whether I should be relieved or upset.

Well, I wasn't going to call him. He wasn't my responsibility. Was he?

I went to English, feeling like I'd swallowed a pincushion. There was a reminder on the board about submitting poetry for the January issue. The deadline was today.

Felicia sat down and placed the December issue on my desk. "Check it out. Anonymous started something. There's a couple of more in there this time."

I turned to the poetry pages. The anonymous ones were

grouped together. Along with mine, there was a poem about bulimia. And someone else had written a poem about a relative who'd committed suicide.

"Wow," I said. "That's great. Isn't it? That more people want to share?"

She nodded as Ms. Bloodsaw started class.

I pulled out a piece of paper and wrote a short poem right there on the spot. It came easily. And afterward I felt a little less guilty about breaking up with Nathan.

What I've Learned

by Anonymous

I'm not the floor
to be walked on
or the hammer
to be used.

I'm not the choir
to sing your praises
or the commercials
to be ignored.

I'm the baby bird
wanting to fly
and the orchid
starting to bloom.

I'm the bonfire
spreading warmth
and the poem
with something to say.

Good-bye, commercials.
Hello, poetry.
It's time to start being
the me I want to be.

from bad to worse

NATHAN NEVER SHOWED UP AT SCHOOL. I DIDN'T WANT TO BE worried about him, but I couldn't stop imagining the worst. After school I had the afternoon off from work, so I got my hair cut before heading home to get ready for dinner with Alix. She'd promised she'd have Santiago swing by Nathan's house to make sure he was okay. What a good friend.

I got home around five, and had planned to tell Dean he'd have to eat dinner early since I had plans. He probably wouldn't like it, but it was either that or he could cook himself dinner. When I drove up, his Bronco wasn't there. I figured he'd gone out again, which was happening more and more often.

So I was surprised when I found him sitting on the couch, a beer in his hand, watching half-naked men pound on each other.

"Where's your car?" I asked.

He took a drink of beer, in no hurry to answer my question. Finally he said, "Sold it."

Though I was pretty sure I knew the answer, I wanted to hear what he had to say. "What? Why?"

He glared at me. "Why do you think? We need the money."

"How are you supposed to look for work then?" He ignored me. I walked over and threw my keys and backpack on the kitchen table. "I'm going to make your dinner now. I have to be somewhere at six."

"Is someone picking you up?"

"No," I yelled as I rummaged around in the kitchen.

"Tonight you'll need a ride." He appeared just inside the kitchen now. "Because I'm gonna borrow your truck. I need your paycheck, too."

I scowled at him. "You're kidding, right?"

"No, I need to borrow it, so just call one of your friends."

I threw my arms in the air. "I'm not going to get a ride! That's *my* truck! God, I already give you most of my paycheck. Isn't that enough?" I turned and opened a cupboard door. It was empty, with the exception of one can of stewed tomatoes, two cans of corn, and few saltine crackers. "What are you doing with my money, anyway, Dean? Because whatever it is, you're not feeding us. There's nothing here to eat. Nothing. Unless you want me to whip up a corn and cracker casserole."

"I'm not hungry," he said. "So don't worry about it. Your

mom said she'll bring groceries home with her tonight. Get your check and sign it."

I went to my backpack and did as he said. I held the check away from him until he pulled two twenties out of his pocket and handed them to me. "Dean, can't you go later? I'll be home by eight. You can use my truck then, how's that?"

He stepped forward. "Look, I've had one hell of a day. I wouldn't take your truck if it weren't real important, all right?"

"Can I give you a ride somewhere on my way?" I asked, my brain scrambling to find a way to make this work for both of us. "I could even pick you up later."

"No. Out of the question."

I followed him out of the kitchen. He grabbed my keys off the table. "Tell your mom not to wait up."

And that was it. He was gone.

I sat on the couch, dazed. What was going on? Whatever it was, it had to be bad for him to sell his Bronco. He loved that thing more than he loved anything else in the world. My stomach rumbled. I had skipped lunch again, comforted by the fact that I'd be having pizza for dinner. I grabbed the phone from the coffee table next to the couch.

I hit talk, but nothing happened. Dead. The pile of bills still sat there on the coffee table, unpaid. I grabbed my cell from my backpack, thankful once again I had a savings account so I could afford my own phone.

I speed-dialed Alix.

"Hey," she said. "I was just about to call you."

"Yeah?"

"Yeah. Apparently, no one knows where Nathan is. His parents are, like, freaking out. He never came home last night."

"Oh no." I leaned forward and put my head in my hand. I felt sick to my stomach. "Alix, what have I done? What if something horrible has happened?"

"Try not to think the worst. I know it's hard. But let's stay positive, okay? We'll find him."

"Have they called the police?"

"No. They can't report him missing until it's been at least twenty-four hours. Santiago and I are going to look for him. You probably shouldn't go. I mean, the last thing we want is a scene when we do find him."

I hated the thought of being stuck at home, but I knew she was right. It'd be better for everyone if I stayed out of the way.

"Will you let me know when you find him? I mean, I care about him, you know?"

"I know you do. We'll do the Mushroom another time soon, okay?"

"Okay. Bye."

I sat there for a few minutes, considering my options. I dialed Nathan's number, but he didn't answer. There was nothing else to do but wait. And have some corn for dinner.

there's more to life than kissing

WHEN I WOKE UP ON SATURDAY MORNING, THE FIRST THING I DID
was check the driveway. Thankfully, my truck was in its usual
spot. Then I checked my phone. The last text had been from
Alix at around eleven p.m. They hadn't found Nathan. I wondered if maybe I should try looking for him, but I had no clue
where to go, and besides, Nina would be expecting me soon.

I showered, got dressed for work, and made myself some
toast. Mom had come home last night with groceries, like
Dean had promised. While I'd put a frozen pizza in the oven,
I'd told her how totally fun it'd been to be stranded at home
with nothing to eat. She didn't say so, but the look on her face
told me she felt bad about everything.

I'd offered her some of the pizza, but she didn't take any of
it. Said she was tired and just wanted to go to bed. Yeah, she
was tired all right. Tired of being in the dark when it came to

her husband. When I told her he'd sold his Bronco, she was more surprised than I'd been.

As I drove to Full Bloom, I told myself Dean was her problem. I kept my eyes peeled for Nathan or his car. Though I had no idea what I'd do or say if I found him, I really wanted to know that he was all right.

At work I found Nina and Spencer surrounded by flowers in the back room, getting ready for the wedding. Nina had hired a couple of temps to help out too. It was a flurry of floral activity.

I poked my head in. "You guys need anything?"

"Coffee!" Spencer called out, his hands tangled in a bouquet of white roses. "Please, Rae, I'm begging you. A bucket of coffee, if you can manage it."

"Take some cash from the register, Rae," Nina said. "Get us all coffees. And you, too, if you want one."

I was happy to oblige. I grabbed a twenty and went next door. It was busy, like every Saturday morning. Leo's mom, Georgia, gathered dirty dishes from a table. Leo, Aaron, and their dad hustled behind the counter, taking orders and filling cups with caffeinated goodness.

I didn't notice him right away. He sat on a stool at the tall counter. As my eyes scanned the room, they landed on his, and a wave of a hundred different emotions rose up inside me.

"Nathan," I whispered as he came over to where I stood, "everyone is worried sick about you. Where have you been?"

"Come outside with me?" he asked, the smell of coffee on his breath.

I was torn. What should I do? Surely he'd tell me the same things he always did, that I was the only one who understood him and nothing else mattered to him but me. He'd probably beg me to go back to him. But while I felt bad for the guy, I wasn't going to change my mind. I didn't want a boyfriend who treated me the way Nathan treated me.

"I'm sorry, but I can't. My boss asked me to get coffee for everyone. We're really busy, and she's expecting me back soon."

He leaned in and kissed my cheek. "I have to talk to you," he whispered in my ear. "I want to make things right."

We inched closer to the counter. How could I get him to understand that what we'd had really wasn't much of a relationship? "Nathan, I'm curious. When I get to the counter, do you know what I'll order?"

"What do you mean? You just said you were getting coffee for your coworkers."

"I mean, what do I drink when I go to a café. Do you remember?"

His eyes narrowed. "I don't know. Who remembers something like that?"

"Okay. What about ice cream? What's my favorite kind of ice cream?"

He bit his lip, thinking for a few seconds. "Uh. Chocolate chip mint?"

"No, that's your favorite. See, here's the thing. You can't claim to care that much about me when you don't even *know* me."

He crossed his arms in protest. "That's not fair. Just because I don't know what kind of coffee or ice cream you like?"

"Tell me one thing I really like, Nathan. Just one. Besides the Foo Fighters."

His eyes dropped to the ground as he thought about it. After a few seconds his head popped up. "Kissing. You like kissing me!"

I might have laughed if I thought he was trying to be funny. But he was serious. And it hurt. I think there was a small part of me that had hoped he'd prove me wrong. "Really? That's all you can think of?"

"What? What's wrong with that?"

"You need to go," I said softly, only one person in front of me now. I looked at him. "It's over. I'm sorry. Go home. Let your parents know you're okay."

His sad eyes searched mine, but I stared back at him with nothing but resolve. I meant what I said. He took a deep breath and turned for the door.

"Hi, Rae, how are you?" Leo asked as the person in front of me moved to the side to wait for his order. I didn't know how to respond. Should I tell him the truth or lie? My face must have told him what I couldn't say. "Hey, are you okay?" Leo's voice was soft and soothing. "Was that guy bothering you?"

"That guy is my boyfriend," I said. "Well, ex-boyfriend.

I broke up with him a couple of days ago. He isn't taking it very well."

He cringed. "Ooh. Sorry. Anything I can do?"

"I don't think so. Sometimes I wish I could get away from my life, you know?"

He nodded, like he understood. "So, here's what you should do. Come and do a video with me. It's a great way to escape. Focus on something else for a while."

I shrugged. "Okay. When?"

"What can I get you, Rae?" Aaron asked, sounding annoyed that Leo hadn't barked out my order yet.

"Four large coffees and a tea for me, please."

Aaron stepped away to get the drinks. I handed Leo the twenty-dollar bill. "What time are you off work?" he asked.

"Two o'clock."

"Perfect. Meet me in the parking lot." He handed me my change. "It'll be fun. I promise."

After two days of drama, I really liked the sound of that.

fishing for answers

I FOUND LEO LEANING AGAINST MY TRUCK IN THE PARKING LOT.

"You mind driving?" he asked.

"Nope," I said, unlocking his door. "I figured you came with your family."

"I just need to stop by my house and get the camera."

"You got it." Although Leo and I had been friends for a while, this was the first time we were actually going somewhere together. Our relationship up until now had mostly consisted of talking during breaks at work. I felt a tinge of nervousness as I got into my truck. I hoped we'd get along the same way we always did—perfectly.

The lingering cigarette smell from when Dean borrowed the truck hit me. I rolled down my window. "Sorry it stinks. I don't smoke, I promise."

"I don't smell like a meadow of daisies myself," he said.

"Compared to this truck, you do."

"Well, now it will smell like coffee and cigarettes," he said, rolling down his window too. "The poor man's breakfast, they say."

It made me think of Dean and my mom, and my hard-earned money they were spending on who-knows-what. I couldn't let myself think about it too much because it made me want to scream. "It's ridiculous. If they didn't buy all those cigarettes, maybe they wouldn't be so poor."

As Leo gave me directions, I realized we lived in the same neighborhood. I didn't say anything—didn't say he lived in the crappy part of town, like me. Maybe he liked it. Or maybe, since he was homeschooled, he didn't even really *know* he lived in the crappy part of town.

"I love this song," he said, tapping out the rhythm on the dashboard with his hands. "My Hero," by the Foo Fighters.

"Yeah, me too." It made me smile, and any nervousness I had initially felt vanished. I already felt better than I had in days.

He stopped tapping. "Do you have a hero, Rae?"

I paused. "Probably Nina. I mean, she runs her own business and works hard to make the people around town happy. I admire her. A lot." I looked at him. "What about you?"

"I'd have to go with my dad. For some of the same reasons. And because, you know, he's my dad."

I felt a tug at my heart, like I did anytime someone talked lovingly about a father. It was a reminder of what I was missing. "Yeah," I said. "I think a lot of kids feel that way about their dads."

"It's that one," he said, pointing to a white ranch style with bluish-gray trim. I pulled into the driveway.

I felt him looking at me. "What about your dad?" he asked.

My chest tightened. I wanted to say my dad was the greatest dad who ever lived. But I couldn't. Because as much as I'd wished he'd come and rescue me, he never had. He was the opposite of a hero. A villain? A coward? A deadbeat dad?

I looked at Leo. "My dad walked out on me and my mom. I'm pretty sure he doesn't qualify for hero status." I turned off the truck and changed the subject. "So, do you want me to wait here? Or should I come in with you?"

"Rae, I'm sorry, I shouldn't have—"

I lightly slapped his knee. "No, don't apologize. It's fine. I don't talk about my family very much, so how were you supposed to know?" I smiled. "Anyway, what now?"

"Come in. I can make some sandwiches for us too, if you want. You've gotta be hungry, right?"

With everything going on at work and with Nathan, I hadn't even noticed. But the toast before work had been the last thing I'd eaten. I'd been skipping lunch so often to save money, maybe I was starting to get used to living in a constant state of hunger. "That would be great."

He led me inside and to the kitchen. It was clean and smelled like lemons. "What kind of sandwich do you want?"

"Something easy? I mean, I'm fine with PB and J."

As he pulled a loaf of bread out of a drawer, I realized this was an opportunity for me to do something nice for Leo for a change. "Hey, why don't I make the sandwiches while you take a shower."

"Are you sure?"

"Yes, I'm sure. Go!" And I meant it. It was the kind of home a person couldn't help but feel comfortable in.

He shrugged. "Okay. Well, the jam's in the fridge and the peanut butter is in the pantry. I'll be back in a few."

I gathered everything I needed and went to work. After I finished making the sandwiches, I poured two glasses of milk and grabbed a potato chip bag from the pantry. I set everything on the dining table and then wandered around the family room. It was filled with family pictures. They obviously did a lot of camping. Or used to. The boys in the pictures were much younger. They probably couldn't get away as much now because they were always working.

"Hey." Leo suddenly appeared. His hair was damp, and even from a few feet away, I noticed how good he smelled. Like coconut. "Checking out the Martin family photos? My hair wasn't so great back then."

"It's definitely gotten better with age," I teased. "You guys still go camping?"

"Nah. Not since my parents bought the coffee shop. Too busy all the time."

"You miss it?"

"I don't think about it that much, to be honest. But, yeah. I guess. I really like fishing. Just me and the water, standing there with a pole, being still."

I had to admit, it sounded nice. Even if I didn't like fish. "I've never been," I told him, moving toward the table.

"Fishing or camping?" he asked.

"Neither."

He took a seat at the table and looked up at me, his eyes big and round. "You've never been camping? Never had a s'more? Never been eaten alive by bugs and scratched your legs until they bled? Never peed in the woods and gotten poison oak for going in too far?"

I opened the chip bag and took a few out. "Wow, you make it sound so fun. We should go right now!"

"Well, s'mores are good. And the fishing. The rest I can take or leave."

I sat across from him. "You're lucky. My mom really isn't the camping type."

He took a drink of milk. "Not everyone is, I guess." He pointed to his sandwich. "You make a mean PB and J, Rae. Best one I've had in a long time."

"It's my specialty. Along with hamburgers."

We ate in silence for a few minutes. Then I asked, "Do you think it's possible to grow up and be different from your parents? I mean, take camping. If my mom doesn't like camping, am I destined to not like camping either? Is it just in my blood?"

He set his sandwich down and leaned forward a little bit. "Your parents may have created you, but they don't define you." He sounded so sure. I wanted to believe him. "Next spring I'm taking you fishing," he said.

I smiled. "I'd love that." I meant it too.

He shook his head. "I still can't believe you've never been camping."

"What can I say?" I fiddled with my potato chips. "I'm a freak."

"No, I didn't mean it like that. You're not a freak."

I nodded. "Yeah. I am. Not just because I've never been camping." I sighed. "I do stupid things, too. Like breaking up with my boyfriend when he's having problems. What was I thinking?"

I felt him staring at me. "Rae?"

"Yeah?"

He didn't say anything. His eyes were soft. Kind. He held his hands out far apart. "Freak? You? Not even close. Sometimes you have to do what's best for you, no matter what. I mean, no one can look out for *you* better than you." He paused. "He'll be okay."

I took a deep breath. "I hope you're right."

"Of course I am. Now finish your sandwich so I can show you what a freak looks like shooting videos of random crap."

"You're not a freak," I said.

He smiled. "Well. Takes one to know one."

muddy boots

AFTER WE FINISHED EATING, WE HEADED OUT ON FOOT, VIDEO camera in hand. It was chilly but not freezing cold like it had been earlier in the week. The clouds rolled by in a parade of white mixed with gray. Leo pointed the camera skyward as he spun around slowly. When he passed under a tree hanging over the sidewalk, he stopped and shot up through the branches. I wanted to see what he saw, so I got underneath the tree with him. A maze of empty branches zigzagged through the air, higher and higher.

"It looks kind of sad without the leaves," I said.

"Lonely," he said.

"Yeah. Exactly."

We started walking again, neither of us talking. When we got to the end of the street, we made our way back toward the cluster of trees. The muddy ground squished beneath my boots.

"Sorry," he said. "You okay with getting a little dirty?"

"Despite the fact I've never been camping, yes. Mud washes off. Or so I hear, anyway."

He chuckled. "Go ahead of me. I want to get a shot of you walking toward the trees."

I stopped. "No way. I don't want to be in the video."

"Okay, fine." He handed me the camera. "You shoot. Just don't show my face. Anything else, fair game."

I stood still, hit record, and watched through the lens as Leo walked on without me. He had a cute butt. Cute, like the rest of him. Okay, so he wasn't the kind of guy who caused girls to stop and stare, like Nathan Sharp. He was your average boy next door, with brown hair and brown eyes. And now, I discovered, a cute—

Rayanna Lynch, stop it.

I zoomed in on Leo's feet and the ground all around them—step, step, step. When he ducked behind a tree and I couldn't see him anymore, I pointed the camera up, like he'd done earlier. The clouds had begun to break, so sunlight streamed through the branches, creating a beautiful portrait of branches and sky. Everywhere I looked, I felt the contrast of darkness and light.

I let the camera roll as I walked, zooming in, zooming out. Everything faded away until it was just me and this lovely place filled with greens and browns, and the smell of earth mixed with the soft scent of pine. I could literally feel the peace seeping into my pores.

I don't know how much time had passed before I felt a tap on my shoulder. I lowered the camera as Leo put his finger to his lips. Then he pointed at a squirrel up in a tree. I giggled and zoomed in on our new subject. He scurried across the branch, to the trunk, and then down to the ground. Leo and I stayed perfectly still, watching him, his big fluffy tail twitching this way and that as he ran.

When the squirrel finally disappeared into the woods, I stopped filming and handed the camera back to Leo. "I love it here," I said. "It's so peaceful."

"No matter how many times I come here, I don't get tired of it. The light and the weather and the seasons are always changing, so it's never the same."

I leaned up against a tree and wondered why I'd never thought about coming here. Why I never thought about going somewhere to just be quiet and let myself breathe.

"Thanks for inviting me today," I said. "It's exactly what I needed."

"You want to talk about it? I get lots of practice listening at the coffee shop. People love to explain their desperate need for a caffeine fix."

"My stepdad's been out of work for a while, and I have to give him some of my paycheck." I corrected myself. "Most of my paycheck. It's so stressful at home, you know? He sold his Bronco because he needed the money, and then last night he took off in my truck. On top of everything else, I broke up with Nathan."

"I'm sorry, Rae. That's a lot to deal with."

I leaned my head back and looked up at the sky. "Some days I wish I could just run away and leave it all behind."

"Where would you go?" The way he asked, it felt like if he could, he'd take me there. His voice sounded so warm and comforting.

"Anywhere."

"Pick a place."

"I'll go with Hawaii. A sunny beach sounds nice."

"Okay, close your eyes." I looked at him. He stood there, a big grin on his face. "Go on, do it."

I closed them.

"Listen. You can hear the gentle hum of the ocean. The waves, lapping the shore. And smell the scent of coconut lotion on your skin."

"Just like your shampoo," I said.

"What?"

I kept my eyes closed. "Your hair smelled like coconut when you got out of the shower."

"Shhh. You are in Hawaii, not in my house smelling my fabulous hair. Now, feel the warm sun on your face and the cool sand on your hands as you lie on your towel. You scoop up the sand and let it fall gently through your fingers."

"Can I get a cold drink with one of those little umbrellas?"

"I'm a barista, remember? But if that's what you want, here you go. You take a sip, the taste of ice and strawberry—"

Just then, my phone rang, startling me. I opened my eyes. "Crap. Sorry."

I checked the number. Alix. She'd probably heard I'd seen Nathan. I sent it to voice mail, but it was too late. The peace I'd felt disappeared. Reality came crashing in, squeezing me so tight, it almost hurt.

"I should probably get home." The reluctance in my voice was hard to hide.

He took a couple of steps toward me. His eyes begged me to trust him. "Are you sure?"

"Yeah. I'm sorry. I have to go."

Leo and I kept quiet until we reached the sidewalk. I smiled at him. "You're sweet, you know that?" He shrugged and his cheeks turned the color of cherry blossoms. I'd embarrassed him. "For a few seconds there I almost believed I was in Hawaii."

He grinned. "Well, you looked smoking hot in that black bikini."

Whose cheeks were a pretty shade of pink now?

no reassurances

IT WAS MOM'S DAY OFF. WHEN I GOT HOME, I FOUND HER OUT
back, sitting at the white plastic patio table, wearing her robe
and smoking a cigarette.

"Mom, I'm home." No response. "You want something to
eat? I can make you a sandwich."

Again, no response. She didn't even look at me.

I shut the door and went to work making her a bologna
sandwich. As I spread the mayonnaise on thick, the way she
liked it, I wondered where Dean had run off to this time.
Mom's car was gone—we could only hope he wouldn't go
completely insane and sell it, too.

I took the plate with the sandwich and some chips and set it
on the table, along with a Coke. "You have to eat, Mom. Okay?"

She looked up at me, then down at the plate. Her tired eyes
blinked a couple of times, and then she reached over and picked

up half the sandwich. I knew that was all the thanks I'd get.

I went to my room and called Alix.

"Hey, sorry I couldn't take your call earlier."

"Nathan's back," she said. "Santiago hung out with him for a while."

"Yeah. I know. He came by the shop this morning." I slumped down onto my bed. "What did Santiago say? Does Nathan seem all right?"

"He saw you with Leo," she said slowly, like she was trying to break the news to me ever so gently. "He was pissed. I'm pretty sure Santiago used the words 'psycho pissed.'"

I sat up straight, my heart beating fast. "Wait. What? When did he see us?"

"He saw the two of you get into your truck. Then he followed you to Leo's house. Fortunately, that's when Nathan called Santiago, and my brilliant boyfriend told him to get the hell away from there before Nathan did something he'd regret. They met up at Mickey D's. Santiago got him some lunch. Said once he got him to start eating, he chowed. It was like Nathan hadn't eaten anything for two days."

"Okay, wait a second. I saw Nathan this morning. Early this morning, like nine o'clock. I didn't leave the shop until two. Are you telling me he sat there, waiting for me, all that time? Because if that's what you're telling me? That's crazy."

"I know." She breathed it softly, as if agreeing with me would make it even worse.

I ran my hand through my hair, trying to figure out what it all meant. And no matter how I spun it around, I could only come to one conclusion.

"Alix?"

"Yeah."

"I'm scared."

I wanted her to reassure me like she always did. I wanted her to tell me Nathan was just a normal boy with overactive hormones and a few personal issues. I wanted her to say everything would be okay and he'd get over it, and things would go back to how they used to be.

But that isn't what she said. Not even close.

"Rae?" Her voice quivered just slightly, and I knew what came next. "I am too."

I dreaded going to school on Monday more than I'd dreaded anything in my whole life.

What would Nathan do? What would he say to me? Would he completely ignore me? Spread a bunch of rumors? Did he think I'd dumped him because of Leo? The questions running through my brain were out of control. I wanted them gone, to disappear like chalk on a sidewalk after a rain shower.

I tried to imagine what might be going through Nathan's head, but I couldn't even pretend to know. Nathan didn't think like anyone else.

Lucky for me, Alix was waiting for me at my locker instead of Nathan.

She pulled me into a hug. Then she said, "His parents took him away. They left early for winter break. You don't have to worry. Nathan's gone."

I collapsed against the lockers. "That is the best news I've heard in probably forever."

She reached over and held my hand. "Rae, I'm really sorry. I feel like it's all my fault, this mess with Nathan. I shouldn't have pushed you so hard."

"No. Don't say that. You didn't know things would turn out like this. I wonder where his parents took him? Are they back together? I mean, last I heard, his mom wasn't even letting his dad in the house."

Alix put her hands on my shoulders so we were looking eye to eye. "Hear me loud and clear, okay? It's not our problem. He's gone, and his parents are taking care of him. Now, let's get through the next two days so we can have a glorious winter break, okay?"

Oh, right. Because after all this fun, there was Christmas to look forward to.

Not.

surprises

WITHOUT NATHAN AROUND, I FELT LIKE MY OLD SELF. THE TWO days flew by and on Tuesday, when the final bell rang, I hugged my friends good-bye and wished them a merry Christmas. Alix and her family were heading to Sacramento to visit her grandparents, while Felicia would be spending the break skiing in Vail. Envy seeped through my pores. I wanted to go somewhere. Anywhere.

"What are you doing?" Alix asked.

"Oh, you know," I joked. "We'll be taking the old yacht out for a spin around the Virgin Islands. Should be a blast, as long as I remember my sunscreen."

Alix smiled, then hugged me again. "I'll miss you. I'll see you when we get back, okay?"

I was going to miss her too. I hated the thought of not

seeing her for two weeks. But it wouldn't do any good to whine about it. I tried to smile. "Okay. See you soon."

When I got to work, I found Leo standing outside the Bean Shack. He looked troubled. Down. We'd been swamped at the flower shop, so I hadn't seen him since our little adventure.

"Hey, Leo. How's it going?"

"Rae, can we just fast-forward through the rest of this month? I swear, all anyone wants to do is bitch about stuff. What happened to peace on earth and goodwill toward man?"

I dropped my backpack in front of me and leaned up against the wall next to him. "Never heard of it. Is that some new-wave band or something?"

He nudged me with his elbow. I looked over at him and was pleased to see half a smile. "I'm done editing our video," he told me. "If you give me your e-mail address, I'll send it to you."

I reached into my backpack and pulled out a pencil and a piece of paper. "I can't wait to see it," I said as I wrote my address down. "Is it good?"

"Better than good. Brilliant."

I laughed as I picked up my backpack and slung it onto my shoulder. "I see modesty isn't your strong suit. Well, I look forward to taking in the brilliance. And now duty calls."

I started toward the shop and then I stopped, remembering something. I reached into my backpack and pulled out the book he'd lent me. I handed it to him. "Thanks a lot. You were right. It was really good."

"So good you might say . . . brilliant?" he teased.

I gave him a little wave as I headed into Full Bloom. Inside, I inhaled the familiar, sweet fragrance of flowers as I gave Mister a few pats on his head.

"Rae," Spencer called to me as he hung up the phone. "Death by guillotine or hanging?"

"Gross," I said, taking a seat next to him. "Hanging, of course. But why are you in such a morbid mood today?"

He took my hand and held it up to his chest. He wore a festive, red-and-green-plaid sweater vest over a long-sleeve white T-shirt. My hand covered his heart. "Kevin and I got in a huge fight last night," he explained. "It was awful. Is my heart still beating?"

I pulled my hand away and gave his shoulder a little shove. "Of course it's still beating. You're stronger than that, Spence."

He sighed. "No. I'm really not. I'm a fragile flower, Rae. An orchid. That's what I am."

I stood up and put my arms around his shoulders, pulling him into a hug. "Well, what do you know? My favorite." He wrapped his arms around me tight. We stayed that way for a while. He needed it. And maybe I did too.

"Thank you," he whispered. "You're the best, my little Rae of sunshine."

I pulled away, my hands resting on his shoulders. "It'll be okay. Take home some flowers. A bottle of wine. And apologize. A lot."

"But—" he started to protest.

I held my finger up. "Doesn't matter. Make it right. That usually starts with sorry. For something. It doesn't have to be for everything, but for something."

"I hate to interrupt, but could I get some help here, please?" Nina called to us as she came through the front door carrying a large box.

Spencer jumped up to help her. "Sorry, darling. I was just getting in a quick therapy session. Rae's quite good at listening, you know."

"I don't doubt it," she said as she placed the box into Spencer's arms. "She's good at a lot of things."

"What'd you buy?" I asked.

"Stupid printer died this morning," she told me, taking Spencer's stool as he carried the box to the back room. "And, good heavens, it's insane out there. You'd think Christmas was tomorrow. Speaking of which, young lady, I made up the schedule last night and I didn't put you on it. I figured you've been working a lot lately, and you needed some time with your family and friends."

I felt panic rising up in my chest. "Wait, what? You took me off the schedule?"

"Yes. Starting tomorrow, the twenty-second through the third of January. You know that once the holiday is past, it'll be dead as a doornail anyway." She patted my arm as she got up. "Spencer and I can handle it. Take some time off, Rae. Have some fun. Do whatever it is kids your age do when they have nothing but time on their hands." She smiled and winked at me.

I didn't know what to say. How could I be stuck at home with nothing to do for twelve days? Not to mention that if I didn't work, I didn't get paid. Dean would throw a fit.

"Nina, look—"

"No buts about it. I'm paying you too. All good employees deserve a paid vacation once in a while."

So that was that. I was taking a vacation, whether I wanted to or not.

I spent the rest of the afternoon helping Spencer put together some wreaths and flower arrangements for the Lutheran church in town. The time flew by, and when the clock struck six, my heart sank a little bit. Home. I had to go home. For almost two weeks. It made me shudder just thinking about it.

As I put on my coat, Nina walked over and handed me an envelope.

"Merry Christmas from me to you." I turned the envelope over in my hands. "Well, go on," she said. "Open it!"

The flap wasn't sealed. I peeked inside. A hundred dollar bill was tied with a pretty red ribbon.

"Nina!"

She waved her finger in front of my face. "Uh-uh. No arguing. It's a little Christmas bonus, that's all. Buy yourself something nice, okay? I'm assuming finances are still an issue, since your planets continue to be in retrograde. It probably won't solve all your problems, but maybe it'll help a little."

I gave Nina a hug. She smelled like lilacs. When I pulled away, I said, "Thank you. For everything. You're the best boss a girl could have."

"Have a great holiday, okay?"

"I'll try. You too. What are you doing, anyway? Please don't say working."

"My friend Linda invited me to spend Christmas Day with her and her family. The rest of the time, I'll be here." She shrugged. "What can I say? It makes me happy."

When she said it like that, I couldn't get upset with her. It made me hope that someday, when I had a full-time job, I'd love it as much as Nina loves hers.

We said good-bye and then I went out to the shop. Spencer was rearranging flower arrangements in the glass cases.

"Bye, Spence. Go home soon and make up with Kevin, okay? And have a happy Christmas."

He turned around and held his finger up, then rushed to the desk, opened a drawer, and grabbed a package wrapped in Christmas paper.

"Merry Christmas, Rayanna Louise Lynch," he said as he handed me the gift.

I felt like such a loser. "But I didn't get anything for you!"

"What? Are you kidding me? You gave me the most amazing hug in the world earlier today." He reached out and squeezed my hand. "The best gift I'll get, I promise you."

"Can I wait?" I asked him. "To open it? Do you mind?"

"Whatever you want to do is fine with me. I hope you like it!"

"I'm sure I'll love it, Spencer. Thank you. Really."

I gave Mister a little scratch behind his ear, and then I walked outside into the darkness. I turned around and took in the brightly lit shop, twinkling like a brilliant star in the night sky. Spencer waved and I waved back. I felt like I might cry, which seemed ridiculous. I'd be away for twelve days, not twelve years.

I drove home thinking about the hundred dollars Nina had given me. It was our little secret, which meant Dean couldn't get his hooks into any of it. It was all mine. I started spending it in my head. I'd get my mom a little something. She loved chocolate, so maybe a box of chocolates. In the next few days, I planned on stopping by to see Maddie and Ella. I thought about them a lot. So maybe I'd get them a little something too. The rest of the money I'd keep, to supplement the measly forty bucks Dean continued to give me every two weeks.

The lights were out and no one was home when I got there. There wasn't a single sign of Christmas, except for the brightly wrapped gift Spencer had given me. I grabbed a maple bar from the box of doughnuts Mom had brought home the night before and went to my room. I stuck Spencer's gift under my bed so Dean wouldn't find it and open it, hoping it might be something valuable. At least I'd have one gift to open Christmas morning.

When I got on the laptop and opened my e-mail account, Leo had already sent the video. I opened the file and watched.

A black screen appeared. Next, soft music from an acoustic guitar and the words IN SEARCH OF FUN appeared. And then images, one after another. Squishy ground. Tangled branches. Swirling sky. Each image was lovelier than the last. Leo's editing was flawless, and the music a perfect accompaniment. When our friend the squirrel took the screen, he took us to new heights, until suddenly, the squirrel and the music stopped simultaneously, and the squirrel stared right at the camera. And then, a giggle, my giggle, edited into the video in that moment, followed by the words I THINK WE FOUND IT against another black screen.

I hit replay, and watched it seven more times.

And then I e-mailed him back with this message:

Best. Video. Ever!

He replied a few seconds later.

In other words, brilliant?

gifts

I GOT UP EARLY ON THURSDAY MORNING AND DROVE TWENTY
miles to the mall. Even at nine o'clock, the parking lot was
packed. I could have gone to one of the stores in Crestfield,
but I was hungry for some Christmas spirit, even if it was the
crazy kind you find at the mall two days before Christmas.

I had no idea what I wanted to get, so I wandered around
aimlessly for a couple of hours. At one point I stopped and listened to a children's choir. A sign said they were called Inside
Voices, and they were so cute. Talented, too. It was exactly the
kind of spirit I'd been longing for. They sang all my favorites—
"Joy to the World," "Silent Night," "Little Drummer Boy," and
"Oh, Come, All Ye Faithful."

I bought three of their CDs. Along with the music, I
walked out with a custom assortment of See's Candies with all
of Mom's favorites, and a couple of gift bags and cards.

When I got back to Crestfield, I stopped at Maddie's apartment first. She looked much better this time and the baby wasn't crying.

"Hi," I told her. "I don't know if you remember me, but—"

"You delivered the flowers. And bought me some formula." Her cheeks flushed a little. "Thanks again for that."

"You're welcome."

She glanced at the bag I was holding. "Do you want to come in?"

She led me to the family room and we sat on the couch. A short and stubby Douglas fir tree stood in the corner of the room, decorated with red and green paper chains and some candy canes. It smelled good. Like Christmas. The baby slept in a baby swing next to the couch.

"I'm Rae, by the way. I don't think I ever told you my name." I turned to look more closely at the baby. He looked so peaceful, his little eyes closed and his tiny red lips set in a dreamy almost-smile. "How's he doing?"

She grinned. "He's doing great. His dad is living here now, so he helps with the night feedings sometimes. He got a job, too, after school. A janitor at the hospital." She paused. "It's a lot harder than I thought it'd be. Taking care of a baby, I mean."

For some reason I thought of my mom. She'd been just a couple of years older than this girl when she'd taken care of me all by herself. My grandma probably helped sometimes, but she didn't live with us. My mom never talked about those days. Maybe she wanted to forget about them.

"Well, I came by to wish you a merry Christmas." I handed her the gift bag.

Maddie reached in and pulled out the CD. She studied the list of songs. "I love Christmas music. Thank you." Then she looked up at me. "But I don't have anything—"

"No!" I said, holding my hands out as I stood up. "Please don't feel bad. You didn't know I was coming. I just, I don't know, sometimes I wish I had a big family. And since I don't . . ."

"You're buying gifts for random strangers?" she teased.

I laughed. "But you're not a random stranger! I mean, I know your name, right? Know where you live. Know you have the most adorable baby boy in the world. That makes us practically friends."

"Hey, do you want to stay for a while? I was about to roll out some dough and bake some sugar cookies. I'd love some help. It'll be fun."

I agreed to stay, so we went into the kitchen. While Maddie pulled out a bag of flour from the cupboard, she asked, "Are you a junior or a senior?"

"Junior."

She reached into a drawer and got the rolling pin. "Do you live around here?"

"Not far," I said. "I actually lived in these apartments once. A long time ago."

"You did? Too bad you don't live here now. We'd be neighbors." She wiped down the counter, then sprinkled flour all over it. "It's hard, being here alone with Eli most of the time. My friends don't come around much anymore. I guess I understand. What are they going to do, ask me to go party with them and have me bring him along?"

I didn't know what to say. As hard as my life was sometimes, hers was probably ten times harder.

"What about your parents? Are they . . . supportive?" She shook her head. "I'm sorry," I said. "That's got to be rough."

"Do you get along with your mom?" she asked as she grabbed the bowl of cookie dough from the fridge.

I shrugged. "Some days we tolerate each other. Other days, not so much. We're so different, you know?"

She set the bowl on the counter. "Yeah. I know exactly what you mean."

I decided it was time to lighten the mood. "All right, let's get this cookie party started!"

Maddie held up two cookie cutters. "Which one do you want? Santa or the lobster?"

"A Christmas lobster? I must have missed that television special when I was a kid."

She laughed. "My aunt, who lives in Maine and has a weird sense of humor, sent it to me one year for my birthday. Sorry, but these are the only two I have."

I took the lobster from her. "It's actually perfect, because

I've heard Santa *loves* lobster. Every year he asks Mrs. Claus to make a lobster dinner before he flies around the world. You've never heard that?"

"No. I thought Santa lived on fudge and sugar cookies."

Now I laughed. "Just think, if we combine his favorites, lobster and cookies, he'll be thrilled when he finds them Christmas Eve. He'll probably give us a spectacular gift, like a diamond necklace or a sports car."

She pretended to look shocked. "How did you get ahold of my Christmas list, Rae?"

After a fun afternoon, I left Maddie's with a plate of cookies and drove to Ella's. Her new place was nice. An old man in a wheelchair sat by the doors, looking outside. I smiled at him as I walked toward the front desk. A young woman with short hair greeted me. "Can I help you?"

"Yes," I said, looking behind her, at a bulletin board full of pictures showing the residents participating in activities like aerobics, music, and bingo. I hoped Ella was joining in and having fun. "I'm a friend of Ella's. She moved in a week or so ago? Could I have her room number, please?"

"Yes. She's in room two forty-two. Take the elevator to the second floor, and it's down at the end of the hall."

I thanked her and proceeded to Ella's room. I knocked softly on her door. She answered almost right away.

"Rae! What a nice surprise."

Behind her I could see the studio apartment that now served as her home. A twin bed was in the far corner, and in the middle of the room, her two La-Z-Boys and a television. Along the nearest wall, just past the door, which I assumed led to the bathroom, was a short counter with a couple of cupboards and a microwave. I couldn't help but wonder if it had felt a little claustrophobic to her at first. And what about all of Ella's books? Where'd they go?

"I brought you a present," I said, handing her the gift bag.

When she pulled out the CD, she looked it over and then, honesty being one of Ella's strong suits, said, "But I don't have a CD player."

Right. That was a problem. My mind whirred as I tried to figure out how to fix it.

"Have you eaten dinner yet?"

"No. I was actually about to head down to the dining hall."

"Do they let you leave this place?"

"Well, sure," she said. "It's not a prison. We're free to come and go."

"Then grab your coat and let's go have dinner. You can listen to the CD on the way."

She raised her eyebrows. "Oh, you don't need to do that. I'm sure I can ask my son if I can borrow a CD player from him."

"But I want to! We'll go to King Kone and get two of their hamburgers to go. Along with fries and chocolate shakes, of course. They have the best shakes."

At the word "shakes," she licked her lips. She really did.

We didn't say one word on the drive there, instead letting the Christmas music fill us up. When we pulled into the drive-through at King Kone, I ordered for both of us (Ella liked plain burgers too). After we got our food, the smell of greasy goodness seeping through the bag, I drove us up a hill and we parked. We ate our hamburgers and sipped on our shakes while the Christmas lights winked at us across the city.

"This is the best kind of gift, Rae. Thank you." She paused. "Life should have more moments like this." It made me so happy, I wanted to hug her, but I wasn't sure if Ella was the hugging type. She continued, "'Oh better than the minting of a gold-crowned king is the safe-kept memory of a lovely thing.'"

"I love that," I whispered.

"Sara Teasdale," she replied. "My favorite poet. From 'The Coin,' one of my favorite poems."

Why didn't it surprise me that Ella liked poetry? I ate my last fry. "After eighty-five years, you must have a lot of safe-kept memories."

"Yes. I do. And now, thanks to you, Rae, I have another one."

And then I watched as she closed her eyes and took a long drink of her milk shake, savoring it so much, when I took a drink of mine, it suddenly tasted better than any other shake I'd ever had.

merry christmas

MOM HAD WORKED CHRISTMAS EVE. I'D SAT IN MY ROOM ALL DAY, reading and writing poetry. Dean had borrowed my truck at some point, and when Mom came home, he still hadn't come back. I didn't feel like hearing her whine, so I'd gone to bed and pretended to be asleep. She'd opened the door and closed it right back up when she saw my light off.

I'd left the plate of cookies and the CD on the counter for my mother, and when I went out to the kitchen Christmas morning, I found them exactly as I'd left them. Well, if she wasn't going to enjoy them, I would. I took them back to my room.

After I shut the door, I popped the CD into my computer and let the now-familiar music fill the room. Then I reached under my bed and pulled out the gift Spencer had given me.

"Merry Christmas, Rae," I whispered as I sat on the floor and listened to "Have Yourself a Merry Little Christmas."

"Why, thank you," I replied. "Same to you."

I peeled back the paper slowly, wanting to prolong the moment. The paper gave way to a plain white box. I felt my heartbeat quicken in anticipation. Inside the box lay a knitted scarf, made of extra-soft yarn. The scarf was luxurious and warm, and such a gorgeous teal. It reminded me a little bit of a chenille bathrobe my grandma used to wear.

I wanted to call Spencer. I started searching for my phone just as Dean opened my door.

"What's this?" he asked. I had to focus my eyes to see what he was waving in front of my face. Panic fell over me when I realized he had my bank statement. I scrambled to my feet. "You've been holding out on me, haven't you?"

It felt like the floor had dropped out from underneath me. "Where'd you get that?"

"Found it tucked away in your glove box."

I reached for the papers, but he held them behind his back. "Give that to me," I said. "It's not yours."

"Well, yes, it is. If you want to keep living under this roof, you'll hand it over. Monday we'll be taking a little field trip to the bank when it opens. Understand?"

"I'm not going." It came out almost like a growl.

"We'll see about that," he said, dangling my truck keys in front of me. "You want these back? It's gonna cost you." He glanced down at one of the papers. "Fourteen hundred and fifty-one dollars. I'll let you keep the thirty-two cents, how's that?"

I lunged at him, but Dean was too strong for me. He pushed me back, and I landed hard against my dresser.

I crumbled up into a ball on the floor, crying.

"What's going on?" Mom asked, appearing in the doorway.

I looked up, trying to explain through the sobs. "Mom, please! Don't let him take my savings. I worked hard for it. It's mine!"

Mom looked at Dean and back at me.

"Don't let him do it," I begged.

Dean turned for the door. "I'm hungry. What's for breakfast?"

Mom's sad eyes met mine. She started to say something, but Dean wasn't gonna have any of that. "Joan?" he said through gritted teeth. She knew better than to piss him off any more than I already had.

"All right," she said with a sigh. "I'm coming."

He headed down the hallway, giving her half a second to whisper, "Merry Christmas, Rae." Mom reached into the pocket of her robe, pulled out a small package, and tossed it to me. And then she left, closing the door behind her.

I grabbed the box of candy I'd bought for her but hadn't wrapped yet, and threw it against the door. The lid flew off and chocolates fell like dark rain, scattering everywhere.

I eyed the gift she'd given me, trying to decide how I felt about it. Then I picked up the package and threw it into the trash can by my desk. With nowhere to go and nothing left to do, I crawled into bed with my beautiful scarf wrapped around my neck and cried.

THE DIFFERENCE BETWEEN ME AND YOU

When I hold a rose,
I see the soft, velvety petals
and smile, because
tucked between
those precious petals
is a special gift—
the one of a fragrance,
pure and sweet.

When you hold a rose,
you see the thorns
along the stem,
and you frown
because those thorns
can bring you pain
and cause you to bleed.

I see the gift.
You see the tragedy.

More and more
I fear that one of these days
someone will hand me a rose
and all I will see
are the thorns.

Talk about tragedy.

the hospital—4:21 p.m.

Circumstances shape who we are and who we become.

    I believe that.

    But I also believe we have choices.

    There are always choices.

    Even now, I can choose who to blame.

    I can choose how to feel.

    I can choose to hold on or let go.

"Rayanna, honey, I'm here."

Mom strokes my hair.

    It feels nice.

"You're going into surgery now."

"You have to stay strong. You're going to be all right."

She is choosing to believe that which makes her feel the best right now.

    The thing about choices, though, is sometimes you choose wrong.

three months earlier

a revolution

WHEN I GOT TO THE BENCHES, EVERYONE HAD THEIR HEADS buried in the latest edition of the *Crestfield High Review*. I went to the rack and got a copy. Alix made room for me next to her on the bench.

"What's everyone reading?" I whispered.

Her pretty green eyes sparkled with excitement. "Rae, you know I'm not big on poetry. But even I teared up when I saw today's paper. Check out the poetry pages. You won't believe it."

I flipped through until I found it. This time "Poetry Matters" was four pages rather than two. Alix moved her finger around the poems on the second set of pages. They were all signed "Anonymous."

I looked at her, my mouth gaping open. "How many are there?"

"Fourteen people submitted anonymously this time. And

some of them are so heartbreaking. I'm not kidding."

I had just started reading when she nudged me with her elbow. Nathan walked by with his new "friends." He'd come back from winter break a completely different person. Gone was the all-American boy and in his place was someone I hardly recognized. First of all, he had a mustache and a scruffy little beard. And he was letting his hair grow out. None of it looked good on him. He looked way older. Darker. He didn't come to the benches at all when school started up again. Santiago had tried to reach out to him when he got back, but according to Alix, Nathan didn't want anything to do with him.

I'll admit, I was relieved at first. But then, a few days later, as I headed to lunch, I saw him sneaking out the back door with a couple of stoners. From that day forward, whenever I saw him, that's who he was with.

Guilt consumed me. Had he turned to them because of me? Was he changing who he was, who and what he cared about, because of me? Had I hurt him that bad?

Alix told me, "He's not your problem anymore. If that's what he wants to do with his life, then let him. We all make choices, Rae. And we have no one to blame but ourselves when we make bad ones."

Now I watched him walk by, his shoulders slumped and his hands stuffed in his pockets, like he didn't want to bring attention to himself. He gave me the slightest of glances, his longish bangs partially covering his vacant eyes. I tried to smile at him. Santiago called over, "Hey, Nathan. Come here, man. You getting excited? Baseball practice starts up soon, right?"

No response. Didn't even turn around. Sadness pressed against my heart.

The bell rang, so we all tucked our newspapers away and scattered like dandelion seeds.

I was one of the first to arrive in English class. Ms. Bloodsaw motioned me over to her. "Did you see the paper, Rae?"

"Yeah, I was just looking at it. I didn't get a chance to read them all yet, but wow. It's kind of amazing, right?"

She winked. "Really amazing." She leaned in and whispered, "It's like you've started a poetry revolution."

I loved the sound of that—a poetry revolution. Troubles at home? Put your pen to the page. Is your boyfriend being a jerk? Instead of spreading lies all over the Internet, whip out your journal and write a poem or two.

Ms. Bloodsaw gave us the period to read *The Great Gatsby*. I had finished the book, so I pulled out my poetry journal and began playing around with a new poem.

Felicia turned around. "Did you see the one Nathan wrote about you?" she whispered.

"No. How do you know it's about me?"

"Because he used your name."

My stomach dropped to the floor.

"Felicia," Ms. Bloodsaw called out. That's all she needed to say. Felicia turned around as I thought back to where things were with me and Nathan a month ago. That was about the time we'd broken up.

Time dragged as I tried to focus on my poem. I couldn't stop wondering, *What did he say, what did he say, WHAT DID HE SAY?*

Finally, the bell rang. I rushed up the aisle and out into the hallway, pulling the newspaper out of my backpack as I went. The bathroom seemed the only safe spot to read the thing without having everyone's eyes on me.

A couple of girls stood at the mirrors, putting on lipstick. I went into a stall and shut the door, leaning up against it as I scanned the poems. The title "For My Girl" jumped out at me. It was a short one, by Anonymous, and Felicia had been right. He'd used my name, although in a very subtle way. Some people probably wouldn't even catch it. But I knew, without a doubt, it was about me. I'd thought he'd say terrible things, like I'd said about him in the poem I'd submitted for this issue. But it was just the opposite. And so it didn't upset me, really. I actually kind of liked it.

For My Girl

by Anonymous

I'm not good with words.
I want to tell you how I feel
when you look into my eyes.
I want to tell you how I feel
when you smile at me.
I want to tell you how I feel
when you kiss me soft and slow.

I try.
But my words,
they're never quite right.

If only you could see my heart.
Know what you'd find?
A million little Raes,
lighting my insides
like a lantern.

That's what I've been
trying to tell you
all this time.

You light me up.

ups and downs

AT LUNCH I GRABBED ALIX AWAY FROM SANTIAGO FOR A MINUTE. They were headed off campus to get something to eat.

"Did you see Nathan's poem?" I pulled the paper out of my backpack and pointed it out to her.

"How do you know that's him?" she asked.

"He spelled 'rays' wrong. It's spelled like my name."

She shrugged. "So? Lots of people, me included, are crappy spellers."

"Why is it capitalized like my name, then?"

"Alix, come on," Santiago called from the doorway.

She touched my cheek. "Rae, do you remember how you wanted him to leave you alone? Well, now he's leaving you alone. If he really did write that poem, it's history now. Just like the two of you. Let it go. He'll be okay. And so will you."

She took off with Santiago, and I stood there, wondering

what was wrong with me. I'd felt something after I read his poem. Flattered, maybe? And perhaps a little sad that things didn't work out between us.

I quickly opened the paper and read the poem I'd written a month ago, when I knew breaking up with him was the right decision.

I didn't miss him. Not really.

What I missed was someone wanting to be with me. Not wanting me in *that* way, but someone who wanted to get to know me and wanted to spend time with me because of who I am. I mean, that's huge. Out of a million things a person could choose to do with his time, how amazing is it when he chooses to spend it with *you*?

I hadn't had many people in my life who made me feel special. You know what happens after a while? You start to wonder if you matter.

I mean, *really and truly* matter.

And the more time that goes by, the harder it is to believe that you do.

After school I went to work, wearing the scarf Spencer had given me for Christmas. I'd thanked him when I came back from vacation, but it had been unseasonably warm so I hadn't worn it.

Today he stood up when I walked in, a huge grin on his face. "Oh, Rae. It looks fabulous on you."

I ran my hand down one side of the scarf. "I know, right? It's like it was made *just* for me."

"You really love it?" he asked.

"Spencer, I adore it. I'm surprised you don't have people lining up outside your home, asking for one. I'm telling you, you're amazing."

Just then, a customer walked in.

"Hi," I said. "How can we help you?"

"My name, Peter, is on your board. I wanted to pick up the free flower to take home to my wife."

While Spencer helped him, I stepped into the workroom where Nina was busy arranging a bunch of lavender and white roses with white minicarnations.

"Hi, Nina. What's happening? Did I miss anything exciting today?"

She chuckled. "You mean like a visit from the Queen of England? Nope, nothing out of the ordinary, I'm afraid." She tucked a white rose into the vase. "Though that reminds me, I forgot to tell you, the floral philanthropist struck again while you were on vacation. Your name was on the envelope, but Spencer delivered it."

"So who was the lucky recipient this time?"

"Well, she's not really so lucky. It was a mom whose teen son is in rehab for drug addiction."

I couldn't help but wonder if it was someone I went to school with. "That's too bad. I hope the flowers cheered her up."

She spun the vase around, giving it a critical eye. "I have to say, it makes all the annoying stuff in my life seem trivial. Last night I went home to find the electricity had gone out. The electric company said they'd send someone as soon as they could. But I'm afraid I've lost a freezer full of pizzas."

I tried not to laugh. "Frozen pizzas?"

"Well, I don't have time to cook."

"I get it. I'd live on pizza too, if I could. I tried to get hired on at the Mushroom just for the discount. But they weren't hiring."

"What? Are you thinking of leaving me?"

I smiled. "No. This was a while ago. Before you hired me."

She held her hand to her chest. "Thank goodness. You about gave me a heart attack, Rae."

"Don't worry. I'm pretty sure you're stuck with me." I paused. "Nina, if I decided I needed a full-time job, could you give me more hours? I mean, would that be a possibility?"

She stood up, with a puzzled look on her face, and rubbed her lower back. "What about school? You're not thinking of dropping out, are you?"

I shrugged. "No. But I—"

"Wait," she interrupted. "Finances still troubling you?"

After Dean cleaned out my bank account, how could I be anything but troubled? I nodded.

"Hang in there, honey. Things will get better. Dropping out of school is not the answer, I promise."

It wasn't like I'd seriously been considering it. I'd just been curious. "I think I need a tea," I told her, ready to change the subject. "You want anything?"

"Yes, great idea. I'd love a coffee. Get some cash from the register and get us all something."

Spencer was on the phone with a customer, so I grabbed a ten and went next door.

Leo sat in one of the comfy chairs, flipping through a magazine. I was so glad to see him. I hadn't seen him since before Christmas.

"Hey," I said as I slid into the chair next to his. "Long time, no see."

He tried to smile, but he looked exhausted. "Rae. How are you?"

"I'm all right. You, however, look terrible. What's going on?"

He set the magazine down. "It's been a rough few weeks. My grandma's been really sick with pneumonia, so we've been taking turns at the hospital with her. We actually spent Christmas Day there. Christmas dinner in the cafeteria is something else. You should try it sometime. The lime Jell-O? Out of this world."

"Oh no. And here I thought I had a crappy Christmas. Yours sounds terrible."

He nodded. Then he raised his eyebrows. "Wanna have a do-over?"

"What do you mean?"

"A Christmas do-over. Me and you. We could exchange gifts. Go out for a ham dinner. Sing carols."

I laughed. "A ham dinner? Really?"

"What, you don't like ham? Turkey, then."

I shook my head and held out my hands. "I don't think so. I'd be up for another video though."

He scratched his head, as if considering the proposition. "Okay. But only if we can do it at the mall. We'll pick gifts out for each other. And the gifts will live on in the video. But nowhere else."

"Gift giving without the expense. I like it. When?"

He sighed. "Yeah. That's gonna be the hard part. I'm basically working full-time and then some right now."

"What about school?"

"Leo!" his brother called as a couple of customers walked in.

He stood up and shoved his hands in his pockets. "It's not exactly anyone's priority right now." He looked around. Then he said quietly, "I told Mom I wouldn't be able to work that much and keep up with my online classes. She told me not to worry about school for the time being. I can catch up later." He leaned in. "To be honest, I'm afraid later will never happen and I'll be working here forever."

Poor guy. He really needed to have some fun.

"Let's do the video tomorrow night," I told him as I stood up. "Six o'clock. We'll leave from here. I'll drive."

"Sounds good." Leo reached out and touched my scarf. "Very nice. I like it."

"It was a Christmas present from Spencer." Without thinking, I said, "The only one I got."

He nodded as his hand moved from the scarf down to my hand. He held it as he said, "I'm sorry. You deserve so much more. You know that, right?"

I didn't quite know how to respond. I cleared my throat and fidgeted a little, so Leo smiled and said, "You really do," before he headed over to help his brother.

As I got in line, I realized why I'd felt so flustered. With just a few words and a simple gesture, he'd made me feel that elusive feeling I'd been thinking about earlier.

For a second I'd felt . . . special.

afraid

MOM'S CAR WAS GONE, BUT SHE WAS HOME WHEN I GOT BACK
that evening. For the third night in a row, she hadn't gone to
work. Dean, on the other hand, was nowhere in sight.

"Can I give you a ride to work?" I asked when I walked in.

She shook her head. "I called in sick."

I sat down next to her on the couch. She had the television turned on to the news. The weatherman said we could
expect a big storm over the next few days. "Stormy" pretty
much described my life lately.

"Are you okay?" I asked Mom.

She sighed. "I don't know, Rae. I think something bad is
going on. And I have no idea what to do about it."

Well, she might not know, but I knew exactly what we
should do.

"Let's leave, Mom. We don't need to stay here. We can get a little apartment and—"

"Stop it, Rae," she said quietly but firmly. "I'm not leaving him. I need him."

I was astounded that she actually believed she *needed* him. "For what, Mom? To make you feel like a piece of garbage? To take all our money and spend it on God-knows-what? To—"

She stood up, her jaw set and her face red. "Stop it! Just stop it! You don't understand. It's complicated!"

I stood up to face her. I wasn't going to let her off this time. She had to see the truth: We'd be better off without him. "It is *not* complicated. It's so simple, I can spell it out for you. He's a jerk with a capital *J* and he gives you absolutely nothing. Not even love, Mom. Don't you see that? He gives you nothing!"

"I said, stop it!" she yelled. "You don't understand!"

"Then explain it to me. Why won't you leave?"

"Because he'll hurt us," she cried, her voice shaking as tears ran down her face. "He's told me at least a hundred times. If we leave, he'll find us. Don't you see? We can't leave."

Her whole body trembled. I held her and tried to calm her. My words came out softer now. "Mom, that's just his sick way of making you stay. Would he be mad if we left? Yes. But he wouldn't try to hunt us down like wild animals."

Her eyes, big and round, stared into mine. And before she could respond, I knew it was a lost cause. Nothing I might say would change her mind.

"He would," she whispered. "He's told me the things he'd do to you, and to me, if we left. And, Rae, I believe him."

She stepped back, twisted her torso, and pulled up her sweatshirt, revealing an ugly purple and green bruise, the size of a baseball, on her lower back. My mouth dropped open as I stared in disgust at the secret she'd been hiding. I wondered how long it'd been going on. Were there others I couldn't see?

"Sweet mother-of-pearl, what are we *doing* here?" I cried.

She didn't respond, just sulked off to her room, leaving me there, angry and confused.

that was close

MOM SHOULD HAVE LISTENED TO ME. WE SHOULD HAVE LEFT while Dean was gone.

That's what I kept thinking as they argued at two o'clock in the morning. She kept asking him where he'd been. He kept telling her it wasn't any of her business. She tried to tell him it was her business because he took her car and her money. He told her to shut up, shut up, SHUT THE HELL UP, making Mom cry.

Yeah, I got a lot of sleep that night. What *was* he doing with all our money? So many scenarios ran through my brain, and not one was good.

I felt like a zombie the next day. An empty shell. Like someone had reached inside me and ripped out my heart.

Most days I managed to leave the darkness behind me. It stayed at home, confined to those ugly walls. Because, unlike my mother, I knew the world was a bright and colorful place, and I wanted to enjoy it.

But that day the darkness followed me. It followed me to my truck. Rode with me to school. I was too tired to shake it. Too worn out to tell it to leave me alone and bother someone else. I think Nathan must have known he was approaching both of us that morning, the darkness and me.

I walked across the gravel parking lot, kicking rocks as I went. It started to rain. The five-minute bell rang. One guy across the lot started running. I would be late if I didn't speed up, but I kept walking at the same, slow pace. That's what darkness does to a person. You don't care about anything.

"Hey, Rae." I hadn't seen Nathan approach me. He was just . . . there.

I looked up at him. He still had the scruffy little beard. The mustache. The ugly, long hair. "You look different," is all I could think of to say.

"I know."

It started to rain harder. We both ignored it. I spun my ring on my finger as I said, "That was a nice poem you wrote about me."

"Yeah," he said softly. His eyes were so blue. Even behind the long bangs, they reached out to me. Color. Bright, beautiful color. "I meant it too."

I nodded. "I know. But, Nathan—"

He didn't let me finish. Because when we talked, everything

got difficult. He pulled me to him and, just like that, we were kissing. Holy sweet and delicious lips, those kisses. Except, this time, it was different. I felt something I'd never felt before.

Need.

A desperate, painful need.

We kissed each other like a person drinks a cold glass of lemonade on a ninety-five-degree day. And I swear, as it rained and we kissed, everything melted away. Everything. Even the darkness.

Especially the darkness.

The bell rang again. I pulled back. He reached out and brushed raindrops from my cheek. "So you do miss me."

I couldn't speak. How could I explain everything I'd been feeling that morning? I couldn't. It would take a lifetime.

I kissed him again. Our bodies pressed together, closer and closer, and I didn't want to stop. He moved his mouth to my ear and whispered, "Let's get out of here."

I wanted to say yes.

I mean, I *really* wanted to say yes.

I probably would have said yes if it hadn't been for Alix coming to find me. I'd texted her before I left the house, something dramatic like, "Today blows and I think I want to die."

The rain came down in sheets as she came to my side. She looked at Nathan. "What is it with you and rainstorms?"

"We were just—"

"No." She shook her head. "You don't have to tell me. I

saw, okay? Five more minutes and I would have found you in the back of your car."

She faced me. "Rae, are you all right?"

I was wet and cold and I couldn't believe what had almost happened. What I had almost let happen. Suddenly, I could barely stand up. Each raindrop that pelted me felt like a knife to my skin. I hurt.

Everything hurt so much.

I fell into Alix's arms.

"Shhh, I've got you. Everything's going to be okay." She looked up at Nathan. "You need to go. Stay away from her, please? She doesn't need you."

I started to lift my head up, to tell her he hadn't done anything wrong, but her strong arm kept my head against her shoulder.

When she finally let me go, Nathan was gone.

"We need to get cleaned up," she said. "Do you want me to take you home?"

I shook my head no as my teeth began to chatter.

She was quiet for a minute. "I'm taking you to my house. No one's there. You can borrow some clothes and tell me what happened. Then we'll come back. Okay?"

I was too cold to speak. Too humiliated. What was I doing kissing Nathan, and why had I wanted more? I tried to make sense of it, but that was the problem. It didn't make any sense. Nothing made sense anymore.

. . .

I sat on Alix's bed with a blanket wrapped around me while she rifled through her closet for some clothes to lend me. I felt better, thanks to my sweet friend.

"I'm sorry," I told her. "I don't know what happened. Something came over me and I just, I couldn't say no."

She turned around and tossed some clothes into my lap. "I know. I get it. Once you've had a boyfriend, it can be really hard to go back to not having one."

I pulled the white T-shirt over my head and then zipped up the light orange hoodie. I couldn't tell Alix about the stuff going on at home. About how totally alone I'd felt this morning. "No, that's not it. I mean, I'm fine on my own. He caught me at a bad time and I didn't have the strength to tell him to leave me alone. And then, when he started kissing me, it's like my brain evaporated. Because, Alix, here's the thing: Nathan may have a lot of issues, but he is one fine kisser."

She laughed. "Okay, then. Good to know."

"Please don't hate me. Please? Because I think I hate myself enough for the both of us."

She went to the mirror and brushed her pretty brown hair. "Don't do that. And you know I could never hate you. But I think that's why sweet girls sometimes stay with guys who are tools. The physical part is great. They love feeling loved. And so they put up with stuff they shouldn't."

I thought of my mom when Alix said that. The way I'd

acted today? It was just like my mom. It made me sick to think I could turn out like her.

"Alix?"

"Yeah?"

"I don't want that to happen again."

"Then it won't. It's all up to you, and you are one strong girl, Rayanna Lynch. I know that for a fact."

I wasn't so sure, but I clung to her words all the same.

A HAIKU FOR THE BOY IN THE PARKING LOT

Don't get your hopes up.
I needed someone today.
Darkness said you'd do.

a mutual acquaintance

"YOU DEFINITELY NEED THESE SOCKS," I TOLD LEO, HOLDING UP a pair of men's dress socks with flying eagles on them.

"Need them for what? To remind myself I'm grateful that I'm not seventy years old?"

"What about these?" I held up a pair of green camouflage socks.

"Right. That way the mountain lions won't see my feet and will bite off my head instead."

We'd been at the mall for an hour or so and had already filmed some fun gift exchanges for our new video. I'd tried on a lavender lace and silk evening gown by designer Elie Saab. It was stunning. I'd felt like Cinderella, going from rags to riches in the space of a minute.

After I'd stepped out of the dressing room, Leo had stared

at me for a few seconds before he said, "Were you a movie star in a different life?"

It'd made me blush, the way he'd looked at me. "Don't you want to record it?" I'd asked. "Before a salesperson comes by and gets upset with us?"

He'd fumbled around, trying to pull the camera out of the bag. "Yes. Sorry."

Once he'd started filming, I'd felt shy, but I did as he asked and spun around slowly, so he could get the dress from all sides. When he'd finished, he said, "I never really understood that saying, 'You look like a million bucks.' But I do now."

Back in the dressing room, it was hard taking off that dress. It seemed almost . . . magical. Somehow I managed to do it, and when I'd walked out, I told Leo it was his turn.

For him I'd found a fifty-five-inch 3-D television with a price tag that made us both gasp. And a super-fancy popcorn maker to go with it. Because what's an awesome entertainment system without snacks to go with it?

"What exactly are we doing in the men's underwear department, anyway?" he asked now.

"It's not the underwear department. It's the sock department. Socks are a must-have gift for every Christmas. Don't you know that?"

"Maybe for you. I've never gotten socks for Christmas in my life," he said. "Not even from my grandma."

My grandma had always given me socks. The soft and

fluffy kind in bright colors. I almost started to tell Leo this, but then I saw how his face had changed at the mere thought of his grandma. No more grandma talk.

"Can we please finish our video?" I said. "I'm starving."

We did a couple more spots before we went in search of food. For a Friday night, the mall wasn't very crowded. January must be the worst month for retailers. Just about every store had a SALE sign in the window or sitting outside the store, trying to lure shoppers inside. But who had any money in January? I sure didn't, although that was primarily Dean's fault.

"What sounds good?" Leo asked as we stood at the edge of the food court, looking around. He reached into his back pocket for his wallet, his camera bag slung over his shoulder. "Not sure we'll find an old-fashioned Christmas dinner here, unfortunately, but I'm buying, so whatever you want."

My stomach rumbled at the words. Lunch had consisted of an apple Alix had given me and a cookie Felicia's mom had packed her but she didn't want because of her New Year's resolution to lose weight.

"Think I'll have a big slice of cheese pizza from the Italian place."

"Okay. I like their calzone."

We'd just gotten in line when my phone buzzed. It was a text from Nathan.

CAN WE MEET UP? WANT TO SEE YOU.

Perfect. Just perfect.

I shut my phone as someone called out, "Rae! Leo!"

It was Maddie with baby Eli. I waved, and so did Leo.

"How do you know Maddie?" I asked after she turned back to order.

"From the coffee shop. She doesn't come in much since she had the baby. But she and her friends used to come in all the time." He looked at me. "Do you know her from school?"

I shook my head. "I delivered flowers to her a while back. We've sort of become friends. She's really nice."

"It must be tough, having a kid so young. Is she doing okay?"

"Yeah. Her boyfriend moved in, and he has a job. I don't know how she was supporting herself before. Welfare, maybe?"

"Hopefully her parents are helping her out too."

"I don't think so. She told me they aren't supportive at all. Which is sad."

"I hate mean parents," he said.

Wouldn't he just love mine, then?

After we got our food, we sat in a corner, eating and talking, having such a good time, we didn't even notice Maddie walking toward our table.

She leaned in, surprising both of us, and said, "I just had to tell you guys, you make the cutest couple!"

"Oh, but we're . . ." I turned to Leo for some help, but he looked like he wanted to crawl under the table. "Thanks," I said quickly. I motioned to Eli, strapped into the baby carrier, smiling. "Not as cute as he is, though."

"I've gotta run. Almost his bedtime." She waved. "See you later."

I reached into my purse to get my ChapStick. "Sorry," I said, popping the lid off. "I didn't want to make her feel bad by telling her we're just friends."

I moved the tube across my lips nervously, wishing he'd hurry up and say something. I tried to read his face, to figure out what he was thinking, but all I could see was some lingering embarrassment as he fiddled with the napkin in front of him.

"It's fine," he said. "And you're right, that is one cute baby."

"Yeah. The cutest."

I couldn't help but wonder if he'd ever thought about us in that way. I had, once or twice. Never for long, because our friendship meant so much to me, but I definitely had.

He stood up suddenly. "You ready to go?" He tried to be funny. "It's almost my bedtime too."

"Oh, yeah. Sure."

We didn't say a word all the way to the parking lot. It seemed like Leo was bothered by what Maddie had said, and I couldn't quite figure out why. It didn't seem like a big deal to me. If it was a big deal to *him*, what exactly did that mean?

I could have asked him. But I wasn't sure if I really wanted to know the answer.

the unexpected

"WHAT TIME DO YOU HAVE TO BE AT WORK TOMORROW?" I ASKED, to break the silence as we drove back to Crestfield.

"Four thirty," Leo said. "Doors open at five."

"That is so early. How do you do it?"

"I don't have a choice. Everyone needs me to do more right now, so that's what I have to do. My dad keeps telling me what a great team we make."

"I can't imagine having a family like yours. You live together and work together, and you still seem to like each other. It must be nice."

He let out a little laugh. "Trust me. It's not all daisies and roses, like where you work. Aaron and I have a code word that means, 'Stay the hell away from me right now.'"

I laughed. "What's the word?"

"Titanic."

"As in, you're going down if you don't stay away from me?"

"As in, at this moment I hate you as much as I hate that movie."

We laughed as I stopped at a red light, and I thought, *This is more like it.* We were on the edge of Crestfield now, just a few minutes from his house. I looked at him. "So you don't always get along. I find that sort of comforting."

"If you're in Full Bloom and you hear coffee mugs breaking against the wall? It's *probably* not a good time to stop in for coffee. Or tea, in your case."

I wanted to say I knew about fights. I knew about meanness and yelling and throwing things. Part of me wanted to tell him everything—beyond the glimpse from the poem I'd shared with him and our talk that day in the woods. But the fear of rejection gripped me, like it always did when it came to the subject of my family.

I kept the conversation focused on Leo. "The stress with your grandma in the hospital has got to be hard. On everyone. Can I do anything?"

The light turned green. "You've already done a lot."

"Yeah, a 3-D TV is a pretty amazing gift, isn't it?" I joked.

"No, really, tonight was exactly what I needed." I felt his finger gently brush my jawbone. It surprised me. I glanced at him and he smiled back. "Thanks, Rae."

I didn't know what to do, what to say. It was such an intimate gesture. I remembered the way he'd held my hand yesterday, ever so briefly, and the way he'd looked at me earlier tonight as I came out of the dressing room.

Was that why he'd been so flustered by Maddie's comment? Did he wish what she'd said was true? I didn't know what to think. I gripped the steering wheel and drove. When I pulled into the driveway, my palms sweaty and butterflies circling my stomach, I wondered how the night would end. Even more important, I wondered how I *wanted* the night to end.

"Do you want to come in for a while?" he asked.

"Oh, no, that's okay, you have to get up early. Maybe I'll see you tomorrow?"

"Yeah." He paused. "You know, I really want to—"

Except he didn't finish. He must have decided it was better to just go for it and see what happened, because as soon as he stopped talking, he leaned in, took my face in his hands, and kissed me.

Kissed. Me.

And I let him, because I couldn't deny a small part of me was curious. It was over quickly, but I liked it. It was nice—smooth and easy, the way our friendship had always been.

Still, I wasn't sure if I could see him in that way. Could he be more than a friend? Did the kiss mean he already was?

"If you get a chance," he said, "come see me on your break tomorrow."

"I will." I thought he might say something about the kiss, or the way he'd been feeling. Maybe he hoped I would broach the subject, but I didn't know what to say.

He started to get out, and then he stopped. "I didn't just ruin everything, did I?"

"No," I said firmly. "It kind of surprised me, that's all. I didn't know—"

"That I felt that way? Yeah. I do. But if you only want to be friends . . . it's your call."

What did I want? I wasn't sure. I liked him. I liked being with him. A lot. Leo made me laugh. And I never felt awkward or uncomfortable around him. I trusted him more than I'd ever trusted Nathan, and yet, I was still kind of scared. More than anything, I didn't want to ruin our friendship. If things ended badly, the way they'd ended with Nathan, I'd lose more than a boyfriend.

My hesitancy hung there between us. "How about a real date?" he asked. "We can see how it feels. Tomorrow night? Dinner and a movie?"

"Oh. Um. I don't know. You really want to?"

"Yes! I think it'll be fun, and if it isn't, just say so. And we'll go back to friends."

"All right. I guess we can try it." He made it sound so easy, like a switch you turn on and off. Friends. More than friends. Back to friends. Didn't he realize it might not be that simple? Still, I could see his point. We wouldn't really know until we tried.

"What time should I pick you up? I'll need your address."

Hesitancy started to creep back in. *Don't do this*, it whispered. I decided not to listen. "You know, maybe we can just leave from work? I'm working from noon to five. Is that okay?"

"Sounds good." He smiled. "See you then."

A date. With Leo. Did that really just happen?

close call

AS I LINGERED IN THAT SWEET SPACE BETWEEN SLEEP AND AWAKE Saturday morning, I remembered Leo's hand on mine. His lips on mine. His admission that he had feelings for me.

Tonight we'd go out on an actual date. The more I thought about it, the more I was happy, although nervous, that I'd agreed to go out with him.

My door opened. And in an instant I'd gone from dreamy to that oh-so-familiar feeling of dread.

I opened my eyes. Dean stood at my desk, ready to reach into my purse. I jumped up, like someone had set a match to my comforter, and grabbed my purse from his hands.

"What are you doing?" I asked.

"Are you holding out on me?"

"What do you mean?"

"Have you got any more money?"

"Are you serious? You left thirty-two cents in my savings account!"

"It's not enough!" He slammed his fist on my desk. "Damn it, I need more. You sure you don't got anything else?" He eyed the purse tucked under my arm. I gripped it like a drowning victim would a life preserver.

If he opened my wallet, Dean would find the money Nina had given me for my time off at the holidays. I'd told Dean she'd made me take an unpaid vacation, since it had been slow at the shop.

I weighed my limited options and chose the riskiest one. "Fine," I said, holding the purse out in front of me. "You obviously aren't going to believe me until you see for yourself. But, Dean, you can't just barge in here and get into my stuff. It's not right!"

I stood there in just a T-shirt and underwear. I was freezing. And scared. If he found the money, it could get ugly. But I stood there like a stone. After a few seconds he let out a big sigh and cussed under his breath.

"You get any tips on those deliveries of yours, you gotta promise to give me the cash." He blinked his eyes really fast as his upper lip quivered a tiny bit. Then he wiped his face with his hands, like he wanted to clear away the desperation. "You understand me? Every little bit helps right now."

"I understand," I said softly as I plopped down on my bed.

"What about Mom? You know she can't get to work because you've been taking her car?"

"I know it, Rae. I'm doing the best I can. God help me, I am."

He stood there for a minute longer, neither of us saying anything. I think maybe he wanted me to reassure him. But those words, they hid from me. Maybe because I'd never heard them when I'd needed them.

After he left, I put my purse on my desk, but then my grandma's voice rang in my ears. *The road to happiness is paved with good deeds for others.*

I reached in, pulled out my wallet, and grabbed a twenty. Then I went out to the kitchen and handed it to him. Surprisingly, Dean didn't get mad and ask where it came from. He simply said, "Thank you, Rae."

I went back to my room, shut the door, and checked my phone for messages. Nathan had left me a voice mail after texting me a couple of more times. He said he didn't want to leave things "unfinished." I muttered mean things under my breath. I'd have to call him and basically break up with him again. I was such an idiot. As if it hadn't been hard enough the first time.

I called Alix.

"Happy Saturday," she said sleepily.

"Did I wake you up?"

"Kind of. Actually, no. I'm just lying here, thinking."

I crawled back into bed and pulled the covers up to my chin. "About what?"

"Strangely enough, all of that poetry in the newspaper. A few words were floating around in my brain about what happened to you yesterday. I'm like, is this how a poem starts? A few words? A feeling? And then you start writing?"

"Yep. Pretty much," I said. "Wait. You're not upset with me about yesterday, are you?"

"No, silly, we're fine. But I'm fascinated by what happened between you guys. You needed someone in that moment. He was passing by. And it's like everything fell away except the two of you. In the school parking lot while rain poured down. Seems like that's a poem waiting to be written right there."

I sighed. "Nathan's bugging me again. Texting me. Calling me. I need to call him back. What should I say, besides I'm sorry and it was a big mistake?"

Alix blew a breath out. "I don't know. Whatever you say, it's gonna sting all over again."

I snuggled deeper under my covers. "What a mess. I should have kept walking. Said hello and kept on walking."

"Yeah. You really should have."

"I'm so glad you rescued me, Alix. Thank you for that."

"You're welcome. Now call Nathan. Get it over with."

"Yeah. Okay. Talk to you later."

I hung up and looked at the clock. If I didn't get in the shower, I'd be late for work. I didn't want to be late.

I'll call him later, I thought. After all, what was the hurry, really?

boys, boys, boys

SPENCER HAD THE DAY OFF, SINCE KEVIN'S PARENTS WERE IN
town. Kevin and Spence had patched things up over Christmas, like I knew they would. We sure could have used Spencer
at work, though. A beloved elementary school teacher had
passed away on Friday, so we'd received a lot of flower orders.
Nina said she had to bite her tongue around the seventh
order, when she wanted to suggest they get the family something else, like restaurant gift cards or a housecleaning service. Still, it was heartwarming to see such an outpouring of
kindness.

I didn't look at the clock once the entire afternoon. When
five o'clock came, I helped Nina take all the bouquets to the van.
She would make the delivery, like she always did when there
was a death. It wasn't that I didn't want to deliver flowers to
the grieving family. I think Nina just felt that as the owner, she

should do the harder jobs. I didn't protest. I had a date, after all.

"Thanks for your help today," she said as we stood by the van in the cool night air. "As usual, I couldn't have done it without you."

"You're welcome. I'll see you on Monday."

As Nina drove away, Leo walked up with his black polo shirt untucked, his tan apron hanging over his arm, and a gym bag slung over his shoulder.

"Hey," he said, smiling. His hair was kind of messed up. And as soon as he got within a few feet of me, I could smell the coffee like he wore it as cologne. "We're gonna have to stop off at my house first. I desperately need a shower."

"Sorry. I should have thought of that."

"Nah, it's okay. I brought a change of clothes, thinking I could wash up in the bathroom, but the stuff is relentless." He motioned to a white Honda. "My dad's. I thought I'd drive this time. We can leave yours here, and I'll bring you back later, if that's cool with you."

"Works for me."

Before we could get in the car, Nathan stepped out of the shadows and into a lit area of the parking lot. My stomach lurched as I wondered how long he'd been there and if he'd been watching us.

"Rae, I need to talk to you," Nathan said.

Leo answered before I could. "It's not really a good time right now. We're just heading out."

Nathan walked over and shoved Leo. "I'm pretty sure I wasn't talking to you, asshat."

"Nathan, stop!"

Leo stood tall and firm. He didn't touch Nathan, though I wouldn't have blamed him if he had. "Well, I'm pretty sure she doesn't want to talk to you. Girls don't like stalkers much."

Nathan got into his face. "Did your girlfriend tell you who she made out with yesterday? Did she?" Leo stood there, like a statue. "Yeah. I didn't think so."

I couldn't believe this was happening. "All right, Nathan, that's enough. Let's talk." I asked Leo, "Can you wait in the car for me? Please? I'll just be a minute."

He gave Nathan a look that said, *Don't even try to mess with her.* And then he got in the car like I asked.

I walked over a few feet and stood right underneath the lamppost. Nathan followed me. "What do you want?" I asked.

He rolled his eyes and chuckled. I could smell alcohol on his breath. "What do I want? First of all, I want to know why you lied to me about him. You're obviously more than friends."

"I didn't lie," I said. "We're just friends. At least for now."

"I don't believe you."

"Nathan, what are you doing here?" I was getting exasperated.

He came closer. "I want to know why we aren't together. What happened yesterday proves we should be together."

"I'm sorry," I said, almost in a whisper. "I shouldn't have let it happen. I was feeling lonely. It was a mistake."

He shook his head. "No. No way. What I felt, what I know you felt, that can't be a mistake."

"Nathan, it's over. I'm so sorry. I don't mean to hurt you again, but it's over. Please don't—"

"Don't what?" he yelled. "Don't hate you? I wish I could, Rae. I really wish I could. Everything in my life is hell right now." His voice got quieter. "When I'm with you, it all disappears." He stumbled back. "But I get it. I'm not good enough for you. So you've moved on to some guy who whips up mochas for a living. Great. You two go and be happy together, okay? You deserve each other." He walked away and muttered, "Bitch."

"You're not driving, are you?" I called after him.

He didn't answer. I watched him as he turned the corner, toward Pacific Road. It looked like he'd walked, though he could have parked a few blocks away, in the Safeway lot.

I made a quick call to Alix. She was with Santiago, getting gas before going out to dinner. She assured me they'd make their way over to look for Nathan and get him home safely.

I hung up and went over to Leo's car.

"You okay?" he asked as I got in.

Was I? My hands trembled as I put on my seat belt. "I'm so embarrassed." I looked at him. "The kiss, yesterday morning, I—"

"You don't have to explain," he said. "Really. It's none of my business."

"But I want to. I mean, I don't want you to get the wrong idea."

He started the car. "Are you two back together?"

"No."

He pulled out into the street. "Do you want to be?"

"No."

"Then that's all I need to know."

And that was the end of the conversation. We zipped to his house, where I'm pretty sure he took the fastest shower in the history of the universe. I stayed in the car, needing a few minutes to myself, listening to the alternative rock station on satellite radio.

Alix texted me: WE HAVE NATHAN. TAKING HIM HOME.

I replied: THX! YOU'RE THE BEST. GOING TO MOVIES W LEO.

She wrote back: ??? !!! HAVE FUN!

When Leo got back in the car, he smelled good. Clean. Like Ivory soap and coconut.

"So, are you hungry?" he asked.

"Starving," I said. "Dealing with messed-up ex-boyfriends really works up a person's appetite, you know?"

"There's this new place on the other side of town called the Melt Bar and Grill. They specialize in grilled cheese sandwiches with different types of cheese and stuff. Want to try that?"

"Yeah. Sounds good." I sat back and finally let myself relax a little bit. "I'm really sorry. About what happened back there."

He reached over to take my hand. His was smooth. Warm. "I wish he weren't making things so hard on you."

"Yeah. See all the exciting stuff you miss out on by being homeschooled?"

He groaned. "Sometimes I wish things were different. But then I remind myself of the cliques, the who's-in-and-who's-out crap, the annoying busywork teachers assign. And suddenly being homeschooled doesn't look so bad."

His thumb stroked my hand. It was so sweet. "But just think," I said. "You could see *me* every day."

"Oh my God. You're right. Sign me up."

I laughed as my whole body tingled. Because Leo really seemed to like me. And the more I was with him, the more I realized the feeling was totally mutual.

urgent

WE ATE OUR GRILLED CHEESE SANDWICHES AND DISCUSSED AD nauseam the movies that were out, what we'd heard about them, and why we might want to see one over another. Finally, we decided on a comedy, even though it'd received mixed reviews. We both agreed that we could use a good laugh.

Leo knew a lot about movies. About the directors, about the actors, about the budgets and what that meant. I was fascinated.

"Do you want to work in film someday?" I asked as we pulled into the theater's parking lot. "Like, for a career?"

"Yeah. I think so. It's what I love doing. What about you?"

I looked out the window at the film titles hung on the marquee. Someday a movie he worked on could be up there.

"I want to be an English teacher."

He turned off the car. "Ever think of being an author?"

"No, I want someone else to write the stories. I just want to get paid to read them."

He laughed as he reached for the glove box and pulled out some Tic Tacs. "Want one?" I nodded, so he tapped out a few and I took one from the palm of his hand. He popped the others in his mouth.

When we got out of the car, Leo took my hand, like he'd been doing it forever. "What are you reading now? Anything delicious?"

I remembered our made-up book titles. It made me smile. We walked slowly to the ticket line. "I got this book from the library that my English teacher mentioned in class. *Eyes Like Mine*? It's really sad. She said it's one of her favorite books. I'm not done with it yet, but it'd better have a happy ending."

"Man, I hear ya," he said. "I am all about the happy ending."

I wondered if he was thinking about his grandma. Even though the worst was over, she was still in the hospital. If anyone deserved a happy ending, it was Leo.

I shivered as we got in line, regretting that I hadn't brought a coat. Leo must have noticed how cold I was, because he slipped his arm around me and pulled me to him.

"Better?" he asked.

"Yeah." And it really was.

Just then, my phone rang. I fished it out of my purse. It was my mom. Leo watched as I turned off the ringer.

"Don't want to take it?"

I shook my head.

"What if it's important? I mean, I don't mind."

Great. He probably thought I was totally inconsiderate, when I just didn't want her to ruin my night. "Okay. I'll be right back."

I stepped a few feet to the side of the line and pressed talk. "Mom? What's up? It's not really a good time."

"Rae? Oh, thank God. I need you to come home."

I looked over at Leo. He smiled. I smiled back before I turned my back to him.

"Mom, I can't!" I hissed. "I'm on a date."

"It doesn't matter—you need to come home now!" Her voice shook. "We need to find Dean."

"Mom, just calm down. Did something happen?"

"Yes. Two men came to the house looking for him. I'm afraid they might hurt him. So we need to find him first. We need to warn him."

At the mention of the two men, I felt my heart speed up. I swallowed hard. "Wait. Who came to the house?"

She started crying. "I don't know who they were! A couple of big guys. Said they had an urgent message for Dean and needed to talk to him."

Sweet mother-of-pearl, what has Dean gotten himself into? I had to think fast. My mind raced, trying to figure out how to help her.

"Mom, I think you should get out of there. Right now. Do you have a friend you can go see? Anybody?"

Through her sobs I heard her say, "No."

"Does Dean have your car?"

"Yes."

Stupid question. Of course he did. I wanted to scream, but I tried to stay calm, for my mom's sake. "Okay, here's what you're going to do. Pack a suitcase with some clothes and anything else we might need. I'll come home and take us to the Motel 6."

"How are we gonna pay for it, Rae? He took all my money."

I shut my eyes, trying hard not to burst into tears myself. "We'll figure it out. I have a little bit. It'll be okay. We can't . . . we can't stay there. I don't think it's safe."

Mom didn't say anything. Her sobs turned to sniffles. "Okay. I'll pack. But what about Dean? Shouldn't we try to find him? What if they hurt him?"

"Remember what he said? He can take care of himself. We need to focus on ourselves right now."

"Will you come soon?"

"Yes. I'm on my way."

"Thank you, Rae."

My body trembled. "See you soon."

Fear clung to her voice. "Bye."

I took a deep breath as I tucked my phone away. Was this really happening? First Nathan and now this. Wouldn't Leo have a great story whenever he was asked about the worst date he ever had.

"What's going on?" he asked as I rejoined him in line.

"Can you please take me back to my truck? My mom needs me at home."

He took my hand and started walking toward his car. "Is she all right?"

I didn't know how much to say. I decided to go with the tried-and-true policy—the less shared, the better. "She's fine. It's just, there's stuff going on with my stepdad and she's worried about him." We reached his car, and he unlocked my door and opened it for me. "I'm sorry, Leo."

He waved me off. "Don't worry about it. Things happen. Believe me, I understand."

We drove for a while in silence as I made a checklist in my head of all the things we needed to take with us to the hotel. When Leo stopped at a red light, he asked, "Rae, are you sure you don't want to tell me what's going on? Maybe I can help."

I looked out my window, watching as a guy and a girl made their way down the sidewalk, talking and laughing like they didn't have a care in the world. How come that couldn't be me? Would it *ever* be me? "Thanks," I said, almost in a whisper. "But there's nothing you can do."

"Rae, I care about you. And I want you to know—"

"Please, can we not talk?" I rubbed my temple. I felt so tired. "I'm not feeling so great. I'd just like to get to my truck, okay?"

Maybe he wanted to have a big gut-wrenching conversation, but I didn't. I couldn't. Not now.

Leo started to protest but stopped himself. Then, in the

darkness, I felt his hand on top of my leg. It stayed there the rest of the way, as if trying to reassure me everything would be okay.

When he got to the now empty parking lot, Leo pulled into the space next to my truck. He put the car in park, and I thought we'd say a quick good-bye, then go our separate ways. But he had a different idea.

Leo reached over and put his hand on my cheek. "Rae," he whispered. "I'm worried about you."

The tenderness in his voice, the softness of his touch, and the concern on his face were almost too much. I felt tears rising up, like a giant wave. I shook my head and closed my eyes, trying to hold back the tears.

And then I felt his lips on mine. More tenderness. More softness. Like a pink cloud lined in silver as the sun sets. He tasted like spearmint, and as his tongue gently met mine, my whole body tingled. There was something about the gentle way Leo held my face in his hand that made me feel so safe and warm. Loved.

I wanted to feel more.

I needed to feel more.

I reached for him, pulling him closer. His hand moved through my hair, down my back, and pressed me closer to him. All the while, our mouths never stopped exploring each other's. Desire filled me, like nothing I'd ever felt before. Maybe I'd kissed before. But I'd never kissed *like this* before. Never.

Minutes passed. Maybe hours. I don't know. Time and everything else disappeared. What I couldn't express in words,

I expressed in my touch and in my kisses. Here, I could be honest, in a way I couldn't be with my words.

You matter to me, Leo. I want to know you, and for you to know me. I want to tell you everything. You'd understand, wouldn't you? You're not the type to judge. You're too good for that.

You're too good.

You're too good.

You're too good. For me.

I pulled away, trying to catch my breath.

What was I *doing*? Had I lost my freaking mind?

"I have to go," I said as I grabbed my purse and opened the door.

"Wait, Rae, hold on." He tried to pull me back, but I pulled harder and got out.

"Rae!" he called into the night air. "Are you okay? I want to see you again. Can we, I mean, would you go out with me again soon?"

He was so sweet, so adorable. And we were good together. I knew that. But none of it mattered. None of it changed the fact that my life was a train wreck, and he needed more drama in his life as much as he needed to work another forty hours a week. Instead of asking to see me again, he should have been yelling "Titanic" so I'd stay far, far away from him.

I did what I needed to do. For him. I shook my head no as tears spilled from my eyes.

And then I got in my truck and drove away.

from bad to worse

MOM AND I STAYED AT THE MOTEL FOR A WEEK. MOM WAS AFRAID to go to work, afraid Dean might find her there and be pissed off that she left. I assured her he wouldn't do anything in public. And if he did harass her, she should call the police. I knew she didn't want to go back to her job. She would have rather stayed in the motel, curled up on the bed, watching television. But I told her she had no choice. It was either go to work or live on the street. We had to save our money and find a new place to live.

So every afternoon Mom got on the bus and went to work. One of the ladies she worked the swing shift with, Carol, gave her a ride to the motel after the store closed at nine and they'd finished their closing procedures. Mom had a new routine, and although I knew we had a long way to go, it felt like we were on the right track to a new and improved life without Dean.

At school, final exams for the first semester gave me a good reason to keep my distance from everyone. I just didn't have it in me to play the part of happy Rae. I spent all my spare time in the library, studying. And no one questioned it. Finals week is the one week where people understand if you walk around like an academic robot, even if it's not really like you.

If only I'd been able to study the way I pretended to be studying. It was so hard to focus. All I could think about was Mom. Dean. Money. A new place to live. And Leo.

Thankfully, Nathan kept his distance. In fact, I didn't see him once that entire week. And with everything else that was going on, he was the least of my worries.

Somehow I made it through and passed all my tests. But my biggest accomplishment was keeping Mom from completely falling apart. One minute she'd be praising the heavens we'd gotten away from Dean, while the next she'd be a sobbing mess, telling me how much she missed him.

What little money I had kept us afloat. Barely. But we made it work. We used the motel coffee cups for dishes, filling them with dry cereal in the morning and Top Ramen at night. I finally broke down and went to the office at school to get the paperwork for free lunches. Mom and I filled them out one night while we watched *Dear John* with Channing Tatum.

"You'd be better off if I died," she said as we watched a sad scene toward the end.

"Mom. Don't talk like that."

She looked at me, tears in her eyes. "I don't deserve you,

Rae. I know that. I just hope someday you can forgive me for everything."

It was probably the closest she'd ever come to apologizing. It'd have to do. As we watched the last scene, I took her hand in mine and held it. When the credits rolled, I got up to wash my face and get ready for bed.

"You might not believe me," she said as I stood in the bathroom, "but I do love you." She paused. "I always have. Even if I never show it."

And then I had tears in my eyes.

At work I stayed busy and avoided the coffee shop. I should have learned my lesson with Nathan. Me and boys who want to be my boyfriend do not mix. Now I'd ruined a perfectly good friendship. Every time I started to think about Leo, it felt as if a huge rock sat on top of my chest. It hurt. Not only losing him, but also knowing I'd hurt him.

It'd been easier with Nathan. We never really clicked. Not in the ways that matter. But with Leo, everything seemed right. A part of me wanted to confide in him—not just tell him bits and pieces, but all of it. Every time I thought about doing that, though, I'd think of his grandma in the hospital. He didn't need another worry. It'd only bring him down. It was better this way. For him, at least.

Monday night, after we'd been in the motel for over a week, I waited up for Mom. I wrote a new poem and read a little more of *Eyes Like Mine*. I thought of Leo, telling me he liked happy endings. I was beginning to completely doubt their existence.

Around nine Alix called me.

"Girl, you are like a ghost," she said. "Where have you been and what's been going on with you?"

I chewed on my pen, looking over the poem I'd written in my journal.

"Been dealing with some family stuff I don't really want to talk about."

"You okay?" she asked with concern in her voice.

"Yeah. I'm okay."

"Nathan been bothering you?"

"Surprisingly, no. Whatever you guys said to him that night I called and asked you to find him, it must have worked."

"You know Santiago, he has a way with words. Hey, how was your date with Leo? And what about that, anyway, Rayanna Lynch? I thought you two were just friends."

"Well, because I'm an idiot, we're nothing now."

She groaned. "That is exactly why you shouldn't date a friend."

I put my head in my hand. "I know. I know!"

"So let me guess. It didn't go well and now it's all, like, awkward between you guys."

"Pretty much."

"So do you *like him*, like him? Or are you hoping to go back to just being friends?"

What did I want? "I don't know. I mean, yeah, I like him. A lot."

"Then maybe you should try again."

I felt so torn. Part of me wanted to and the other part wanted to stay far away, because that way I couldn't mess things up for him.

We said good-bye shortly after that, promising to hang out sometime soon. When it reached midnight and Mom still wasn't home, I was worried. So I went out looking for her. I drove to Rite Aid, but the store was dark and the parking lot was empty. Next I drove past our house. It was dark. I didn't know where else to look. Mom wasn't the type to go to a bar. At least she'd better not be, after I'd drilled it into her head all week that we had to save every single penny if we wanted to avoid a shelter or the street.

I finally decided she must have gone home with some guy who could help her forget all her troubles for a few hours. So with nothing else to do but wait, I went back to the hotel and tried to sleep.

It didn't go very well.

I skipped school on Tuesday and waited all day for her to come home.

She never did.

I called Nina and told her I'd be late for work. Then I hung out in the Rite Aid parking lot, waiting for Mom to show up for work.

She never did.

STONE

Let my heart
turn to
stone.

Maybe then
I can sleep
without
nightmares.

Maybe then
I can eat
without
a stomachache.

Maybe then
I can read
without fear
of an unhappy ending.

Take the knife
out of my heart
and, please,
let it
turn to
stone.

the hospital—8:56 p.m.

"Rae, can you hear me?"

Yes. I can hear you, Mom.

"The doctors said everything went well.

"Now it's up to you.

"Honey, you rest and get strong.

"That's all you need to do.

"It'd be real nice if—can you open your eyes for me?

"Let me know you're going to be all right?

"Please?"

Silence.

"It's okay. I'll be here. Take your time.

"We'll all be here.

"Lots of people have gathered over at the school, to hold an all-night vigil for you. I'm going over there to tell them you made it through the surgery.

"But I'll be back.

"I promise, I'm not leaving you, Rae. Never again.

"You have my word."

two months earlier

painful

FOR ALMOST A MONTH I WAS ON MY OWN.

According to Carol, Dean had come to the store at closing time that Monday night. He'd brought Mom a box of her favorite cookies and apologized for treating her so badly. After they'd locked up the store, Carol told Dean he needed to go, because she needed to get home and needed to get Mom home too.

But Dean clung to Mom, squeezing her tightly against him, kissing her cheek and telling her how much he'd missed her. When he asked her if she missed him, Carol said, she'd nodded and started crying.

Carol tried to convince Mom to ask Dean to come back the next day, when they could talk things out over lunch or a cup of coffee. But Dean sweet-talked her into leaving with him. Carol felt bad for me. I knew she'd tried her best to keep Mom away from him. It wasn't her fault. Dean had a hold on my mother that seemed impossible to break.

Carol said she'd left a note for me with the night manager of our hotel, letting me know my mom had gone off with Dean, but I never got it. I found out what'd happened on Wednesday, when I showed up at Rite Aid again.

After Mom disappeared, I checked the house multiple times each day, before and after school, and a couple of times each evening. But it stayed dark. I finally checked out of the motel and moved back into the house. It was scary living there by myself, but what else could I do? I didn't have enough money to stay in the motel. Besides, if the two of them came back, I wanted to be there.

The day I moved back home, I checked the mailbox. It contained only a few days' worth of mail, which surprised me. Dean must have come home while we were at the motel. And if he'd been back before, then most likely he'd be back again.

The only question was—when?

The weeks before Valentine's Day were insanely busy at work. In a way, I was glad. My brain got a break from the constant worrying. Nina put me in charge of decorating the shop with as many hearts, cupids, and teddy bears as we could find.

At school, when the big day arrived, it seemed everyone had been bitten by the lovebug except me. I went to the benches before the bell rang and found myself sitting alone. After all, there were Candygrams to open and lockers to decorate.

Mrs. Knight, the assistant principal, walked by with a

bunch of newspapers in her arms. "Would you like a copy?" she asked me.

"I'd love one."

I said thank you as I took it, and then immediately flipped it open to find the poetry pages. There were about the same number of anonymous poems as last time. The poems with names attached were, once again, less personal. There were poems about cupcakes, about coffee, about stars, and about kittens. In contrast, the poetry that people had submitted anonymously was generally darker. Much more personal. There were poems about the pain of losing someone, the pain of watching your parents split up, the pain of struggling to fit in.

So much pain.

As I sat there reading, something didn't feel right. What was it? Weren't all these poems a good thing? Hadn't Ms. Bloodsaw said I had started a poetry revolution?

And yet, there were people around me right now who hurt. And I couldn't do a single thing about it, because I didn't know who they were.

That's when it hit me. We were sending a message that said, Fine, if you want to cry, just make sure no one can see you.

Your pain is not something I want to see.

It hit me like a punch in the stomach.

I stood up and rushed to Ms. Bloodsaw's classroom.

"Hi, Rae," she said when she saw me. "What can I do for you?"

"You have to stop allowing anonymous poetry," I said. "Please. I think it's sending a bad message."

She gave me a funny look. "I don't understand. You're the one that started it."

"I know. But what if kids feel like they have to hide when things are bad? What if they should get help and they don't?"

Ms. Bloodsaw shook her head. "I'm not quite following you, Rae. It's just poetry. If it gives kids the freedom to share their feelings without being ridiculed, certainly that's a good thing, yes?"

"Ridiculed?" I asked.

"Some teens can be very cruel. I'm sure you know that. If everyone had to give their name, they might get picked on. Or they wouldn't submit anything in the first place. Isn't that why you wanted to submit anonymously, after all?"

Was she right? "I don't know. The issues we have to deal with are personal, and, yeah, it can be hard to share them with others, but maybe we should. Maybe we could help each other, you know? Because the thing is, not everyone is cruel." I paused. "I'm not. You're not."

The bell rang. In a minute students would start streaming in.

She stood up. "Rae, I think you're overthinking this." She reached over and gently squeezed my arm. "Feel free to put your name on your next poem if you'd like. That's your choice. But I will still allow the anonymous submissions."

Felicia bounced in then, carrying a bunch of Candygrams.

She was one of the members of the Key Club, which sponsored the Valentine's Day fund-raiser.

I gave her a puzzled look as she handed one to me. "Do you know who it's from?" She shook her head. "Are you sure it's for me? Because I don't think anyone—"

"Yes," she said, interrupting me. "I'm positive. Your name is right there. See?"

She pointed to the name on the folded note, which was attached to a box of candy hearts. "I gotta go. Lots of deliveries to make and I'm only supposed to miss twenty minutes of class."

Maybe it was from Alix. Girls sent them to their best friends all the time. Although Alix and I had discussed it, and we both agreed it was kind of stupid. Why use Valentine's Day to tell your best friend she matters? You should say that anytime, for any reason—and on more than one day a year.

I opened the note slowly, my eyes scanning the signature first. My heart sank to my stomach.

> Rae,
> I miss you. Every day, I miss you. So much has happened that I want to tell you about. Can we talk? Maybe have coffee or get together at the Mushroom? Hey, remember our first date there? It was so much fun.

I'd really love to see you. Even if it's just as friends. To talk. You said we could still be friends. Remember?

Happy Valentine's Day.

Love,

Nathan

Scars

by Rae Lynch

When a wound
is fresh,
my pen is
the ointment
and my paper
the gauze.

What a surprise.
I'm not the only one.

We write
to remind ourselves
we have a voice.
That what we
feel,
think,
worry about,
matters.

Scars form
and we try
to hide them,
as if they define
who we are.

They don't.

Like it or not,
hurting is a part

of the human experience.
Maybe we shouldn't
be so afraid
to let the world
see our scars.

Sharing brings people
together.

It's secrecy that can
tear people
apart.

special delivery #3

ON THE WAY TO WORK, I THOUGHT ABOUT HOW NATHAN HAD reached out to me. Was I being a hypocrite, saying one thing but doing another? Hey, everyone, share your pain because maybe we can help each other, but sorry, Nathan, that doesn't apply to you.

No, I'd given him lots of chances, and each time, he'd blown it. I couldn't be there for him the way he wanted me to be. I just couldn't. Like Leo had said, I needed to look out for myself. And Nathan needed to find someone else to talk to. I had to get him to see that.

In the parking lot at work, I noticed Leo's white Honda, and I felt a sting in my heart. I hadn't talked to him since our date, the night everything fell apart. He'd come around the flower shop a couple of times, once to borrow something and a second time to order some festive Valentine's Day arrangements for the coffee shop. I didn't help him either time. I'd let Spencer do it. I think Spence figured out something had happened between us. But he didn't ask, because Spencer's cool like that.

Mister gave me his usual happy greeting when I walked through the door of Full Bloom. "Aw, look at you, Mister," I said, admiring his heart-covered bandanna. "Even you're celebrating Valentine's Day."

Spencer hung up the phone and called out, "Would tomorrow just hurry up and get here already?"

I laughed. "But, Spencer, it's the day of *love*. Bask in it."

"I want to bask in my bed is what I want to do. I think Nina and I did something like sixty-seven deliveries between the two of us. And there are still more to do."

"I'll go tell her I can do the rest." I headed toward the workroom. "Hey. What was your best delivery today?"

He stood up, grinning. "Oh, that one's easy. The only place busier than Full Bloom is probably the courthouse downtown, where people are getting married right and left. Anyway, a lady from Missouri called and said her daughter was getting married and asked if we could make up a special bouquet for her to carry. Oh, Rae, you should have seen the girl's face. She was literally tickled pink. Her guy is in the military and ships off in a few days. Super-sweet couple."

It made me smile, because I knew how rewarding it was to be a part of deliveries like that one.

"But you know the best part?" he asked. "The bride asked

me to stay for the ceremony. I was one of their witnesses!"

"Aw, that's great, Spence. Did you cry?"

He dabbed at his right eye. "You know me. More senti-mental than Mr. Hallmark."

I patted his shoulder as I walked past him toward the door. I could see Nina putting the finishing touches on a few more bouquets.

"Oh, Rae, wait a second. This came for you today too." Spencer handed me an envelope. As I took it, images of Maddie and Ella flashed before my eyes. With everything going on, I hadn't thought about them much lately.

I opened the envelope and pulled out the card and fifty dollars cash. I read it out loud to Spencer.

> *Please deliver a bouquet to the following address:*
>
> *The Crestfield Hospital, Room 1241*
>
> *The flowers are for George. Sign the card "From a Friend."*

Nina stuck her head out the door. "Rae, if you don't get started like *right now*, we're not going to get all these flowers delivered. Come back here so I can show you what's what, okay?"

"I'll be right there."

"I don't want to worry Nina about this today," I told Spencer.

"There really isn't any time to make a new bouquet. Can you pick one out of the case for me?"

"You bet. I'm sure I can find something George will love."

I went to the back, where Nina ran down the list before she helped me load the van with all the flowers. Spencer brought me a beautiful bouquet to take to George that wasn't pink and red like most of the others. It had wild grasses, gerbera daisies, roses, and peonies in a pretty woven basket.

Nina had provided me with a route that would take me through our town quickly and efficiently. I decided before I got started on her list, I'd stop at the hospital and deliver George's flowers first, since the hospital was close by.

When I got there, I parked and made my way to the twelfth floor.

"Can I help you?" asked the woman behind the desk.

"I have a delivery. For George? He's in room twelve forty-one. Should I take them to him or would you like to do it?"

The nurse took the flowers from me. "Thank you. I can take them to him."

"Is he going to be okay? I mean, what's he here for?"

"I'm sorry, I can't share any patient information. But, yes, he is going to be fine."

"That's good."

"Thanks again," she said as she whisked the flowers away.

As I spun around to make my way back to the elevator, I practically ran right into Leo.

missing you

"HEY," LEO SAID. HE BUSTED OUT HIS WARM, ENDEARING SMILE. Man, I'd missed that smile. Man, I'd missed Leo.

"Hi."

After a few seconds of awkward silence, he raised his eyebrows and said, "Happy Valentine's Day?"

I squeezed my hands together nervously. "Yeah. Wow, what a day. I think everyone and their dogs are getting flowers today." Then I remembered the reason he was probably hanging out at the hospital. "Wait. Is your grandma still here?"

"Well, she was here. Then she went home. And then she came back. She gets to go home again today. Hopefully for good this time."

"Are your parents here?" I asked.

"My mom is with her, getting her ready to go. I went and

brought the car around to the front entrance. That's where I was coming from."

"I'm glad she's doing better."

"Yeah. Me too."

"Well"—I gestured toward the elevator—"I should get back to those deliveries." I hated how strained it felt between us. I wondered if it would ever feel comfortable again.

"I know you must be really busy," he said softly, "but do you have just a minute? To talk?"

It made me think of Nathan. Whenever I agreed to talk, it only seemed to make things worse. I couldn't take another roller coaster of emotions.

"I can't." My eyes met his for just a second as I walked past him. "I'm sorry, Leo. I have to get going."

And then I continued on with my afternoon, spreading love through the town of Crestfield. To everyone, it seemed, but me.

When I got home, I went right to the kitchen to make myself the last of the Top Ramen. Tomorrow was payday. The grocery store would be my first stop, right after the bank.

As the microwave did its magic, I went through the mail. In the past week we'd gotten second and third notices from all the utility companies, asking for payment. And just as I wondered what, if anything, I should do about that, the electricity went out.

"Perfect," I muttered. I pulled my Top Ramen out of the microwave and put my finger in the bowl. Warm, but not hot. I fumbled around in the drawers, first for a flashlight and then for a fork.

Set with food and light, at least for the time being, I went to my room. Thankfully, my laptop was fully charged. I opened it and checked e-mail first. I kept hoping Mom would get in touch somehow. Dean probably had her on a tight leash, wherever they were. That's what I really wanted to know—where were they? But there was nothing from Mom. Not that I'd really expected her to find a computer and send me an e-mail. She probably didn't even know my e-mail address.

I did have an e-mail from Leo, though. He'd sent it just a few minutes ago. I opened it and found a video, along with a note that said:

> Rae,
> Consider this my Valentine's card. Even
> though it's all about Christmas. I know,
> that's confusing. But since our date, I'm in a
> constant state of confusion.
> Leo

I hit play and slurped my noodles as I watched the two of us being silly at the mall, before we'd found the evening dress that he'd insisted I try on. Leo handed me a cashmere sweater with a price tag of $229. I accepted the gift with gratitude and adoration all over my face.

"It's the perfect color," I said to the camera. "And so unbelievably soft. I can't thank you enough."

"Yes, Rayanna, the periwinkle looks perfect against your skin. And the blue in your eyes, it makes them look so . . ."

"Blue?" I quipped.

We laughed.

He'd added some soft, breezy piano music behind the film, cutting out when one of us said something cute or funny. It was good. More than anything, I noticed how genuinely happy we looked. Maddie had been right. We made a cute couple.

At the end, Leo used the clip of him and me, arm in arm, as he held the camera in front of us. He looked at me. "Best Christmas ever, Rae. Thank you." I remembered how I'd felt when he said that. Because he'd said exactly what I had been thinking. And I didn't know what to say after that. So I'd just smiled at him and said, "Yeah. Best Christmas ever." Then we looked back at the camera as Leo had said, in a very deep voice, "Be sure to tune in next time, when we go diving for buried treasure at Pirate's Cove!" I raised my eyebrows, and then the screen went dark. Just as I was about to close the window, white letters slowly scrolled across the black screen.

I MISS YOU, RAE. YOUR FRIEND, LEO

Was the message supposed to make me feel better? Because

it had the opposite effect—I felt such incredible sadness as I realized how much I missed him.

I desperately missed him.

And there, in my room, where I sat alone in the dark and cold, the pain came crashing down on me.

It sliced up every inch of my body.

Every breath was excruciating.

For days, weeks even, I'd been pushing all the emotions away, over and over again. All of it—the stuff with Dean, feeling abandoned by my own mother, dealing with Nathan, and losing Leo. Just stay busy, I'd told myself. Go to school, go to work, come home, keep a smile on your face, and don't let anyone know you're hurting.

I pretended the pain away.

Now the pain had become a monster, and there was no escaping him.

I crawled into my bed and sobbed into my pillow. The darkness filled me up so completely, I wondered if I'd ever see light again.

I cried and cried. With every tear, the monster only seemed to get stronger. His grip on me was tight, and never had I felt so helpless. It went on for a long time, until it felt like I was being smothered. I couldn't take it anymore. I jumped out of bed, ripping the covers off and throwing them on the floor.

"What am I supposed to do?" I screamed. "What do I DO?"

Now fury boiled inside me. I tore posters off the wall.

I pulled dresser drawers out and flung them on the floor. I threw the small trash can at the closet doors.

Something bounced out. Something small. And that's when I remembered. Mom had given me a gift.

Holding the flashlight, I frantically searched the floor until I found it. As I tore the paper off the small box, my breathing loud and erratic, I wished for something good. I couldn't bear to be hurt again.

For once, I got my wish. As I stared at the gift, it comforted me, and I felt the monster retreat. I breathed easier. It was a small, round, silver picture frame with a photo of me, my mom, and my grandma. Grandma, healthy and alive. Mom, her arms squeezing me tight, a smile on her face. And me, a little girl who, in that moment, smiled big and bright because she felt loved.

My grandma—such a light in my life, and so full of wisdom. Like my friend Ella.

"Life should have more moments like this," Ella had said that night we ate hamburgers in the car, watching the lights in town.

Why *couldn't* there be more moments like that? Why did it always have to be so hard?

My thoughts circled back to Ella having to move out of her home. To Maddie, a teenage mother. To George, in the hospital. All of them facing tough situations. And somewhere, out there, a person sent them flowers, hoping to light up their world momentarily.

I crawled to my bed, clutching the picture frame to my chest. Every muscle ached. My eyelids felt heavy, like I hadn't slept for weeks. I picked up a blanket off the floor and clambered into bed. As I flipped off the flashlight, the darkness returned, but I didn't panic. I told myself to hang on. A little bit of beautiful light had eventually found all those people.

Maybe, just maybe, it'd find me too.

A NEW DAY

Soft,
warm,
golden
light
reaches
through my
window
and wraps
its arms
around me
as if to say
you are
loved.
I smile,
caressing
the golden
light,
remembering
all that is
good
in my life.
Friends.
Work.
Flowers.
It's amazing

how a little
light
changes
the
perspective.

a good reminder

I STOOD NEXT TO MY TRUCK AFTER SCHOOL, RUMMAGING AROUND in my backpack, trying to find my keys. A hand squeezed my upper arm. It was Nathan.

I took a deep breath and, as nicely as I could, said, "Hi. How's it going?"

"Did you get my Candygram yesterday?" he asked. He didn't look very well. He'd lost weight, and he had dark circles under his eyes.

"Yes, thanks, but you really—"

"It's true, Rae. I can't stop thinking about you. I miss you. I miss us. Is there any chance we could try again? Or at least be friends?"

I stared at him, trying to figure out what to say. Maybe at one time I'd believed we could be friends, but not anymore. I didn't know how to help him. And I didn't have room in my life for one more person to worry about.

He continued. "Things are so messed up. My mom and dad, they've separated. And it's hell. My mom won't stop crying. And I don't know what to do, you know?" He looked up toward the sky as he ran his hand through his hair. "I need someone to talk to." His eyes looked back at mine. "Don't you get it? How much I *miss* you?"

I opened my truck door. "I'm sorry about your parents. But, Nathan, you need to find someone else to talk to. Can you call one of your friends from New York?"

He shook his head in disgust. "You don't understand. I don't have any friends there. Not anymore. She turned them all against me."

Who was "she," I wondered? Maybe he'd been Mr. Psycho with someone else, too. I wasn't about to ask.

"Look, I have to go, or I'm going to be late for work."

He reached behind me and slammed the door closed. I managed to pull my hand away just in time or it would have been smashed.

"Why won't you talk to me?" he yelled. "That's all I want to do, I swear!"

"Do you see what you're doing right now?" I said. "This is why. You scare me when you're like this, Nathan." My voice got quieter. "It's over. I'm sorry. Nothing's going to change my mind."

His jaw tightened and he grabbed my arm. "I need you! I can't . . . I don't know what to do."

People were looking at us. I tried to be calm. "Just . . . do your best. Take it one day at a time. Some days, one hour at a time. That's what I do. That's all anyone can do. Sometimes life sucks. Believe me, I know. We just have to get through the best we can." His grip loosened. I tried to smile. "You can do it, Nathan. You can. Look. You're already doing it, right? Give yourself some credit."

He dropped his hand and took a deep breath. I backed into my truck, fumbling for the handle. "I really have to go. Maybe you should go see the school counselor. She could help you."

His eyes turned hard again. "I don't want . . ." His voice trailed off for a second. "Never mind. Obviously you don't care."

"I do, but I can't—"

"No. You don't. And, God, how I wish I didn't." And then he was gone.

At work we took down the Valentine's Day decorations and gave the shop a good cleaning. With a few bouquets left over, Nina told Spencer and I we should take one or two and find someone to give them to, so they didn't go to waste.

After I finished up my shift, I went to the bank to deposit my check and then I took a bouquet to Ella. I hoped she'd be happier about getting flowers this time around.

The lady at the front counter gave me an *Oh, isn't that sweet look* as I made my way to the elevator. When I got to Ella's room, I knocked. It took her a while to answer, and when she did, she had her robe on.

"Oh no," I said. "Were you sleeping?"

She shook her head slightly. "In bed. Trying to sleep. Not doing a very good job of it."

"I'm sorry. I wanted to bring you these. A late Valentine from me to you."

Her hands reached up, shaking slightly. As I placed the bouquet in them, our hands touched. Hers felt cold.

"Are you okay?" I asked. "Do you want me to call someone?"

"I'm fine, dear." She set the flowers on the counter a few steps behind her. Then she came back to the door. "I haven't been feeling very well, but there's nothing anyone can do. It's just old age, I suppose. You know what I was thinking about while I tossed and turned?"

I leaned on the door frame. "What?"

"Poetry."

"Sara Teasdale?" I asked.

"Yes. My son took all my books. I wish I'd asked him to leave my old copy of *Flame and Shadow*. Do you know I've had that book for more than sixty years? Her poetry has always been such a comfort to me."

I smiled. "I love poetry as well. I actually write my own. Sara Teasdale I'm not, but I love writing it. And reading it too."

"That's wonderful, Rae. I find poetry so comforting. A dear friend, Ruth, gave me *Flame and Shadow* during an especially difficult time in my life. It meant the world to me, and when I told Ruth as much, her response really stuck with me. She said, 'I'm glad you like the book. The joy on your face is like a poem, and I'm happy to have played a part in writing it.'"

"Yes. You know, my grandmother always said, 'The road to happiness is paved with good deeds for others.'"

It made her smile. "She taught you well, Rae."

"You remind me of her, actually." I wanted to ask Ella if I could come in and sit with her for a while. Make her some chamomile tea and tell her a story, so she might sleep.

But then she said, "I think I can sleep now. Thanks for the flowers. You're a good girl."

"So are you, Ella."

She reached out and stroked my hair before she gently shut the door.

"Happy Valentine's Day," I whispered.

welcome home

AFTER VISITING ELLA, I STOPPED AT THE GROCERY STORE BEFORE heading home. When I pulled up to the house, the lights were on and Mom's old Buick sat in the driveway.

I flew through the door, grocery bag in hand, anxious to see Mom. She and Dean were watching television, like they'd never left.

"Where have you been?" I asked, trying desperately not to sound as angry as I felt. "And why didn't you call?"

Mom sat there, cuddled up next to him. She rubbed his arm and gave me a weak smile. "I'm sorry, baby. We had some business to take care of in Vegas. We were gone longer than we thought. But we're back, and everything's all taken care of. Right, Dean?"

He grunted and then shushed her. Using the remote, he turned up the volume a couple of notches. He disgusted me, and I almost started to tell him so. Mom got up off the couch and waved at me to follow her into the kitchen.

I set the grocery bag on the counter. "Mom, do you know how worried I was? It was like you'd vanished from the face of the earth. I didn't know if you were dead or alive!"

She craned her neck to check on Dean, then pulled me farther into the kitchen. "I'm sorry," she whispered. "He wouldn't let me call. He got himself into some huge gambling problems. But he's paid the men off now, and Dean swears he's done. Said he's gonna go out and look for work tomorrow."

I crossed my arms over my chest. "That's what he did with my money? Spent it gambling?" I felt like I might throw up. "So, what, he went to Vegas and fixed his gambling problem with more gambling? Great, Mom. And you really think he's going to stop now? After he's had a winning streak?"

She narrowed her eyes at me. "I believe him, Rae. Let's give him a chance, all right?"

"What about your job? What are you gonna do?"

A look of satisfaction crossed her face. "All taken care of. As soon as we pulled into town, I went and talked to my manager. They gave me my job back, starting Monday."

I didn't know whether to laugh or cry. I should have felt happy that things were suddenly looking up, but it felt like the universe was rewarding them for running off and leaving me in the dark.

I pointed to the pile of bills on the counter. "Who's gonna pay those?"

"I don't know," she said. "We have to figure that out, I guess. At least we had enough to get the electricity and cable back on, right?"

Dean came into the kitchen then. "Rae, what's for dinner?" He started rummaging through the grocery bag. "Oh, good, you got some hamburger and buns. Fry some up for us, would ya?"

All I could think of to say was, "You'll have to eat it without onions. I thought I'd be eating alone again."

"It's good to have us back, isn't it?" he said as he pulled Mom to the couch with him.

Good? While I was thankful to have my mom back, it felt like one nightmare had abruptly ended only to have another one take its place. And this time I didn't simply dislike the darkness. I was frightened by it.

the hospital—8:04 a.m.

Fingers touch me.

Cold fingers. Like plastic.

Where am I?

Mom, are you there? Who's there?

I hear beeping. And footsteps.

There's pressure on my arm.

My eyes don't want to open.

"Can you believe all of those people?" a woman with a high-pitched voice asks.

"Isn't it incredible?" a man replies, his voice smooth as sherbet. "I caught the news early this morning. The footage they showed? It was one of the most moving things I've ever seen."

"Temp's ninety-nine point three," the woman says. "BP a hundred over seventy. I know. A sea of people, far and wide, holding candles. So amazing."

"Apparently students at the high school organized the whole thing," the man says.

"I think half the town must have kept vigil last night."

"It's all up to her now," the woman says.

A cold hand squeezes mine.
Did he say half the town?
So tired . . .

one month earlier

the pink house

IT WAS A WARM MARCH DAY WHEN I GOT THE NEWS. SHORTLY after I arrived at the flower shop, Nina handed me an envelope with my name on it along with Full Bloom's address. It was stamped, "From the Law Offices of Steel, Lawson, and Greer."

I turned the envelope over in my hands, trying to imagine what could be inside. It looked so official. My instincts told me it was bad news.

Nina and Spencer stood close by, waiting to see what I'd do. "I'm afraid to open it," I told them.

"Would you like me to?" Nina asked. I nodded. Slowly and carefully, she opened the envelope, while Spencer held my hand. It took only a few seconds before she said, "Oh dear. Rae, I'm so sorry. It says Ella Perkins has passed away."

It took a second for the news to hit me. Ella? Ella was

gone? Spencer leaned into me and I let him wrap me up in his arms.

While he held me, I tried to get it to sink in. Ella. Dead. I'd never see her again. It made me so sad, because I'd only begun to get to know her.

"Who was she, Rae?" Nina asked when Spencer finally let me go.

I wiped a tear away from the corner of my eye. "I met her when I delivered flowers to her a while back. She sort of reminded me of my grandma. I stayed in touch because I liked her so much."

Spencer moved aside and let Nina give me a hug. "Do you want to read the letter?" she asked. "I didn't read very far, but there must be a reason why they're notifying you."

I shook my head. "I can't right now. Maybe later."

"Oh, Rae," Spencer said. "I hate to see you so sad. I'm really sorry. But what a lucky lady she was to have you as a friend."

"I'm the one who felt lucky. She had dinner with me. Shared poetry with me. She reminded me of what's important in life, you know?"

"I wonder if there will be a service for her," Nina said. "Spencer, why don't you see what you can find out online?"

"Great idea." He scurried off, and I stood there, not sure what I was supposed to do next.

As if reading my mind, Nina said, "Maybe you should go home. Or would you like to call a friend?"

"I think I might take a walk," I said. "If that's okay? Then I'll come back and get to work. It'll be good for me to stay busy."

She patted my back. "Take as long as you need."

Outside, I took in a deep breath of air. Spring didn't officially arrive for another week, but with the sunshine and clear blue sky, you wouldn't have known. Without even thinking, I turned toward the Bean Shack. And there was Leo, standing by the door, taking a break.

"Hey," I said.

He smiled. "Hi, Rae. How's it going?"

I could have just said "fine" and kept walking. But I didn't want to. I wanted to talk to my friend. "I just got some sad news. A sweet old lady I knew passed away. I didn't even know her that well, but . . ."

And before I knew what was happening, tears filled my eyes again. I pursed my lips together and blinked fast, trying to keep them back. Leo didn't even hesitate. He reached out and pulled me to him, wrapping his arms tightly around me.

"I'm so sorry," he whispered as his hand stroked the back of my head. I breathed in the smell of him, a mixture of coconut shampoo and coffee. I'm pretty sure it was the best thing I'd smelled in a long time.

"Your hair smells delicious," I said as I pulled away.

"Looks even better, right?" he joked.

I laughed. I'd missed him so much.

"Do you want to walk with me?" I asked. "Maybe to the park?"

"Yeah. I'd love that."

Not far from old downtown was a little park near the elementary school. That's where we headed. The sun felt amazingly good. I held my head back and let the warmth wash my face.

"I'm really sorry about your friend," Leo said as we walked.

"Yeah. Me too. Spencer's checking to see if there will be a funeral. If there is, I want to go."

"You sure? They're really sad."

"Yeah. I want to say good-bye." I paused. "How's your grandma doing anyway?"

"Really well. Things seem to be back to normal." He turned and looked at me. "For the most part, anyway."

I knew he was referring to us.

We passed a little house painted bright pink. In the front flower bed, some daffodils had started to bloom, a sure sign of spring. Nina told me once that daffodils and tulips are Mother Nature's gift to us for making it through the dark, cold winter. Ever since she said that, I've had a love affair with daffodils and tulips. Nina gave me a bunch of bulbs last year to plant. The stalks were up and were about to bloom, and I couldn't wait to see all the bright-colored flowers in my own yard.

Leo stopped at the white picket fence and stared at the little pink house.

"Think the store had a sale on pink paint?" I asked.

"You know what I love about it?"

In the sunlight, the freckles on his nose stood out. I couldn't stop staring at them. At him. How many times had I thought about him, about that kiss we'd shared in his car before I'd ended things so harshly? I'd played it over and over again in my head, like a scene from a movie. And here I was. With him. I so didn't want to mess it up.

"What?" I asked.

"It takes guts to do that. I mean, obviously, whoever lives here loves pink. But people don't usually paint their houses pink. But Miss Daffodil here, she loved this pink paint. She probably went back and forth, should she or shouldn't she? Finally, she said, 'Screw it,' and painted the house pink." He looked at me. "That's what I love."

It was as if Leo was telling me to be brave. To stop with the back-and-forth in my head, say "screw it," and tell him everything.

I took a deep breath. "I'm sorry about that night. At the movies." His warm, kind eyes encouraged me to go on. "My mom, she's kind of a mess. Dean, my stepdad, is a horrible person. And that night, things were really bad. Some men were looking for Dean, and it was like something out of a mobster movie. I didn't know what to do. No one knows what it's like for me at home, you know?"

"I knew when you showed me that poem, things weren't good. But I didn't want to push you to share more if you didn't want to."

"I was afraid. Because if people knew—"

"What?" Leo interrupted firmly but kindly. "If people knew, they'd what? Think you're a mess too?"

I shrugged and looked down at my feet. The boots I'd gotten last fall at Goodwill were scuffed pretty bad. I needed to go shopping. I hadn't been in so long. With no money, I couldn't.

Such a mess.

He lifted my chin with his hand, until my eyes met his. "Rae. Life hands us things we don't want. Nasty things. Terrible things. It's how we handle those things that matters. That's all."

"But—" Tears started to rise up. "If people knew—I mean, he swears at me, pushes me around, takes my money, and gives me and my mom absolutely nothing but grief. It's completely humiliating."

"Rae," Leo said, his voice still filled with kindness. "You're doing the best you can with what you've got. You're still in high school. It's not like you can leave."

I let the tears fall as I finally handed over some of the mixed-up emotions I'd been carrying around for so long. "But I feel like I should be able to! Like I should have figured out a way to get out of there. I mean, who in their right mind stays somewhere like that?"

He reached for my hand and held it in his. "It's not your fault."

I studied my boots some more, feeling nervous about what

I was about to ask him. "It doesn't bother you? Knowing all of that about me?"

"Not at all. I don't want to go out with your mom. Or your stepdad. I want to go out with *you*."

He took my face in his hands and held it there, his eyes telling me everything would be okay. I wanted to live in those eyes.

"Can we go to Hawaii again someday?" I asked.

"Close your eyes."

I did as he said.

"The sun is warm. A soft breeze brushes your cheek. All you can see is ocean. And all you can feel is this."

Then he kissed me. A long, soft kiss.

I'm pretty sure I heard the daffodils sing.

in the garden

ELLA'S FUNERAL WAS SCHEDULED FOR THE FOLLOWING DAY. Leo offered to go with me, which I appreciated so much. We agreed he'd pick me up at one o'clock, since the service started at two.

I opened the envelope from Ella's lawyer before I went to bed. Inside was a letter from the executor of the will, letting me know I had been named a beneficiary of his late client, Ella Mae Perkins. It had been her wish for me to receive her book of poetry by Sara Teasdale, along with a check for five hundred dollars. The money, it said, was so that I may continue my mission, in Ella's words, "to do good in the world for yourself, Rae, as well as for others." To receive the items, I was told to schedule an appointment with the lawyer, and then bring the letter along with proof of identification to the lawyer's office at the agreed-upon time.

I held the letter to my chest, humbled that Ella had chosen to leave me one of her most treasured items—a book of poems. It meant more to me than the money, though I couldn't deny I was thrilled about the money, too. I vowed to keep it out of Dean's hands.

The funeral was held at the Lutheran church. Leo and I found seats near the back. We watched little old lady after little old lady come in and sit down. Once in a while a little old man, too. A couple of them patted Leo's shoulder as they walked past.

"Coffee shop regulars," he whispered to me.

And then a middle-aged man and woman, looking somber and dressed all in black, and their three kids, all older than me, walked up the center aisle to the front row. Ella's family. I wondered what they were thinking. How they were feeling. If I felt sad, I couldn't imagine how they must feel.

A minute after they were seated, the organ began to play and we all stood and sang "In the Garden." I thought of Ella and her beautiful backyard, and how much she'd loved it. They'd chosen the perfect song, and it made me smile.

When we finished, the pastor told us to be seated and he began to talk about Ella and her life. As he talked, I read her obituary on the back of the program. There was so much I hadn't known about her. She loved the outdoors and used to fish and ski with her husband and son. She'd been a librarian for almost forty years, working part-time after her son was born and then returning to full-time work when he went into high school. Her husband had died fifteen years earlier. Gardening was Ella's passion, along with reading. She had been a longtime member of the Literary Legion, a book club for women over seventy.

As he talked, I found myself wishing I'd had more time with her. More time to learn about the kinds of books she liked and why. Just more time. At least, I thought, there's one book I knew she'd loved. I couldn't wait to pore over its pages.

"Ella's son, Paul," the pastor said, "had this to say about Ella Perkins. 'My mother could make friends with anybody. She had this rare combination of honesty and kindness that people liked. I often think our world would be a much better place if there were more people like her.'"

It made me cry. Because I'd been lucky enough to be her friend for a short time. But also because I desperately wanted to be more like her.

nobody's perfect

THE NEXT DAY I LEARNED MY POEM "SCARS" HAD BEEN THE TOPIC of conversation at school. Ms. Bloodsaw even brought it up in class for a bit of a discussion.

She asked the class if we thought we were ultimately hurting people by letting them submit poems anonymously. Were we telling them we didn't want to see their pain, and encouraging them to hide it?

It seemed that the majority of the students didn't agree with me.

Felicia basically said what Ms. Bloodsaw had said earlier to me. "If we don't let people submit their poems anonymously, people simply won't submit anything personal. And that's even worse. At least this way they're doing something positive with their feelings."

I raised my hand. "What if kids knew for sure they'd be

safe when they signed their names? That's what we need to do; we need to assure people that this is a safe place to share what they're going through."

Ms. Bloodsaw narrowed her eyes. "I'm afraid that's difficult to guarantee, Rae."

I leaned forward, my arms resting on my desk. "Maybe alongside a poetry revolution, we should try to start a kindness revolution. Why are we so cruel to each other, anyway? Why aren't we more empathetic when it comes to the stuff we're all dealing with? We should be lifting each other up when things are hard instead of knocking each other down."

No one said anything. I looked around the room. Kids were doodling in their notebooks or trying to hide the fact they were checking their phones.

Dale, a scrawny, quiet kid, raised his hand. I don't think he'd said anything in class the entire year. "It's like everyone thinks they have to portray this image of perfection. Like online, at social media sites, people love showing off their cool stuff and pictures of their cool friends, as if to say, be jealous of me. So over and over, I see snapshots that say, 'My life is awesome.' Pretty soon it feels like I'm the only one having problems. But if you stop and think about it, there's no way all those people don't have problems too."

I looked around again. Now people were paying attention.

Another guy, Markus, responded. "It's no fun reading

negative stuff all the time, though. Personally, people who complain a lot bug the crap out of me."

"I'm not saying we should all whine and complain," Dale said. "But a little more honesty—a little more reality—would be good."

I swallowed hard and then I spoke. "My friends think I get all my clothes at the City Girl. That's what I've told them. That's what I've wanted them to believe, because I didn't want them to think I was less than them, somehow. But the truth is, I can't afford expensive clothes. I shop at the thrift store most of the time."

Felicia swiveled in her seat to look at me, her mouth gaping open. I continued. "Why does it matter what we wear? What kind of car we drive? Or where we live? I don't get it. I'm beginning to realize that all the energy we spend on trying to be as good as or better than everyone else would be better spent elsewhere. So, personally, I'm not gonna hide stuff anymore. Everyone has problems. You may feel alone, but you're really not."

I scanned the room, and a few people were nodding their heads. Whether anything would change their behaviors remained to be seen, but at least I'd tried my best to get my point across.

"Does anyone have anything else to add?" Ms. Bloodsaw asked. When no one spoke up, she continued. "What I'd like to do now is give you some time in class to write a poem. The topic is entirely up to you. This is a class assignment that will be graded, with the option of submitting it to the paper, name or no name, whatever you're most comfortable with."

She went back to her desk and sat down. "Thank you for the great discussion, class. You certainly got me thinking."

I hoped she wasn't the only one.

Bloom
by Rae Lynch

In the dark,
the flowers hide.
They wait
for the right time
to come up.

Warmer temperatures
and sunshine
encourage them
to come out,
to reach,
to grow.

They are proud
of who they are.
They bloom,
giving the world
color and joy.

In the dark,
the people hide.
They wait
for the right time
to speak up.

Compassion
and kind words
encourage them
to come out,

to reach,
to grow.

They are proud
of who they are.
They bloom,
giving the world
light and hope.

Sometimes it's dark
where I am.
I don't want to hide
anymore.

confessions

FELICIA DIDN'T SAY ANYTHING TO ME AS WE LEFT CLASS. WE met Alix in the hallway, since we had chemistry together next period.

"Hey," Alix said to me, "what's wrong?" She pulled me into a hug. "You okay?"

Did I look upset? I didn't feel upset. Anxious, maybe? I took a deep breath and let it out. "I told a secret last period. I'm hoping Felicia isn't annoyed with me."

"What happened?" Alix asked.

"I shared with the entire class that I buy my clothes at the thrift store." I laughed nervously. "I'm a real pro at it. You should come with me sometime. You'd be amazed how much money you can save."

Alix considered this for a second and then said, "Really? Everything you own?"

"Pretty much."

"Huh. Well, fine with me. I don't care." She shrugged. "It's fine, right, Felicia?"

"I guess." She gave me a puzzled look. "But I don't get why you lied to us. We're your friends."

"I know. I'm sorry. Please don't take it personally. I think it says more about me than you. I can be insecure, that's all."

"I'll bet we all have stuff we don't tell each other," Alix said. "It's okay." Now she put her arm around Felicia. "Like she said, we shouldn't take it personally."

"Is there anything else we should know?" Felicia asked. She didn't say it in a mean way, but still, I kind of wished she'd let it go.

I started walking toward class. "Mostly, life is a lot worse at home than I let on. But you guys know I don't like talking about it."

Alix looped her arm with mine. "You know we love you no matter what. Tell her, Felicia."

Felicia's face softened. "Yeah. Of course. I'm sorry. It just . . . surprised me, that's all."

"There's a lot more where that came from," a voice broke in from behind us. I knew who'd said it before I'd even turned around.

"Don't start, Nathan," Alix said, pivoting around, causing us to stop in the middle of the hallway.

He ignored Alix and glared at me. "Why don't you tell

them what a prince your stepdad is, Rae? How he tries to recruit innocent kids like me to do his dirty work for him?"

"I don't know what you're talking about," I said.

Nathan's hair was really long now. I could hardly see his eyes behind his bangs. "That night I went over there? He tried to pull me into his gambling ring. Said they could use someone like me. Someone with a rich daddy who wouldn't miss a few bills taken from his wallet now and then."

I could feel my face turning red. "I'm sorry he did that. I didn't know."

"Yeah, well, I'm a big boy. I can take care of myself. I told him to go to hell."

When he said that, a chill went down my spine. He sounded exactly like Dean.

"Stop trying to make trouble," Alix told Nathan.

As the bell rang, Alix pulled Felicia and me into chemistry. I turned and watched as Nathan walked down the hall, flanked by two of his buddies. Clearly, they weren't going to class.

Oh, Nathan. What's happened to you?

the last special delivery

"HOW WAS THE FUNERAL YESTERDAY?" SPENCER ASKED ME WHEN I got to work.

"It was nice," I said. "I loved the song they started the service with. Have either of you heard the hymn 'In the Garden'?"

Nina stepped away from the shelf of plants she was arranging. "No, I don't think I have. Did you like it?"

"I loved it. I think I want that played at my funeral."

"Don't talk like that," Nina said. "It might be bad luck or something."

"I want mine to be a big party," Spencer said. "I hope they play some ABBA. Or Pointer Sisters. Something that makes people want to get up and dance."

"Okay, can we stop talking about this, please? It gives me the creeps," Nina said as she returned to the plants. "Rae, we're glad you're back."

An older man stepped into the shop holding an envelope. "Just found this by your door," he said. "For someone named Rae?"

I took the envelope from his hand. "That's me. Thanks a lot."

"No problem. Don't know why the person didn't bring it in to you."

I smiled. "Yeah. I'd love that, actually." The man left as I tried to analyze the handwriting like I'd done every other time. I still had no idea what I had to do with these anonymous deliveries, and I was beginning to think I'd never know.

It was like Spencer read my mind. "Any idea who it might be? It's been going on for a while now. Seems like we should be able to figure it out."

I stared him down. "Spencer, it's not you, is it?"

His eyes got big and he put his hand to his chest. "Me?" He laughed. "Oh, that is funny. Remember, I'm the selfish one. I want credit where credit is due."

It did seem like it would take a special someone to do something so incredibly kind and not want any recognition for it.

"So let's see it," Spencer said as he put his arm around me. He smelled good, like Altoids and rose petals. "Who's the lucky person today?"

I opened the envelope. Spencer read it out loud, over my shoulder.

Dear Rae,

Please make yourself a flower arrangement.

Make it the bouquet of your dreams, with your favorite flowers.

It's your turn to smile for a change.

Signed,
A friend

Tucked in the envelope was fifty dollars, just like the others.

"This doesn't make sense," I told Spencer. "I'm supposed to deliver flowers to myself?"

"Even better, Rae," Spencer said as he pointed to the work-room. "You get to create the bouquet of your dreams! What are you waiting for?"

Before I could respond, Leo walked through the door.

He had a big smile on his face. Something about it was different. And his eyes, they lit up with excitement. What could possibly make him that happy on a boring March afternoon?

And that's when it hit me. Why hadn't I thought of it before?

Maddie had known both of us.

Lots of people in town knew Leo. He even told me he was a good listener because people loved sharing personal stories while he made coffee.

It had to be Leo.

Still holding the envelope, I walked over to him and whispered, "Can I talk to you outside?"

"Sure. Can I see if you guys have some ones first?" He looked at Spencer. "My mom's going to make a bank run, but would you have five or ten dollars' worth to hold us over?"

After Spencer gave him the change, I led Leo out the door and over to the bench outside Cutting Edge. He took a seat and patted next to him, gesturing for me to sit too. But I couldn't. I felt on edge, my heart beating fast as I wondered if my suspicions were right. I waved the envelope at him.

"Why have you been doing this?"

At first he tried to play dumb. He looked confused and asked, "What?"

"You know what! I've figured it out, Leo. It's you. You're the one who had me deliver flowers to Maddie. To Ella. To George. Why? Please, tell me, why?"

He started to protest again, and then stopped. A smile spread across his face and he said, "Okay. You got me."

I pressed my hand to my stomach as a mixture of relief and confusion rushed through me. "It's really you?"

Again he gestured for me to sit, and this time I didn't refuse. "I hope you're not mad that I didn't tell you."

I laughed nervously. "No, I'm not mad, but I don't understand at all."

He put his hand on my thigh. "In high school, kids are supposed to do community service projects, right? My mom wanted me to do something to make a difference in someone's life as part of our homeschool curriculum.

"For the longest time, I couldn't figure out what I could do. Because of work, I don't have a lot of free time. And then, after you showed me that poem you wrote, I wanted to help you. It felt to me as if you were carrying around your secrets like a deadweight.

"I came up with the idea to have you deliver flowers to cheer up a few people. I figured it'd help them, and maybe it'd help you, too. And before you say I was crazy for spending that kind of money, my mom agreed to help me. She really liked the idea. She called me the flower fairy." He narrowed his eyes. "Please let that be our little secret."

I smiled. "Spencer called you the floral philanthropist. As for me, you were the ninja of nice."

He laughed. "Now we're talking."

I still was confused about one thing, though, and I really wanted to understand how I fit into the equation. "But, Leo, I deliver flowers every day, because it's my job. How did you think this project of yours would help me?"

An older lady walked by us. He waited to reply until she'd gone inside Cutting Edge. "The people I chose came into the shop and liked to talk. I hoped the people I chose might be willing to open up to you, even a little bit, as you stood on the porch with their flowers. You have such a big heart, and I knew if they started talking, you'd want to know more. And in getting to know them, you'd meet nice people having a hard time, like yourself. I wanted you to see that people do the best they can, and in the end, you don't judge them. You come to like them because of the good people they are, which is completely separate from their crappy situations."

It was pretty sweet what Leo did. Kind. What he'd said was exactly what I'd hoped to get across in Ms. Bloodsaw's class this morning. Basically the same message, just a different method.

Leo took my hand in his. "That delivery for George? At the hospital? That one was completely selfish. I wanted to see you. To get a chance to talk. I missed you so much."

I cringed. "And I blew you off. I'm so sorry. Okay, what about that delivery over winter break? I wasn't here for that one."

He nodded. "Right. I didn't know you were on vacation, so that didn't exactly go as planned. But it's okay. At least you got to know Maddie and Ella."

It was kind of unbelievable, how much he'd given me with such a simple idea. "What's the deal with today's envelope?" I asked.

He scratched the back of his head, like he was trying to

figure out how to explain himself. "I needed to end my little project, and I wanted to tell you, but I didn't know how. I figured maybe you'd catch on if I sent you a bouquet. I almost chickened out of coming clean, though, if you couldn't tell." He put his arm around me and pulled me close. "Thanks for understanding."

Understanding? I was blown away by what he'd done to try to help me. I leaned in to kiss my ninja of nice.

"Leo!" his brother called from the door. "Did you get those ones? I need them now, man!"

Leo groaned as we both stood up and I handed him the envelope. "Take it. I don't need a bouquet of flowers. I get to enjoy them every day for free. Really."

"Can I take you to a movie instead? We need to have a do-over date, don't we?"

I smiled. "Yeah. We definitely do."

He quickly kissed me on the cheek and said, "I'll call you later, okay?" And then he ran off toward the coffee shop.

I collapsed on the bench. The mystery was solved, and it would probably take me days to fully understand and appreciate what Leo had done.

No one had ever done anything like that for me before. I felt like the luckiest girl in the world. For a little while, anyway.

at the park

OVER SPRING BREAK, LEO WENT WITH ME TO THE LAWYER'S
office. I got teary when the man handed me the tattered blue
book with the faded cover. The book had been well loved and
I couldn't wait to start reading it. I felt close to Ella, just holding it in my hands, like she'd left me a small piece of herself.

After that we went to the bank, and I opened a new savings account. I planned to be much more careful this time.
Dean would never know about the money or the account. As
we left the bank, I realized Ella had given me more than a
book and money. She'd given me hope. I had a new confidence
in myself and what the future might hold. I sent up a soft
whisper of thanks.

For the first time in a long, long time, life felt good. I
couldn't remember the last time I'd been this happy.

With our errands done, we headed to the park, where Leo

pushed me on the swings until it felt like I was flying. We went down the slide over and over, a couple of times with me sitting on his lap. I leaned back and tried to kiss him as gravity pulled us to the ground, making him laugh because it wasn't easy, kissing and sliding at the same time.

After we took a spin on the tire swing, we collapsed on the ground underneath a big oak tree. Leo lay flat on his back and pointed his video camera up at the branches, the leaves, and the big blue sky.

"You love the sky, don't you?" I asked as I lay down next to him. "You always seem to point that thing toward it."

"I guess I do. It's rarely the same sky twice. It's always changing, always different. And yet, always beautiful."

He looked over at me. "No way," I said. "Don't go all cheesy on me and say the sky is like me. The sky is *nothing* like me!"

"What are you like, then?"

I pointed to the seesaw. "I'm like that thing. Up one minute and down the next. Constantly trying to find my balance."

He smiled. "Always changing. Always different. Always . . ."

"No. Don't say beautiful. Nathan used to call me that."

"Okay. Always interesting? Or, I know, always spectacular, how about that?" he teased.

"Constantly trying to find my balance is not spectacular. It's awkward and painful, that's what it is."

"Well, then, I think you're pretty much like everyone else in the world."

I sat up and plucked a handful of grass, then slowly let the blades fall into my lap. "Some days, when I'm down, it's hard to get back up again. I wonder sometimes if something's wrong with me. Like I should be stronger and have the ability to push myself up faster."

He pulled me into his arms. I lay on his chest, our faces inches apart. "I promise, there's nothing wrong with you," he said as he tucked my hair behind my ears. "The fact that you try so hard to get up when you're down says a lot about you. Not everyone does that, Rae. I wish you'd see that. You're an amazing girl."

"Really?" I asked, running my finger along his jawbone. "Spectacular and amazing?"

He leaned in closer. "Yes. Absolutely, yes."

I wanted to believe him. I put my lips on his, and I kissed him over and over and over again, wanting, so desperately, to believe him.

from the poem THOUGHTS

by Sara Teasdale

When I am all alone
Envy me most,
Then my thoughts flutter round me
In a glimmering host;

Some dressed in silver,
Some dressed in white,
Each like a taper
Blossoming light;

I love this poem. I especially love the image of "blossoming light."

Being alone can be dark. Sad. Or it can be an opportunity to think and dream lovely things.

It's all in how we see the world. And what we hold within our hearts.

I think I've realized that through words, through stories, through poetry, we can change the way we see the world.

And even more important, we can change the way we see ourselves.

the hospital—9:17 a.m.

I hurt.

Everything hurts.

I moan.

I feel hands on me and hear voices around me talking about dosages and vital signs.

What did the nurses say earlier?

People holding vigil.

What does that mean?

It's so hard to think.

Do they know all the ugly details?

Half the town. That's what they said. Half the town knows?

The pain is almost too much to take.

I moan again.

Make it stop.

Please, just make it all stop.

one day earlier

twelve hours or else

THERE'S NOTHING QUITE LIKE WAKING UP TO A YELLING MATCH from the bedroom next door. So much fun. I rolled over and opened one eye to see the time on my clock radio. Four thirty. In the morning.

"Dean, I told you," Mom yelled, "I don't have anything to give you. You took it all!"

"There's got to be more around here. You're holding out on me. I know it." Then came the sound of drawers dropping to the ground, one after the other, as he dumped stuff onto the floor. I could picture him going through Mom's panties and bras, hoping to find a stash of cash she'd tucked away. I hoped for her sake she was telling the truth. I didn't know what he'd do if he found out she'd been lying to him.

After a few minutes he stormed into my room. I sat up as he flipped on the light. With squinted eyes, I watched him as he went to my desk, looking for my purse. I'd learned my lesson, though. I didn't keep it there anymore.

"Where is it?" he demanded.

"I don't have any money either, Dean. Are you seriously in that much trouble again? So much for your promises."

He marched over and slapped me across the face. He hit me so hard, my head slammed against the headboard and made a loud cracking sound. I squeezed my eyes shut, not wanting to cry, and held my hand on the spot, wondering if it was going to bleed.

Mom stood in the doorway, crying. "Dean, what's going on? Why are you acting like this?"

"They are going to kill me, Joan. If I don't come up with some kind of payment, those thugs are going to kill me. Is that clear enough for you?" He looked at the clock as he ran his hands through his thinning hair. "I have about twelve hours to figure out how to come up with some cash or I am a dead man. It's that simple."

Mom pleaded. "Rae. Don't you have anything? Even just a few dollars might help him."

No way. I wasn't giving Dean anything else. Along with my money, he'd taken my dignity, my confidence, and, at times, any hope I had for a better future. I shook my head and started fiddling with my ring. My stupid, nervous habit. "I'm sorry," I told him. "I don't have anything."

Dean stormed over and grabbed my hand. "The hell you

don't." He practically tore my finger off my hand as I tried to pull away from him. He was too strong for me.

I held my naked finger, screaming. "No! Please, not that!"

"Someday you'll regret not trying harder to help me!" he yelled at the top of his lungs. "You worthless piece of shit."

He stomped off, making sure to slam the front door as he left.

As I cried, I checked my head for blood again. Nothing, though I was starting to get a bump. It hurt. Not as much as my heart, though, as I thought about losing Grandma's ring forever.

My mom melted onto the floor, her hands on her face as she let out big ugly sobs. I got out of bed and wrapped my arms around her, rocking her back and forth, telling her everything would be okay.

I hoped they did kill him. I knew I shouldn't think like that, but I did. We needed Dean out of our lives for good so we could finally have some peace.

I took her back to her room and tucked her into bed.

"I'm sorry, Rae," she whispered.

"I know, Mom. I am too."

She rolled over and I tiptoed out, shutting the door behind me.

Back in my room, I looked out my bedroom window. Dean had taken Mom's car, thank goodness. I'd have my truck to get to school.

Still, it was too early to get up, and I'd never be able to go back to sleep. I grabbed my laptop, put on some Foo, then pulled out my journal. It lay next to the book I'd finally finished, *Eyes Like Mine*. The book was way overdue, but I'd taken a long time finishing it because I'd been so worried about the girl in the story. I wasn't sure the main character was going to get the happy ending I desperately wanted for her. She had to fight for it. Really fight.

But in the end, she got it.

She got exactly what I wanted.

CHERISH

In books
we watch
as characters
go through
hard times.

We pull
for them
as they
struggle
to survive.

In our hearts
they deserve
the happy ending.

I haven't always
rooted for myself.
Haven't always
believed in my heart
that I deserve
the happy ending.

While I've always
cherished words,
books and poetry,

I haven't always
cherished my
own story.

I realize now
my life is worth
cherishing.

And I'm going to fight
for my own
happy ending.

kindness revealed

AT SCHOOL PEOPLE WERE ALL ABUZZ ABOUT THE LATEST POETRY
pages. I grabbed a newspaper, went to my locker, and flipped
it open. A letter from Ms. Bloodsaw caught my attention, so
I read it first.

From the editor

I'll admit, the idea of a poetry anthology worried
me. And the idea of poetry in the newspaper worried
me even more. I didn't know if students would be
receptive to the poetry section and whether we'd get
any submissions.

As an English teacher, I knew I would regret it
if I didn't at least try. Poetry is good for the soul, as a
reader, as a writer, or as both.

"Poetry Matters" far surpassed my expectations.
Honestly, I had hoped we'd get enough poems for
one page. In this issue, you will see poetry now fills

six pages. The panel of teachers is now reviewing the year's poems to select the entries for the anthology. We definitely have our work cut out for us.

I mentioned to one of my students, as the number of anonymous poets grew every month, that it felt like we had started a poetry revolution. She started to wonder if we were perhaps sending the wrong message to students who were having troubles. How could we help each other if we didn't reveal our true identities?

That student decided to start signing her poems with her own name.

As you will see, she wasn't the only one. We discussed the issue in my classes and what came out of those discussions was a desire, I believe, on most everyone's part, to be empathetic to our fellow students. Instead of being a harsh critic, we will try to be an encouraging friend. I'm afraid, at times, it is easier said than done. Still, I am impressed with all of you who have promised to try. And even more impressed with those of you who are putting yourselves out there through your work, exposing parts of your life you may not have ever let anyone see before.

May the truth set you free.

Lorraine Bloodsaw
Editor in Chief

I turned to the poetry section. Like she'd said, there were more pages this time than ever before. But, surprisingly, of the six pages, only one page contained anonymous poems.

Dale, the quiet kid in English, had written a poem about

being sexually abused by one of his relatives when he was younger, and how he still had nightmares about it. I scanned the pages, looking for other names I might recognize. Felicia wrote one about struggling with an eating disorder. She had never said a thing to us. But there it was, her insecurities about appearances shown in a whole new light.

The last one I read before the bell rang was by Alix. It talked about how she'd lost her grandma to cancer three years ago, and how she still missed her. It made me tear up, because I understood the pain she spoke of that occurs after a memory unexpectedly surfaces, often triggered by the simplest thing, like a smell or a special song.

It's hard to describe how I felt after reading what other people were going through. People I knew. People I called friends.

I felt more connected to them.

I felt changed.

shine

MY STOMACH HURT ALL DAY. I FELT ANXIOUS. WHAT IF SOMETHING actually happened to Dean? Would I feel guilty? What about Mom? As much as I hated the guy, I knew she needed him in a way I didn't understand. She'd be devastated if she lost him.

And yet, I kept thinking Dean had been exaggerating. This wasn't New York City or Chicago. Men didn't come busting down your door, fill you with holes, and dump your body in the river if you owed them money. This was nice little Crestfield. Where grandmas and granddaughters walked to the library and made tomato soup for lunch. Where couples went to the park to play and kiss under the oak tree. Where a little old lady left a special book to a girl she hardly even knew.

I reassured myself that Dean would be fine. We'd all be fine. Whatever was going on, maybe he'd wake up, stop gambling, and finally get a job.

I could only hope.

After school I found Nathan leaning against the hood of my truck. He looked so gaunt that he almost looked sick. Rumor had it he'd been kicked off the baseball team for using drugs. Thankfully, after our last encounter, he'd left me alone. And I'd made it a point to stay clear of him.

"I hear you and that guy are hot and heavy now." He stood up straight, his words slurred a little bit.

"It's nice to see you too, Nathan." I felt the knot in my stomach tighten as my hand instinctively went to fiddle with my ring, only to find a lonely finger. His body was tense as his eyes glared at me. Why was he so angry with me? Hadn't I done everything I could to help him?

"I just want to know one thing. You did care about me, right? I didn't imagine it all, did I?"

It felt like we were standing on a tightrope way up high. Like if I made one wrong move, we'd both go crashing to the ground. I knew I had to tell him what he needed to hear. I stepped closer, and with a soft, soothing voice, I replied, "Of course I cared about you, Nathan. I still do. And so do lots of other people."

"It's not true. No one gives a shit about me," he said, his voice hard and cold. "Look around, Rae. Who cares?" His eyes scanned the parking lot, so I did the same. Kids walked past us, their heads down, phones out. They were oblivious. "Nobody. That's who."

The way he looked, the way he spoke, something was really off. I'd never seen him like this. "That's not true. Your friends care. Your parents care. And I care too."

He kicked a rock with his foot. It was like my words passed right over him. Why should he believe me, after all? I suddenly hated myself for not doing more for him. When his eyes met mine again, the intense pain I saw there sent a shiver down my spine. He stuck his hands in the pockets of his jacket, and as he stared at me with those hurt and angry eyes, fear coursed through my veins, and I had a sudden urge to turn around and run.

But a little voice inside me told me to stay. He needed me to stay. I had to believe he wouldn't hurt me. So I didn't run. Because I knew Nathan felt like everyone was against him. In his mind, everyone was running away from him, and more than anything, he felt alone.

I knew that feeling all too well.

Where light shines, darkness disappears.

I put my arms around him and gave him a big, long hug. At first he resisted. Then he took his hands out of his pockets and wrapped his arms around me. Soon he was sobbing into my hair.

Now people looked at us. But I didn't move.

I don't know how long we stood there. A long, long time. And when he finally pulled away, even with his face all red and blotchy, he looked a little better.

"I think you need to talk to someone," I whispered, wiping

away a tear with my thumb. "Can I walk you inside? To find someone who knows more than I do?"

He didn't answer for a while, as he tried to get his breathing back to normal. Finally, Nathan gave me the slightest of nods. That was all I needed. I took his hand and led him into the school.

"It'll be okay," I told him when we reached the counseling office.

Those words played on repeat while I drove to work, as I tried to calm down.

It'll be okay.

My head buzzed with Dean's words and then Nathan's. Two people at their breaking point, and it felt like I'd let them down. Like it was my fault, somehow, that their situations had gotten so bad. I should have done more.

It'll be okay.

But I knew I couldn't wish it to be so. When I got to work, I practically ran to see Leo. I needed to feel normal. I needed Leo to tell me it'd be all right. If anyone could make me feel better, it was Leo.

His dad was helping a customer. I noticed for the first time how much Leo looked like his father. They had the same warm smile. I felt myself relax a little, finally.

After the customer got her coffee, I went to the counter. "Hey, Mack. Is Leo around?"

"Hi, Rae. Didn't you see him? I just sent him over to the shop to see if Nina has some scissors we can borrow. I have looked everywhere and I can't find them. Georgia probably put them somewhere for safekeeping, which means we'll never see them again." He smiled, causing his eyes to crinkle around the edges. "I'm kidding. I'm just terrible at finding things."

I returned his smile. "I am too. Thanks, I stopped here first, but I'll go find him."

I waited outside the café for a minute, wanting to see Leo alone, not in front of my boss and coworker. But he didn't come.

What was taking him so long? *Nina has scissors on every available surface*, I thought. Finally, I headed over to Full Bloom, and when I walked in the door, it became very clear why Leo was taking so long.

always love

I GASPED AT THE SCENE IN FRONT OF ME.

Nina stood behind the counter, her entire body shaking.

Spencer stood next to her, his hands in the air, talking in a calm, soothing voice, saying things like, "This isn't the answer, sir," and, "Can't we talk this out?"

And Leo. Leo stood just inside the doorway, next to the guy holding the gun. With the gun pressed against his rib cage.

As I took it all in, three pairs of eyes reached out to me. And what I saw in my friends' faces surprised me. It wasn't as much fear as it was love. Love for me.

And in that moment I realized family isn't necessarily who you live with.

Family isn't necessarily the ones you wake up to every morning.

Family isn't necessarily the one you cook for night after night, without even a simple thanks.

Family is the person who makes you a scarf for Christmas.

The person who says, "I'm glad you're back. We missed you yesterday."

The person who arranges opportunities to meet wonderful people who can give you a new perspective on life.

Three of these people were my family. And I promised myself I couldn't let anything happen to them.

"Well, look who's here," Dean said, clearly loving the power he held over us. "Welcome to the party, Rae. I'm glad you're here. You can make up for ignoring my pleas for help this morning and bag some cash for me. These coworkers of yours seem to have trouble following instructions. But you know me, don't you? When I tell you to do something, you sure as hell better do it."

"Where's my grandma's ring, Dean? I want it back."

He moved the gun off Leo, took a few steps, and pointed it at me. "Don't think I won't do it," he growled. "It's gone. Now let's focus on what we need to do here." Leo was now out of Dean's full line of sight, so Leo took the opportunity to ease the phone out of his pocket.

My mind was spinning. I had to say the shop's name. If a dispatcher came on the line, she'd need our location. They might be able to trace the call, but that would take a long time.

"This doesn't make a lot of sense, Dean. Are you really so

desperate that you're stealing from Full Bloom? A tiny flower shop? We don't get a lot of cash. Wouldn't a bank have been a better choice?"

"Banks are prepared for robberies. But a place like this"— he waved his gun around—"I figured I could just walk in, take some cash, and walk out. Except you're talking too damn much!" Now he pointed the gun at my face. "Get over there and get me some money. Right. Now."

I didn't move. The only sound I could hear was the ticking of the clock on the wall. Dean, clearly exasperated, turned the gun toward Spencer as he walked to the counter. My hands flew to my mouth as fear gripped my racing heart.

"Okay, okay," I said as I somehow managed to make my shaking legs move. "Put your gun down, and I'll get you the money. I can't do it with you waving that thing around."

I thought of all those times I'd followed his orders. Dinner at six thirty on the dot. Handing over my checks on payday. Lending him my truck more times than I could count. Something always told me to do as he said, even when I didn't want to. When I hated doing it with every fiber of my being.

Now I knew why. It all led to this moment. Right here.

Because now, when I asked him to put his gun down, and told him I'd get him the money, he believed me.

Thank God, he believed me.

Dean did exactly as I asked, and lowered the gun.

I heard the faint sound of police sirens in the distance. I'd been listening for them. In a minute Dean would hear them too. Who knew what he'd do then? I kept my eyes on Spencer and Nina. I felt their love. I really didn't have to ask the question. But I wanted Dean to hear the answer—and to cover the sounds of the sirens for as long as possible.

"Love or hate, Spencer?" I asked. We'd played the game a hundred times.

A tear rolled down his cheek, but when he spoke, he spoke with pure conviction. "Always love, sweetheart."

Spencer knew what Dean would never know.

Time was running out. I remembered the words I'd told myself earlier.

It'll be okay.

I would have no more regrets. I had to do the right thing for the people I loved.

It'll be okay.

So I struck, with everything I had.

Guided by light. By love. By what mattered most to me in this world.

I hoped to take him by surprise, and knock the gun from his hand.

I didn't expect the gun to go off.

The pain shook like an earthquake inside me. I held my hands to my chest, felt the blood, thick and wet. The bell over the front door jingled. Of course I knew who'd left. I'd been right all those months ago. Dean really would let me bleed to death.

The sirens grew closer. "It's going to be all right," Nina said, her hand pressing hard on mine while Leo put my head in his lap. "We're not going to let anything happen to you, honey. Just hang on."

Before I blacked out, I smelled roses. The ones that say, *I love you.*

the hospital—1:02 p.m.

"Have you ever seen so many flowers?" It's the kind man's voice again.

"How many bouquets do you think we have?" the woman asks.

"The woman from the florist shop said she's made thirty-two so far, and has orders for at least twenty more."

"I wish we could bring them in here, so she could see them when she wakes up. I bet that'd lift her spirits."

Footsteps.

"Can I try again? Can I try talking to her again?"

Mom. She's still here.

"Sure. You never know when she might be listening."

A cool touch on my arm.

"Honey? I wish you could have seen all the people last night. It was incredible, all the support for you. The kids at your school, they went door-to-door and asked people to go to the stadium with their candles and think good thoughts.

"They sang songs and held their candles for hours. All for you, honey.

"I have some messages. People wrote them down and gave them to me. I thought maybe I'd read some of them to you, all right?

"Alix wants you to know how very much she loves you. She said you are the best friend a girl could ever have."

Sniffles.

"Maddie wrote, 'The day you brought me formula was one of the worst days of my life. I was hurting bad. But then you showed me you cared, that someone actually cared. It gave me new hope. Thank you for that, Rae. Please get better.'"

She pauses. There's a rustling of tissues. Mom blows her nose.

"Ms. Bloodsaw's message is short. I'm not sure I understand what it means. But maybe you do? She wrote, 'It's happened, Rae. I believe the revolution you hoped for has happened. If only you could be here to see it. I hope you feel it.'"

A tear slides from the corner of my eye.

"I just saw Leo. He sends you his love and wants you to get better because you two have plans. He also said to give you this."

I feel something cool on my finger. It can't be, can it? Leo, how did you . . .

"It's your ring, Rae. Grandma's ring. Leo went to the pawnshop this morning and bought it back for you."

I slowly open my eyes. Everything's blurry. Mom brushes my cheek with her hand. "Oh, baby. There you are. Thank heavens. Can you feel how much people love you?"

I blink my eyes.

"I'm going to get the doctor," one of the nurses says. "Rae, don't try to talk, okay? You have a tube in your throat we need to remove."

"Do you want to hear more?" Mom asks.

I give her a little nod and blink my eyes again. Mom gives my hand a little squeeze, as if to tell me she understands.

"Nina says she loves you, honey. Says you're the closest thing she's ever had to a daughter. And Spencer said to tell you how much he adores you and he wants an answer to this one when you come back to work. New scarf: pink or purple?"

More tears fall from my eyes. I am overwhelmed by the kindness. By the love. Mom gets a tissue and wipes them away.

"And now I need to give you my message, which is that I'm

sorry. I know I've made more mistakes than a mother should be allowed to make. But I want you to know Dean can't hurt you anymore. You and me, we're gonna make a fresh start. Everything is going to be okay. Please believe me, Rae."

My eyes have finally adjusted. I hold my mother's gaze as I realize the worst is over.

Everyone makes mistakes, I guess. We do the best we can with what we're given. I think that's what I did. What I've always done. Leo told me exactly that, the day we admired the pink house with the daffodils and tulips.

Just like the flowers, Mom and I have made it through the dark, cold winter.

It's time for us to bloom.

two months later

cherished

WHEN MY SHIFT IS OVER, I HEAD TOWARD THE DOOR OF THE
flower shop. My first day back at work, and it went well.
Mister comes over to say good-bye. I bend down and hold
his face close to mine. I'm so glad he's here with us. Spencer
hadn't brought him to work that awful day. Lucky dog.
Missed out on all the excitement. To him, the flower shop is
the same wonderful place it's always been.

I was a little nervous, coming back to Full Bloom. But any
anxiety I might have felt disappeared when I saw the sign.

IF YOUR NAME IS RAE, COME IN FOR A FREE FLOWER.

I knew that Spencer and Nina were waiting for me, and
that I would love my job, and my friends, the same way I
always had. Inside the shop, a big banner hung from the ceil-
ing. "Welcome back, Rae—we missed you!"

Nina greeted me with the most gorgeous orchid I think

I've ever seen. "For you," she'd said. She gave me a gentle hug, with Spencer right behind her.

When he pulled away, he said, "So, what will it be? Pink or purple? If I get started now, I should have it finished by the fall."

"I can't have both?" I teased.

"You know the rules," he said with a smile. "You have to pick one."

"Better go with pink," I said. "My friends say pink is my color."

"Smart friends you have," he said.

"Good ones too. Thanks, Spencer."

The phone rang, and as he went to answer it, I glanced down at the floor. The floor where I'd lain, bleeding, as we'd waited for an ambulance. Any evidence of that day had been washed completely away.

Thanks to Leo's quick thinking and dialing 911, the police and ambulance arrived quickly.

Dean had shot me in the chest, causing my lung to collapse. It hurt so much and made it really hard to breathe. When I got to the hospital, Dr. Lamb, the trauma surgeon, assessed me and I was prepped for surgery. By all accounts, the surgery went well. They were able to remove the bullet and repair my lung. I was on a ventilator overnight and had a chest tube for a few days. After that, I did respiratory therapy, which, while not exactly fun, wasn't too bad.

It could have been so much worse. I can't even count the number of people who have told me how lucky I am.

I'll admit, I didn't see it at first, when things seemed so bad. But I do now.

As for Dean, he tried to run, but the police caught up with him. He's in jail now.

People ask me why I did it, why I didn't just give him the money and let him go on his way. They weren't there. They didn't see the desperation in his eyes. I knew, with what little cash we had on hand, it wouldn't have ended at the flower shop. Dean wasn't going to stop until he got what he wanted. Right or wrong, I did what my gut told me to do.

As I recalled that terrible day, Nina was the one to pull me back to the present. "We have a wedding tonight," she'd told me. "We have a lot of work to do. You ready to get started?"

It had been a long two months. "Ready" didn't even begin to describe it.

And once we got started, it was as if I'd never been gone. We joked, we laughed, and we made lots and lots of lovely flower arrangements. I almost didn't want to leave. But everyone had agreed that for my first week back, it'd be best to take it easy.

Now I turn the doorknob as Spencer and Nina call out goodbye, and I yell, "See you Monday!" I'm so happy about those ordinary words, it's almost funny.

Leo is waiting for me outside the Bean Shack. "The car is

all loaded up. I've got everything we need. I even stopped at the market earlier and picked up some night crawlers."

I scrunch up my face. "I don't have to touch them, do I?"

"Why not? It's part of the experience. You aren't a real fisherman until you put a worm on a hook. Oh, I brought the video camera, too."

"Is it too late to change my mind? Can we go to Hawaii instead?"

"No," he says. "No way. We're doing this. You're going to love it."

"I don't know about that."

"Hey, in case you haven't noticed by now, anything is possible, Rae."

He's right. It is.

I figure this is a good time to tell him. "By the way. I found your channel. And I've watched your videos about ten times. Each."

He smiles, leans in, and kisses me. "My secrets are revealed, huh? Well, I'm glad you told me."

"No more secrets, remember?"

The world certainly knows all of mine now. They know about Dean and his problems, and how they became my problems too. I wasn't sure how people would respond, but they have been so nice to my mom and me. Nicer than I ever could have imagined. People have sent us cards and money and notes of encouragement.

It makes me happy to know I was right when I wrote my poem "Scars," which was selected for the anthology. Sharing brings people together.

Leo takes my hand and we start walking to his car. "I'm curious," he asks. "Which video is your favorite?" I think on that for a moment, but I don't have to think very long. "The one we're going to make today. And tomorrow. And the next day. And the day after that."

So much fun to be had. So much life to be lived.

He starts running, pulling me along behind him. "Well, come on, then. We'd better hurry. We don't want to keep those fish waiting."

"Hold on a second, Leo. We're going to throw them back after we catch them, right?"

He laughs. Then he stops, picks me up, and spins me around. "Rae, do you know what I love about you?"

I kiss him. "What?"

His smile almost blinds me. "Absolutely everything."

acknowledgments

THIS BOOK WAS NOT AN EASY ONE TO WRITE, AND I'M SO VERY grateful for the people who cheered me on and helped make the book what it is today. Suzanne Young was one of the first people to hear the idea, on a spring day as we ate sandwiches at a park and tried to get inspired. Thanks for saying the four magic words: "You should write it." Cheryl Renee Herbsman, who read an ugly first draft, gave me great direction while also giving me what I needed most at the time: encouragement. And Annette Pollert, my fabulous editor, saw the potential amid the mess and sent me off in a new direction that made the book a hundred times better.

The team at Simon Pulse is a great one, and I want you all to know how much I appreciate the work you do! Cupcakes for everyone!!

Sara Teasdale's poems included in this book are in the public domain. I am very thankful for the ability to use them in my book, and I can only hope Sara would approve. Her book of poems I chose to reference, *Flame and Shadow*, was published in 1920, and readers who might like to read more of her work can search online or check the local library.

I'd like to thank Eric and Carol Taylor for their generosity, as it was at their home where I worked on this book not once, but twice, surrounded by snow and blue skies and friends. And thanks to Becca Fitzpatrick, Rachel Hawkins, Irene Latham, Lindsey Leavitt, and Emily Wing Smith for being fun snow bunnies and friends.

Thanks, as always, to my family.

Librarians and booksellers who talk up my books, nominate them for lists and awards, and are simply awesome for putting books into the hands of readers, thank you so much!

And finally, thank *you*, dear reader. Where light shines, darkness disappears. My hope is that this book might be a source of light for you.

One moment can change everything.

The Day Before

beautiful boy

He stares
at the tank
of jellyfish.

I stand on the other side
and watch
the pale pink parachutes
            glide
through the water.

They are

hypnotic.

He moves
slowly,
circling the
round tank.

Moving closer
to me.

I realize
I'm not watching
the jellyfish anymore.

                I'm watching him watching them.

He stares
with such intensity,
I can't help but wonder,
What is he thinking?
Feeling?
Wishing?

While he's under their spell,
I take him in.
He's wearing a black knit beanie
with bits of black hair
sticking out,
a gray hoody,
and skinny jeans.

Only skinny people
can get away
with wearing
skinny jeans,
which is why
I don't own a pair.
Short-and-stocky jeans
are more my style.

So, he's skinny.
But not gross skinny.
Good skinny.
Cute skinny.

His warm voice
tiptoes into the
quiet room.

"Did you see that movie?" he asks.

I did.
Without asking,
I know he's talking
about *Seven Pounds*.

My mom is crazy
for Will Smith.
She dragged me along
like a box of Junior Mints
as soon as it hit
the theaters.

I was haunted
for days.

"Yes," I tell him.
"A crazy way to die."

He's standing right next to me.

We both watch
the glowing jellies,
perhaps imagining
reaching in and touching them,
threads of fire
burning our skin.

"I don't know," he says.
"They look so delicate. Pretty.
Prettier than a gun.
Or a rope."

I look at him.
"Didn't anyone tell you
looks aren't everything?"

like

"Cade," he says, sticking out his hand.

"Amber," I say, accepting his offer.
The warmth is a shock.
A tremor scurries
down my spine.

"You from around here?" he asks.

"Salem."

He nods.

"You?" I ask.

"Portland."

He smiles.
"So. You like jellyfish?"

I bite my lip
to keep from laughing.
Is he going to order me one
like a cheeseburger?

"I love them."

"Me too."

What is he,
a great white
circling his prey?

                    I don't think I care.

something special

Cade motions
with a nod
to follow him.

He's holding the pole,
and I'm the
fish on the line.

Just how far
will he pull me
in?

Around the corner
only a few kids
are at the
tidal pool touch tank.

My heart's racing,
but not from what's
in the tank.

With names like
pencil sea urchin,
scarlet hermit crab,
and chocolate chip sea star,
the creatures
all sound friendly.

I reach into the cold water.

The back of a starfish
feels like wet sandpaper
against my fingertips.

Cade pets it too, his
fingers almost
touching
mine.

"When I was little," he says,
"I wanted to take them home.
Turn my bathtub into a touch pool."

It makes me smile because
I was the same way.

Sea stars
are

m*a*g*i*c*a*l.

We wish on stars,
millions of miles away, and
yet here we can *touch* them.

I've never wished
on a sea star before,
but I want to try it.

I hold my breath and make a wish.

As he gives the
starfish a final pet,
his fingers graze mine.
Just barely.
But they do.

And the way I feel
when it happens,
I know I made
the right wish.

Please don't let me go quite yet.

Some bonds just can't be broken.

LOOK FOR LISA SCHROEDER'S

I heart you, You haunt me

Colorless

And then,
beyond the flowers,
beneath the stained-glass window,
beside the cross,
I see
the white casket.

I see
red, burning love
disappear
forever.

Broken Promises

My mom reaches over
and pulls my hand
from my mouth
where I chew on
the little flap of skin
along the side of my thumb
since I have no more nails
left to chew on.

An ugly habit.
One I promised Jackson
I would break.

I wonder,
do you have to keep a promise
to a dead person?

Mom holds my hand
in hers as the
music starts to play.

Jackson's
smiling face
appears on the screen
as we hear Eric Clapton's
haunting song
Tears in Heaven.

It's not long
before tears in heaven
make their way

to my eyes,
so I close them
for a second.

From out of nowhere,
I'm in his car, by his side.
Music playing.
Windows rolled down.
I kick off my shoes,
put my bare feet on the dashboard
and put my hand in his.

"Never leave me, okay?" I say to him.

"Okay," he tells me.

He squeezes my hand,
like that seals the deal.

My gaze
returns to the
beautiful boy
on the screen
while
my thumb
returns
to my mouth.

He broke his promise.
I can break mine.

I Will Always Remember

The minister speaks.

"It is hard when a young life is tragically cut short.

"But we must celebrate the life that was Jackson's.

"Look around at the friends and the family
who loved Jackson Montgomery.

"You will keep the memory of him alive."

There is *one* memory
that floods my brain
every five minutes.

It reminds me
over
and over
and over again,
I'm the reason
my boyfriend
is gone.

Memories might keep him alive.

But they might
kill
me.

about the author

LISA SCHROEDER is the author of *I Heart You, You Haunt Me* and numerous other books for kids and teens. When she's not writing, she enjoys walking the dog, baking delicious treats, and reading books other people write. Lisa lives with her family in Oregon. You can visit her at lisaschroederbooks.com.

SiMON TEEN

Simon & Schuster's **Simon Teen**
e-newsletter delivers current updates on
the hottest titles, exciting sweepstakes, and
exclusive content from your favorite authors.

Visit **TEEN.SimonandSchuster.com** to
sign up, post your thoughts, and find out what
every avid reader is talking about!

ATHENEUM FICTION

Margaret K. McElderry Books

SIMON & SCHUSTER BFYR

SIMON PULSE

THERE'S A FINE LINE
BETWEEN *bitter* AND *sweet*.

bittersweet

SARAH OCKLER
AUTHOR OF *TWENTY BOY SUMMER*

EBOOK EDITION ALSO AVAILABLE

From *Simon Pulse*
TEEN.SimonandSchuster.com
SarahOckler.com

Smart. Funny. Romantic.

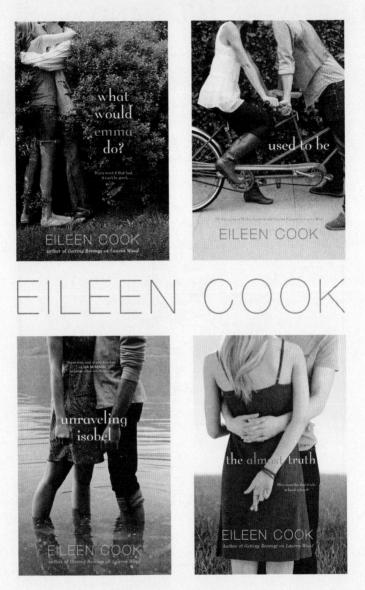

what would emma do?

If you want it that bad,
it can't be good...

EILEEN COOK
author of *Getting Revenge on Lauren Wood*

used to be

EILEEN COOK

EILEEN COOK

unraveling isobel

EILEEN COOK
author of *Getting Revenge on Lauren Wood*

the almost truth

EILEEN COOK
Author of *Getting Revenge on Lauren Wood*

www.eileencook.com